"THAT'S NOT WHAT I WANT," LONGARM HEARD HIMSELF SAY . . .

He reached out both arms to her. "It's you I want."

"Oh my!" she said.

"Now," he told her, his voice sounding unnaturally harsh.

With a delighted cry, she melted forward into his arms. He kissed her on the lips and then kissed a patch of flour that dusted her chin. "Mmm," she said, pulling him gently out of his chair and leading him toward the bedroom. "We were wondering how long it would take for us to get you back . . . to yourself." She laughed softly, seductively. "We were beginning to lose hope . . ."

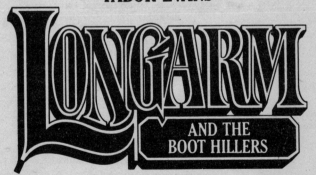

TABOR EVANS

LONGARM

AND THE BOOT HILLERS

A JOVE BOOK

LONGARM AND THE BOOT HILLERS

A Jove Book / published by arrangement with
the author

PRINTING HISTORY
Jove edition / July 1981
Second printing / November 1981
Third printing / September 1982

ISBN: 0-515-06584-6

Jove books are published by Jove Publications, Inc., 200 Madison
Avenue, New York, N.Y. 10016. The words ''A JOVE BOOK'' and the
''J'' with sunburst are trademarks belonging to Jove Publications, Inc.

PRINTED IN THE UNITED STATES OF AMERICA

Prologue

The Pinkerton and the marshal reined in their mounts as soon as they topped the ridge, then stared solemnly down at Antelope Junction. This was the place they were looking for, all right.

It was a tank town in the middle of nowhere, a good half-day's ride from Salt Lake City. Both men were following trails that were now getting as warm as the fireboxes in the steam locomotives that stopped here to get their boilers flushed. At the moment a steam engine—looking like a toy in the shimmering distance—had pulled to a halt beside the water tower. Puffs of steam were drifting skyward as the engine's boilers were topped with soft water. Even from this distance the two men could hear the locomotive panting as it slaked its thirst. In the switching yard beyond it, the tangled web of iron rails gleamed fiercely in the late-afternoon sun.

The Pinkerton's name was Charlie Halwell. He was a bluff, heavily built fellow with a deceptively cherubic face, flushed now from the long ride over the blistering salt flats. As he sat his gelding, he mopped his florid face with a polka-dotted handkerchief. He was dressed in a dusty frock coat and checked pants. A battered bowler hat was perched on his head. Only the gleaming Smith & Wesson riding in the holster on his hip seemed free of dust and ready for action.

His companion was Deputy U.S. Marshal Pete Baker, a tall, gangling, white-haired oldtimer who had thrown in with the Pinkerton after the two had met in the lobby of a Salt Lake City hotel the night before and begun comparing notes. The Pinkerton was after Weed Leeper, a train robber whose chief operating principle was to shoot down in cold blood any witnesses who might later be able to testify against him, a vicious maxim that caused him to leave behind an awesomely bloody trail. The marshal was pursuing Smiley Blunt, a killer who had thrown in with Leeper just before their last job—the notorious Tipton Train massacre, in which six innocent men, women, and children had been cut down mercilessly in the course of a robbery that had netted a paltry five hunrdred dollars.

A deputy U.S. marshal had spotted Blunt on his way through Salt Lake City on another assignment, and had notified the local U.S. marshal's office, which had in turn notified Washington. When Marshal Baker had arrived a few days ago in the city to follow up this lead, and had begun making inquiries with the local federal marshals, he got precious little help until he found himself talking at last to the Pinkerton, whose own sources had spotted Weed Leeper in a small town outside the city less than a week before. It was the marshal's hope that Weed Leeper and Smiley Blunt were still together, and still in Antelope Junction.

The two men could have taken the train, but they had decided to enter the place with as little fuss as possible, and they wanted their own mounts handy in case they had to scour the outlying country for their quarry. More than once, however, during the hot ride, they had cursed their decision. Now, as both men gazed down at the mean-looking tank town before them, they felt a slight chill despite the hammering heat that leaned heavily on their dusty shoulders. Neither Weed Leeper nor Smiley Blunt were men they would choose to meet willingly, but each had come a long way to collar these two vicious renegades, and it was not their intention to turn back now.

Baker turned his pale blue eyes on the Pinkerton, his lean face somber. "Ain't nothin' we can do but ride on down there, Charlie." He smiled bleakly. "We come this far anyway, and my whistle's as dry as a lizard's belly."

"You reckon we ought to ride in together?"

"I been thinking on that. Maybe we better separate, then

2

wait till sundown and come in from opposite ends of the town. Raise as little dust as possible."

"Good idea. I'll come in across them tracks. You can ride in from the west, along that trail leading from the pass."

Marshal Baker nodded as he glanced in the direction of the pass, then looked back at the Pinkerton. "We could meet in one of the bars—by accident, of course. Then we could go see what the local law can tell us."

Charlie Halwell smiled ironically. "*If* we can count on the locals telling us much of anything, Pete—which I am beginning to doubt, from what I've heard of this place."

Without further discussion, the two lawmen nodded good-bye to each other and pulled their mounts apart, Halwell leaving the ridge to circle toward the tracks, Baker angling down the far side of the ridge in the direction of the trail snaking out of the dark hills to the west.

Weed Leeper sat on the porch of the Lucky Seven Saloon, his chair resting back against the saloon's wall, his ankles crossed and resting on the porch railing.

Weed's face was covered with a scraggly beard, which had in fact given rise to his nickname. Beneath his shaggy brows, two red-rimmed eyes blazed out hatefully at a world he loathed. He wore a black, floppy-brimmed hat, a faded red woolen shirt, and greasy Levi's. Two gunbelts sagged across his gut. Both weapons gleamed immaculately in sharp contrast to the rest of the man, for these two Colt Peacemakers were the tools of his trade, and like all good craftsmen, Weed kept them in mint condition.

At the moment, Weed was watching a lone horseman riding into town from the direction of the railyard. The rider was a heavyset fellow with a single, well-kept sidearm, and he rode with the brim of his bowler hat slanted down to shade his eyes from the setting sun.

Weed chuckled. The man had the smell of a Pinkerton about him. As Weed pondered idly who the poor fool was after, he felt a delicious glow of anticipation deep in his gut. Hell, it had been so quiet around here lately that he had been reduced to beating up on the whores for excitement. This was more like it. As the rider rode on past the saloon toward the livery, Weed smiled contentedly, uncrossed his ankles, and got to his feet.

3

He watched the rider dismount, tie up, and disappear inside the livery down the street, then he strode heavily into the saloon to find Smiley.

Marshal Baker left the livery stable close to an hour later, having already noted the Pinkerton's gelding in one of the stalls. Now, moving through the dusty gloom of the main street toward the Lucky Seven, he became aware of a sullen, watchful silence that seemed to have fallen over the street. Of course it could have been just his imagination but it seemed to him that quite a few of the loungers in front of the saloons and other places of business were following his progress down the street with more than casual interest.

The marshal's spare frame moved lazily, but his long legs ate up the distance with deceptive speed. While he walked, his sharp eyes noted the usual shops to be found in a tank town: a beanery-saloon for passengers, a blacksmith shop, a large general store, Western Union, an impressive and fairly substantial switching yard and roundhouse beyond the train station. But the marshal's keen eyes noted something else as well. There appeared to be an unusually large number of saloons along Main Street, all of them operating at a pace that seemed surprisingly brisk for a sleepy tank town in the middle of this barren country.

He passed by the beanery, despite his hunger, and mounted the boardwalk in front of the Lucky Seven. What he wanted more than food at the moment was something to wet his whistle and flush away the dust of too many miles. The moment his tall frame strode through the saloon's batwings, he felt the place go silent. It was an expectant silence, as if his entrance had been awaited eagerly. The bartender leaned forward onto the bar, a grin on his face. A few of the patrons turned about to stare at the marshal coolly, speculatively, like customers at a sporting club waiting for the entertainment to begin.

For a fleeting instant, Baker considered turning about and leaving the place to return when he had found Charlie Halwell. Then he spotted the Pinkerton sitting at a table in the rear, his head resting back against the wall behind him, his bowler hat pulled down so far over his forehead that Baker could not see the man's eyes. A nearly full glass of beer was clutched in his right fist.

He was probably asleep.

This is what Baker told himself as he started across the sawdust-covered floor toward the table. The trouble was, he didn't believe it. He was a man who had stumbled into a waking nightmare, and as he neared the Pinkerton and cleared his throat to greet him, he felt a cold shudder pass up his spine.

Charlie Halwell was sitting too goddamn still.

"Charlie?" he said softly, as he straddled a chair and sat down. "You all right, Charlie?"

There was no reply.

Baker reached over and pushed the Pinkerton's bowler hat up off his forehead. A neat black hole had been stamped in the center of Charlie's broad forehead, and for the first time Baker noticed the dark stain on the wall behind Charlie's head. Baker gasped—the sound coming out like a despairing cry in the silent saloon.

He turned swiftly and saw every man in the saloon watching him eagerly, the slavering grins of wild animals on their unshaven faces. At once Baker realized that it was they who had propped Charlie's dead body up like this and then waited for him to come in and discover the dead man! And now that he had found Charlie, the fun was about to begin. What the hell kind of a place was this? Who were these animals?

Terror slipped like a cold knife into his gut.

Someone sat down at the table behind him. He turned and found himself looking into Smiley Blunt's amused face. Standing behind Smiley was a man Baker recognized at once from Charlie Halwell's description as Weed Leeper. There was a sixgun in Smiley's right fist, its enormous bore staring up at Baker's face.

"Charlie didn't want to die, deputy," Smiley told him. "Bleated like a stuck pig, he did. Said you'd be along to kill me if I didn't let him go. Is that right, deputy? You going to kill me 'cause I blasted this here Pinkerton?"

Pete Baker moistened dry lips. He was a dead man, and he knew it. But somehow he managed to control his voice. "I come a long way to collar you, Smiley. And now I got a better reason than I had before. You give me a fair chance, I'll take you."

"Guess maybe if I gave you a fair chance, you would take me, at that." Smiley's grin broadened. "But I ain't goin' to give you that chance."

Baker saw the man's finger tighten on the trigger. He

5

jumped to his feet, clawing for his sixgun. The Colt in Smiley's hand roared. Baker felt his face expanding, filling the universe. A red tide, then darkness washed over him. He tried to grab for something as he was flung violently back. He felt himself floating through the air, twisting slowly toward the floor. . . .

Deputy U.S. Marshal Pete Baker was a dead man before he came to a sprawling rest on the floor, his shattered face buried in the crimson sawdust.

Chapter 1

It was a Monday morning and it was raining—which didn't bother Longarm all that much, since the rain cleaned the Mile High City's pungent air and gave him a chance to breathe again. Longarm was weary of his long hiatus in Denver, sick of the swarming crowds, the air filled with the essence of horse manure and coal smoke—and that odd but persistent smell of burning leaves.

Longarm chuckled ruefully as he looked down at the narrow street below his window. He was getting edgy, all right. Any agent who finds himself cheering for rain is about ready to pull up behind the nearest funeral procession.

Longarm left the window, padded stark naked across the threadbare carpet to the dressing table, and peered at his reflection in the mirror. He was a big man, lean and muscular, with the body of an athlete. His seamed face had been cured to a saddle-leather brown by the raw sun and cutting winds of many a long trail. His eyes were gunmetal blue, his close-cropped hair the color of aged tobacco leaf. He wore a neatly trimmed longhorn mustache proudly on his upper lip, adding much to the ferocity of his appearance. It was a ferocity he counted on at times. He started to turn away from the window when he heard the rustle of bedsheets behind him, followed by the padding of soft feet. He smiled and turned easily, catlike, in time to enclose the tall, red-haired woman in his arms. Dressed only in a filmy gown, she sighed eagerly as she pressed herself hungrily against him.

Longarm sighed also as he bent and kissed her on the lips. Then, reluctantly, he pulled back. "It's too early, Rose," he told her. "Or too late. I have to be at the office on time this morning."

"Why? You said yourself that Vail hasn't had anything for you in a week." She leaned back, pressed her supple loins against his, a wicked gleam in her hazel eyes. "Stay here for the morning. I'm off today. I could have breakfast sent up. We could eat it in bed." She chuckled throatily. "Afterward."

Longarm shrugged. What the hell, he thought, as he felt himself responding to Rose's nearness. Vail could wait. It might make the man angry enough to send him out of this accursed city.

Longarm reached back for the bottle of Maryland rye on the dresser, then ducked under Rose, lifted her gently over his shoulder, and moved across the floor to the rumpled bed. It was still warm from Rose's body, he noted, as he dumped the laughing woman down beside him and pulled the bottle up to his mouth.

Longarm's breakfast in bed took somewhat longer than he had anticipated. Glancing at his pocket watch as he passed the U.S. Mint on the corner of Cherokee and Colfax, he saw that it was almost eleven o'clock. He would catch hell from Vail, he realized, but it did not bother him; he was still remembering the glow of Rose's eager body beside him in the bed.

He was also remembering the tears that followed, that always followed of late, whenever he was goaded into reminding the woman that his job came first and that marriage was at best a long way off for the likes of him. It was getting to be a problem with Rose, and it was one more reason why he was getting desperate for an assignment that would take him far from this city's complications.

He turned the corner and started for the Federal Building, just ahead of him. Once inside, he strode across the lobby, through swarms of officious lawyers who were already sweating themselves into such a fine frenzy that their oil-plastered hair was coming unstuck. At the top of a marble staircase,

Longarm came upon a large oak door. The gilt lettering on it read: UNITED STATES MARSHAL, FIRST DISTRICT COURT OF COLORADO.

Longarm pushed the door open and entered the outer office. The clerk glanced up from his typewriting machine, a look of terror mixed with joy on his pink, beardless face.

"Ah, Mr. Long!" the clerk cried. "It's you!"

"That's right, Custis Long. I'm glad you remember. Is the chief in?"

"He certainly is!" the fellow fairly sang. "You are late, Mr. Long! Very late indeed. Marshal Vail has already sent Deputy Marshal Wallace to your rooming house. He is most anxious to find you."

"You mean he's as hot as a cat's ass on a stove lid," Longarm said, leaning close to the clerk. "Is that it, sonny?"

The clerk nodded, pulling back anxiously, obviously acutely aware of the Maryland rye on Longarm's breath. "Yessir, Mr. Long. The Marshal is very angry. And I must say I don't blame the poor man. You really should get in here on time."

"That so?"

"Yes, Mr. Long, it is. After all, you've never heard of me being late, have you?"

"Sonny, I never hear much of *anything* about you."

The clerk sniffed haughtily and returned to his precious typewriter. "I suggest you go right on in, Mr. Long."

Longarm straightened, swept past the clerk's desk, and, with a short knock on Billy Vail's door, opened it and marched in. Billy Vail was pacing his small, cluttered office. He halted his pacing when he saw Longarm, his normally florid face even redder than usual.

"Where in hell you been, Longarm? You already missed the morning train north."

"Was I supposed to be on it?"

"You sure as hell were!"

Longarm slumped into the red morocco-leather armchair across the desk from his superior and tipped his head slightly as he regarded the marshal. "Maybe you better tell me what this is all about, Billy."

"Goddamn right I'll tell you," the man said emphatically as he sat down in his swivel chair and began poking anxiously about for a file folder among the blizzard of paperwork cluttering his desktop. "And I'll thank you to show me a little

9

more respect. You can start by not calling me Billy and by getting in here on time!"

Longarm leaned back in the chair. He was impressed. Billy Vail was really hot under the collar this time—which meant he had something for Longarm that demanded immediate action. The tall deputy smiled contentedly.

"All right, Marshal Vail, sir," he said, reaching into his coat pocket for a cheroot. "Where am I headed?"

"Salt Lake City, dammit! If I can find that—" With a grunt of satisfaction, he pulled a file closer to him and flipped it open. "Ah, here it is," he said, squinting down at the directive he had received from Washington.

Billy Vail probably needed glasses. He also needed exercise. After half a lifetime of chasing outlaws, gun runners, and assorted hardcases all the way to hell and back, he had been set down behind this desk and promptly gone to seed; it was a fate Longarm vowed he would never let overtake him.

Vail looked up at Longarm. "Salt Lake City is old territory for you, Longarm. You should have no trouble handling the authorities in that polygamous paradise, and of course that's important. We don't want another war with those damn Mormons."

"What's the problem?" Longarm asked, lighting his cheroot. "The Avenging Angels back to their old habits, are they?"

"I'm not sure. Washington's not sure, either. All we know is they are missing a federal officer who was last seen two weeks ago in Salt Lake City. He was on the trail of Smiley Blunt, a hardcase who had joined up with a pretty mean son of a bitch, name of Weed Leeper. Leeper's specialty is robbing trains, then killing any witnesses in cold blood. I recognize the name of the deputy U.S. marshal. Pete Baker. He's an old sidekick of mine. Tough as a railroad spike back when I knew him, but maybe a mite too old now to be chasin' high-line riders. If he's dead, as Washington fears, I'd like to see you take care of the gunslick responsible."

"Be my pleasure, chief."

Billy Vail looked at Longarm solemnly for a long moment, then nodded curtly, as if that settled it. "Well, I'd sure appreciate it. I'm hogtied to this here desk, so I'm leaving it up to you."

He pushed the folder across the desk to Longarm. "Look this over. Something spooky's goin' on thereabouts. Seems like too damn many no-accounts have been traced to this tank town outside Salt Lake City. This ain't the first peace officer who's disappeared after heading for it."

"And no one can get the Mormon authorities to get off their duffs and investigate."

"You got it. We're lucky they even bothered to inform Washington of Baker's disappearance after he set out for the place. Since it's inhabited by Gentiles, as far as the authorities in Salt Lake City are concerned, they can pave their way to their own hell and be damned. Besides, the town apparently serves as an excellent source of amusement for those members of the Church who can afford the short train ride out there."

Longarm opened the folder and glanced down at it. "Antelope Junction," he said. "Has a nice ring to it, at that."

"Just see what the hell's going on out there, Longarm. And see what you can do to find Pete Baker. I'd like one more drink with that cussed beanpole before I toss in my spurs."

Longarm stood up. "I'll do my best, chief."

"Oh, hell," said Vail. "You can call me Billy."

Longarm smiled.

"If you don't make a habit of it, that is."

Longarm was still smiling as he passed the pink-faced clerk. The timid little jasper was obviously unhappy that he had not heard more of an explosion when the tardy Longarm entered Billy Vail's office, and he did not look up from his typewriting machine as Longarm passed. If he had, Longarm would have swatted him smartly with the file folder he was carrying.

As Longarm rode the hack from the train station and looked out at the broad, neatly paved, well-laid-out streets of Salt Lake City, he was impressed once again. Most of the construction he had noticed on his earlier assignment had been completed, though work was still going on at the site of the Temple. When he saw the huge blocks of granite waiting to be lifted into place, he wondered if the Mormons would ever get their Temple completed during this century. Still, even if they did not succeed in completing it during Longarm's lifetime, there was no denying the remarkable stamina and devotion to their faith that such a mighty project represented. The Mormons would not be driven from this settlement. Not this time. They had come to stay.

If only, Longarm reflected, the Mormons could invest their

city with a little more joy. The stolid faces of the women, the grim countenances of most of the men, together with the drab, no-nonsense garb affected by both sexes, seemed to cast a pall over the city, despite the undeniable impression of prosperity that met Longarm's eyes on every hand. Perhaps these Latter-Day Saints should seriously consider easing some of their restrictions on alcohol, coffee, tea, and other stimulants.

The hack pulled up in front of Quincy Boggs' impressive, three-story residence. Longarm paid the hackman, mounted the front steps, and rapped smartly on the heavy oaken door. A tall butler pulled the door open.

Longarm stepped inside. "I'm Custis Long. I believe Mr. Boggs is expecting me."

"Why, yes he is, Mr. Long," the butler replied, closing the door. "He is waiting for you in the library. I trust you had a pleasant journey."

"Nobody shot at me or tried to cheat me at cards, if that's what you mean," Longarm replied as he handed the man his hat and traveling bag.

"Yessir," the butler said. "Very good, sir."

Quincy Boggs, his lean figure still trim, strode quickly toward him, hand outstretched, as Longarm entered the library. The man looked hardly a day older, Longarm commented to himself as he shook the man's firm hand. Waiting in the library with him was the youngest of his three daughters, Audrey. She smiled impishly as Longarm shook her father's hand. Longarm went over to greet her. Taking her slim hand in his, he gallantly brushed it with his lips. If her father had not aged much in the many months gone by, Audrey had certainly grown up considerably. She had been an impish sprite before; she was a boldly provocative young woman now—and what he read in her eyes almost intimidated him.

"Welcome back to Salt Lake City, Longarm," Audrey said. "We do hope you'll be staying longer this time."

"Yes indeed," said Boggs. "It is just Audrey and myself inhabiting this big house now. Emilie and Marilyn, as you have probably guessed, have only recently married. Audrey and I would be delighted to have you consider this your home during your stay in Salt Lake City."

Longarm thanked him and the two men sat down, Longarm in an armchair, Boggs on the leather sofa against the wall.

"I'll get something to drink," Audrey said, darting for the door.

"Apple cider, I'll bet," laughed Longarm.

"Wait'll you see!" Audrey cried, disappearing from the room.

"Well now, what nefarious business brings you to Salt Lake City, Longarm?" Boggs asked. "Your telegram said only you'd be visiting as soon as you arrived."

"What do you know of Antelope Junction, Quincy?"

"Seems to be a fine place to go if you want to spend money in a sinful fashion. That's all I know about it for sure. It's a deadly place for those who live there, I understand, but it's no skin off my nose—or that of any other devout Mormon—how these children of Satan assassinate each other."

"After all, they're just Gentiles," Longarm commented. "Is that it?"

"Unfortunately, yes." Boggs threw up his hands in mild resignation. "We have heard of the bloodshed and have sent our people out there to check on it every now and then, but all they have ever found is another grave in boot hill, which is certainly nothing out of the ordinary, Longarm. Not for Antelope Junction. It is a rowdy, sinful place. Prostitutes. Gambling. Drinking. Brawling. A devil's brew. But it is out of our jurisdiction."

"And besides, there might be a few devout Mormons anxious to use the place now and then for blowing off steam."

"Alas, Longarm, the sins of the flesh are with us always. It does no good to deny this lamentable fact."

Boggs looked at Longarm with just the trace of a smile on his lean face, his mild blue eyes barely suppressing a twinkle. It was enough for him, obviously, that the Church kept primarily to its mission of looking after its own flock—at least those of its members who would accept its guidance. It could not do much more than that. Man's unregenerate nature was simply too powerful to whip to a standstill, even by the Latter-Day Saints. Antelope Junction was the escape valve, the compromise the Mormons were willing to make in light of this lamentable fact.

With a weary shrug, Longarm settled back in his chair. "I'll want to talk to this local federal marshal of yours, since he's the one who sent in the report of Deputy Baker. What kind of man is he? Can I count on him to back my play?"

Boggs shook his head doubtfully. "His name is Walt Deegar. A large, florid man with a belly to match his enthusiasm for food—and multiple wives. The man is up for reelection.

He will not be too eager to rock the boat. And as I said, too many devout members of the Church want nothing at all to do with that hellhole out on the flats. 'Let the cursed Gentiles stew in their own damnation' is their motto—a motto that Walt subscribes to wholeheartedly.''

Audrey entered, carrying a bottle of Maryland rye, glasses, and a small flask of tomato juice on a silver tray. Audrey joined them with her juice while Longarm asked no more questions about the business at hand and joined Boggs in a noble attempt to punish the bottle of rye, while the three of them recalled Longarm's earlier visit and his successful joust with the deadly Avenging Angels and their terrifying leader—the Elder Wolverton.

"Emilie will be sorry she missed you," said Audrey at last, getting to her feet and stretching her young, lithe body. "But I will tell her that you are in fine health . . . and just as handsome."

Putting his empty glass down on the silver tray, Longarm smiled up at Audrey. "Thank you, Audrey. And you tell her how sorry I was to have missed her, as well."

"Good night, you two," Audrey said, starting from the room as she stifled a yawn. "I'll leave you both to your fuddled memories."

Then, with a delighted laugh, she disappeared through the door. Longarm heard her light, swift feet on the stairs—and yawned mightily, aware for the first time just how tired he was.

Boggs smiled indulgently and got to his feet. "Forgive me for keeping you up, Longarm. You have had a long day. And I imagine you'll have another dreary train ride ahead of you tomorrow. I'll have the butler show you to your room."

Longarm nodded and got gratefully to his feet. Even as Boggs spoke, the butler had materialized in the library doorway, and was now waiting patiently to show Longarm to his room. Wishing momentarily that it was Audrey instead who was taking him to his room for the night, Longarm bade Boggs goodnight and trailed the butler up the stairs.

Longarm's long train ride from Denver had left him pretty nearly exhausted. The Maryland rye had warmed him agreeably—as had the visit with Boggs and Audrey—and now he was more than ready for bed. He sighed contentedly as he climbed in between the immaculate sheets, turned down the lamp on the night table, then rolled over to face the window. The city below was quiet, the moonlight just beginning to flood in through the large, multipaned window. He stretched luxuriously and closed his eyes.

The door squeaked as someone entered. Longarm opened his eyes and turned to see a ghostly figure in a long white nightgown turning to close the door firmly. Even in the dim light, Longarm had no difficulty recognizing Audrey's bright, eager face as she swiftly approached his bed, a finger held against her lips.

"Emilie and Marilyn told me I'd have my turn someday," she said, unceremoniously flinging back Longarm's covers and laughing softly. In the moonlight, Longarm's long, naked flanks stood out clearly—as did his dark thatch of pubic hair. "Mmmm!" she cried. "Look at that!"

Wasting no more time, she stepped out of her nightgown and flung herself into the bed alongside Longarm. Pulling the covers up over them both, she snuggled happily against him.

"Audrey," Longarm said softly, caressing her long curls and holding her tightly against him. "I ain't sure I'm in any condition to pleasure you. It's been a long day for me. I'm pretty near dead."

Her hand snaked down between his legs and took hold of him. At once Longarm felt himself responding. Audrey giggled and pushed herself still closer. "You're not dead yet, Longarm. Besides, I hear tell a woman in heat can revive the dead. If she has a mind to, that is."

With a sigh, Longarm clasped her to him and kissed her on the lips. Their tongues entwined. Audrey thrust herself still closer, moaning slightly. Then she pulled her lips away from his and kissed his shoulder. He felt the moist heat of her tongue sliding along the slope of his shoulders to the strong cords of his neck. She bit him suddenly. He almost cried out. And then she began nibbling delightfully on his earlobes. All the while, the fingers of her right hand had been working their magic on his back, while her left hand continued to massage his growing erection gently. Abruptly she pulled her lips from his ears and kissed him again—passionately, her tongue darting, her scented hair spilling over Longarm's shoulders.

A flame of hot desire lanced upward from his groin. His exhaustion vanished magically, and he felt his pulse quickening. Pulling away from her teasing tongue, he laughed softly, then hauled her over onto him, his massive erection disappearing with effortless ease into the warm moistness of her. It was her turn to laugh now as she flung the covers back and sat up on him, grinding him wildly into her. It seemed as if her body were trying to devour his erection. He grasped her hips and started rotating her fiercely. As they built surely to a climax, she flung herself forward onto him, her corona of straw-colored hair falling over him, her tongue pressing boldly, wantonly past his lips and deep into his mouth to embrace his own tongue—a wild, passionate counterpart to his own thrusting erection.

That did it. He clasped both of his arms around the small of her back, lifted himself mightily under her—and came to a shuddering climax. As he clung to her, he felt her uncontrolled pulsing as she too reached her climax. She came more than once, and each time she tried to pull away, to cry out in her passion—but he kept his mouth firmly on hers until, at last, satiated completely, she collapsed limply onto his long frame. After a moment she sighed and, kissing him slowly, tenderly, pulled her mouth from his and rested her cheek on his chest.

"Mmmm," she said. "That was nice. Now what shall we do?"

Longarm stroked her long blond tresses and said softly, "Sleep."

"But Longarm, the evening is young yet."

"Not for me, it ain't."

He closed his eyes and almost at once felt himself drifting off. Only dimly did he hear Audrey's soft voice in his ear. "All right," she said, her lips drifting with the softness of moonlight over his cheek. "Sleep. But I'll be in early to wake you up."

Thinking of that promise, Longarm fell into a deep, delicious sleep—one that was almost as filled with delight as was the lovely, wickedly imaginative way in which Audrey roused him from sleep in the still, cool hour before dawn.

Chapter 2

Marshal Walt Deegar was exactly as Boggs had described: overweight and reluctant. The fact, however, that Longarm was being introduced to him by Quincy Boggs—a member of the Mormon Church's First Council of Seventy—at least aroused the man to push himself out of his chair with some alacrity. Wheezing slightly, he moved around his desk to shake Longarm's hand.

"Anything I can do to help," the man told him heartily. "Anything at all, deputy."

Boggs turned to leave. "Let me know how things go, Longarm," Boggs said, reaching for the doorknob. "And I am hoping we will have the pleasure of your company for supper tonight."

"I'm afraid not, Quincy," Longarm told him. "As soon as I'm finished here, I'll be on my way to Antelope Junction."

Boggs smiled. "When you get back, then."

"Thank you," said Longarm. "It'll be a pleasure."

As the door closed behind Boggs, the marshal wheezed his way back around his desk and slumped gratefully back into his chair.

"Did I hear you say you was goin' out to that hellhole of a town, deputy?" the big man asked.

Longarm took out two cheroots, handed one to Deegar, then

17

sat down in the chair by Deegar's desk. Deegar's small eyes lit up as he contemplated the cheroot. With a conspiratorial wink, he tucked it away safely in his inside coat pocket. In the privacy of his own home, away from prying eyes, he would take out the smoke and enjoy it as heartily as he enjoyed his many other indulgences, Longarm had no doubt.

Lighting up, Longarm nodded at the man. "You heard right. I'll take the afternoon train out to Antelope Junction today. I'm getting a mite curious about the place. Seems like it might be just the place for a man to visit if he wanted to get rid of any barnacles he might have picked up from too much sitting around."

Deegar nodded solemnly. "It will do that, all right. The place has been getting a fearsome reputation of late, and that's a fact."

"What can you tell me about this missing deputy, Pete Baker?"

"Last I knowed, he picked up with a Pinkerton, name of Charlie Halwell—and the two of them decided to ride out to Antelope Junction. Pete was after Smiley Blunt and the Pinkerton was after Weed Leeper. Pete had got word that Blunt might be holed up in the tank town. The Pinkerton figured that where Smiley was, there would be Weed Leeper as well."

"So that's why they teamed up."

Deegar nodded.

"You say they rode. They could have taken the train."

"Guess they didn't want to get off the train together, or something like that. It was a fool way to go, I'm thinking. Them salt flats are mighty hot this time of year."

"You think they could have gotten lost?"

"The Pinkerton maybe, but not that Pete Baker. One look at that beanpole, and you knowed that in his time he'd been to the other side of Hades and back. He had white hair, but he was spry enough—and his eyes were still sharp. I'd figure him to be a good man to have beside me in a pinch."

Longarm remembered Vail's fervent hope that Baker would be found alive, so that Vail could have one more round with the man; this Baker was becoming someone Longarm was getting quite anxious to know himself. "So you figure both men reached Antelope Junction safely."

"It's likely."

"And that was how long ago?"

"Better than a couple of weeks ago."

"And since that time there's been no sign of either man?"

"That's right, deputy."

"I don't like it."

"Me neither. You can understand now why I wired the office in Washington."

What about the town marshal in Antelope Junction? Can I expect any help from him?"

"Don't know much about the new feller."

"He's a new man?"

"Yup. Tommy Dorner used to be the town marshal until he caught a fatal dose of lead poisoning a month or so ago. The town's elected themselves another town marshal, I understand. Name's Sanders, I hear. Some call him Big Bill Sanders. A bad one, from all accounts, but I reckon the townspeople figured they needed poison to fight poison."

"Big Bill Sanders, huh? Name sounds familiar."

"Should be. Couple of years back, I remember seeing a dodger on a feller with the same handle."

"You mean he's wanted?"

"Couldn't find the dodger to make sure."

"Not that you were all that anxious to find it."

"The big man shrugged. "I guess that puts it fairly enough, deputy."

Longarm got to his feet. "Thank you, Marshal Deegar. I guess I'll be on my way."

The man made a movement to get out of his chair, but he was too well fixed and contented himself with nodding his head briskly and waving a pudgy hand. "You take care, Long. You look big enough, for sure. But that place has a real mean reputation."

Longarm touched the brim of his hat to Deegar, turned, and left the inner office. When he reached the sidewalk a moment later and started to stride through the bright sunlight toward the train station, he pondered what lay ahead of him with a curious mixture of pleasure and anxiety. If ever a place held a fascination for him, this Antelope Junction now did. The town sounded like the original anteroom to Hell. As a result he found that he was looking forward to reaching the place. But concerning the fate of Pete Baker and that Pinkerton side-kick of his, Longarm was more than a little anxious. Though he hated to admit it to himself, it looked to him as if both men were already dead.

And that, he pondered grimly, was a shame. He would have

liked to have had a chance to raise a few with that oldtimer, Pete Baker.

Swinging down from the train, Longarm walked down the platform to the baggage car, picked up his saddle, and went looking for a hotel. The selection in Antelope Junction was not too choice, but he found what he considered a reasonably clean place, the Antelope House, and entered the small but neat lobby. A thin-faced clerk, wearing a green eyeshade, was poised warily behind the front desk. As Longarm dropped his saddle and carpetbag on the desk, the clerk swallowed nervously and opened the hotel register.

"A room for the night, mister?"

"No," Longarm said caustically. "I came in here to rent a horse. You mean this ain't the livery stable?"

"That's . . . that's down the street, sir."

Longarm gave up. "I'd like a room, sonny. Second floor in back, if you've got one."

The clerk reached back for a key and handed it to Longarm. "Number twelve, sir."

Longarm signed the register. There was no bellboy, so he lugged his gear up the stairs to his room, let himself in, and dumped his saddle in the corner. There was still plenty of light left in the day, he noted, as he poured the water from the pitcher into the bowl and proceeded to wash the train soot off his face and neck. A moment later he left his room to seek out some Maryland rye. His tonsils needed tickling.

He found the Maryland rye in the Lucky Seven Saloon a moment later. It was a place crowded with noisy, unwashed patrons, over which a surly bartender—a powerfully built fellow with a head as bald and shiny as a brass doorknob—presided with unquestioned authority. He slapped the bottle of Maryland rye down onto the bar before Longarm, but refused to let go of it until Longarm paid for the bottle in full. The price was at least two bits more than Longarm was used to paying.

"Pretty steep, ain't it?" Longarm asked idly, slapping the coins down on the bar.

The bartender swept the coins off the bar and into his broad palm. "If you don't like it, mister, you know what you can do."

Longarm nodded and took the bottle and the shotglass with

him to a table along the wall. Sitting down with his back to the wall and his eyes on the door, he poured himself a drink and looked the place over. The sawdust on the floor was reasonably fresh, the smell of unwashed men and horse manure strong in the place, the air thick with coils of blue smoke from the many cigars. Bedraggled but valiantly cheerful, the saloon's girls did their best to drum up business of one kind or another. There was a steady stream of men coming down and going up with their female partners. Longarm noticed how tired, dirty, and bruised the girls looked. He did not wonder at it. The men they were taking to their cribs came from the same mean, brutal barrel, it appeared.

On more than one occasion, Longarm was certain he recognized someone as a man wanted for one crime or another, only to find that a beard—or lack of one—made it impossible for him to be absolutely sure. One thing was certain, however. These men were all hardcases, outlaws of one kind or another—and they did not belong in this tank town. For every store owner, clerk, or railroad worker who labored in the railroad's switching yard or manned the water tower, there seemed to be three whose only employment was to keep the girls and the barkeeps of this town busy.

He was pouring himself another drink when one of the bar girls sat down at his table and smiled uncertainly at him. Her thick auburn hair was shoulder length, her eyes dark and sad. She could not have been older than twenty and looked very frightened. There was a fresh welt on her right cheekbone, and as soon as she tried to smile, he saw that one of her teeth was missing.

"My name's Marie," she said uncertainly. "Do you want some . . . fun?"

"Depends, Marie—on what you have in mind."

She glanced over at the bartender. He was watching her closely, Longarm noticed. "You know what I mean," Marie said, attempting what she hoped was a seductive smile.

"Yes," Longarm admitted, smiling back at her. "I know what you mean." He reached over and placed his hand on hers. It was trembling slightly. He squeezed it gently until the trembling ceased. "Why don't you just sit here and join me in a drink? You've been a mite busy, it looks like."

"You mean just sit here . . . and talk?"

"How's that sound?"

"I'll get a glass," she said eagerly, leaving the table.

After she had sipped away more than half of her glass of rye, swallowing the whiskey with no trace of satisfaction, Longarm allowed Marie to tell him her story. She seemed anxious to explain to him her presence in the Lucky Seven. Longarm could easily have gotten from the girl a copy of the story that most soiled doves brought out whenever a customer asked the inevitable question: *What's a nice girl like you doing in a place like this?* This time, however, when Longarm heard the girl's story, he knew she had not manufactured it for his benefit. It did not have the sound of fiction—only the ugly, bitter ring of truth.

In order to get the money he needed for seed, Maria's father had sold her to Clinton Holloway, the owner of the Lucky Seven. The price had been fifty dollars. Longarm shuddered involuntarily when he heard the figure.

"He wasn't my real father, Mr. Long," Marie added hastily, as she tried to brush an errant lock of hair off her forehead. "And besides, it didn't do him much good. He had to sell out anyway. Some fool bought his section from him and gave him just enough so he could pull out. He took my ma with him to California. Last I heard, he was just as broke out there as here."

"That's some comfort, I reckon."

She nodded her head unhappily. "Besides, I couldn't have lived with him much longer anyway. You see, he . . . he'd had me already . . . taken me whenever he wanted to, and I was fearful Ma would find out."

"So you feel you're better off here, is that it?"

"Not really. These men are awfully dirty, Mr. Long. And they . . . want me to do all kinds of things." She shuddered and sipped more of the whiskey.

"So they beat on you some when you refuse."

Marie nodded miserably.

Longarm finished his glass of whiskey and poured himself another. He hadn't come to Antelope Junction to rescue soiled doves from a Fate Worse Than Death, and he knew there was little he could do for this poor, forlorn creature huddled over her whiskey beside him—but he sure as hell *wished* there was something he could do for her, nevertheless.

An ill-shaven, staggering imitation of a cowboy approached their table. The weight of his sixgun dragged his cartridge belt

22

down past his thighbone. His Levi's, shirt, and vest were filthy, the red bandanna around his neck encrusted with dried sweat and dirt. Only one of the man's spurs was functional, and his flat-brimmed hat rested on his back, suspended by its cord, revealing a shaggy growth of unkempt hair that hid his ears completely, along with most of his forehead. Someone had broken his nose in a fight and the mean, squinting eyes that now peered at the two of them reminded Longarm of the eyes of a wild pig he had disturbed once in a box canyon.

The moment Marie saw him approaching, she shrank back fearfully.

Longarm pushed himself a little ways out from the table and unbuttoned his frock coat as the dirty cowboy came to a halt beside their table. He did not bother greeting Longarm; it was Marie he was after.

"If you ain't busy with this gent, Marie," he told her, his voice surly, rasping, "I got business with you upstairs."

Involuntarily, Marie put her hand up to her bruised cheekbone. Then she looked almost desperately over at Longarm. "I . . . think Mr. Long and I . . . are going upstairs soon, Pinky."

"You *think*?"

Marie nodded unhappily.

"Well shit, It won't take me all that long. While this here feller decides if he's man enough to satisfy you, I'll just boost your sweet little ass upstairs."

Pinky reached down, took her by the wrist, and pulled her roughly out of her chair.

Longarm said, "Let her go, cowboy. I just made up my mind."

"You telling me what to do, mister?"

"You heard me."

Pinky flung Marie back into her chair with such force that it almost went over backward with her in it. At the same time he drew his sixgun and held it on Longarm. "Thought maybe that'd get your blood up, lawman," he snarled.

Longarm cursed himself for his stupidity in not seeing this coming. Marie had not been a party to it, but she had been used by this uncouth bully in masterly fashion. He had the drop on Longarm, for sure. There was no way Longarm was going to be able to draw his own iron now without getting his head shot off.

"You ain't welcome in this town," Pinky told Longarm.

23

"Take that sixgun out of your holster and put it down, handle first, on the table. Then get up, nice and slow-like, with your hands in the air."

"I don't care if I'm welcome or not," Longarm said. "I'm staying right here. This town looks like it could use a rat-catcher."

With a vicious snarl, Pinky kicked the table into Longarm's gut; then, reaching down, he flung Marie away from the table as the crowd in the saloon pulled back to watch. The edge of the table dug cruelly into Longarm's gut and the force of it slammed him viciously back against the wall. But it was just what Longarm had hoped for; as he rolled free of the table and slid to the floor, it gave him time to draw his Colt.

But Pinky's boot came up swiftly, its sharp toe crashing into Longarm's wrist, sending his sixgun spinning away. Pinky fired down at Longarm and missed. As the round slammed into the floor, Longarm grabbed Pinky's boot and yanked it toward him. With a startled cry, Pinky slammed down onto his back, his sixgun detonating when he struck, the slug shattering one of the lamps in the chandelier. Before Pinky could fire again, Longarm flung himself onto the downed man, knocked the sixgun out of his hand, then began punishing him with a series of brutal, sledging blows to his chin.

Somehow, Pinky managed to pull free and scramble to his feet. But Longarm followed after him, tracking him carefully as he continued to lash out at the man with sledging blows to the face and head, until Pinky was brought up suddenly with his back to the bar, his arms held up before his head in a futile effort to protect himself from Longarm's relentless punishment. Abruptly, Longarm stood back, paused a second, then drove a massive blow to Pinky's solar plexus. Pinky fell to his knees, fighting for breath.

Breathing heavily, his arms pulling on his shoulder muscles like dead weights, Longarm heard the barkeep order him to stand back away from the bar and put his hands over his head. Turning, Longarm saw the barkeep bringing a sawed-off shotgun up from behind the bar, its two bores yawning at him like twin gates of hell.

"Pinky needed a comedown, sure enough," admitted the barkeep with a mean chuckle. "But that don't mean you're any more welcome than he said you was." The man cocked both

24

barrels and steadied the shotgun. "You done considerable damage to this place, so I guess I'll just have to blow you in two—teach you a lesson."

The man was not kidding, as Longarm could tell from the frantic haste with which those standing behind or close to him hastened to get out of the line of fire.

"Now hold it just a minute," Longarm said to the barkeep. "I'm expecting a contingent of army troopers in here in just a couple of minutes. I advise you neighborly to hold off any more fireworks, or this town is liable to find itself under martial law."

The barkeep frowned, lowering the shotgun an inch or so. "What's that you say? Troopers?"

"Yes. Troopers. In a matter of minutes."

Abruptly, Longarm lifted his watch from his vest pocket and peered at it. Then he frowned and held it up to his ears, shaking it. The frown still on his face, he turned to the hardcases, who were now watching him in some puzzlement.

"Any of you fellows know the correct time?" Longarm asked.

Someone in the back laughed harshly, derisively, and then a voice barked, "It's too late now, lawman!"

"That's right!" cried another. "Time's up for you, lawman!"

But as Longarm had turned to ask for the time, he had palmed the double-barreled .44-caliber derringer, which was attached to the other end of his watch chain, from his right vest pocket. Turning back to the barkeep, he held up the watch and strode toward him. "My watch has stopped," Longarm said. "But I warn you, the army will soon be here."

"When they get here," the barkeep drawled contemptuously, "they won't find you running around with that fool watch in your hand." He laughed then and hauled up the shotgun again.

"You can't shoot me down for disturbing the peace," insisted Longarm, pulling up inches from the shotgun. "Here. Take this watch. It's worth more than any furniture I've damaged."

Longarm laid the watch down on the bar, his right hand still closed over the derringer. As the barkeep lowered his eyes to the watch, Longarm brought up his derringer and discharged both barrels into the man's face. The two slugs punched a single ragged hole just below his right cheekbone. Instantly a bloody maw appeared to open and swallow the man's entire face. The barkeep dropped the shotgun and grabbed at his disintegrating face with both hands, then sank out of sight behind the bar.

Snatching the shotgun up off the bar, Longarm swung around and trained it on the surly ring of men closing about him. "Freeze!" he barked. "I'll kill the first one who moves."

They knew Longarm's capabilities by this time, and froze obediently in their tracks. Marie emerged from the ring of men, eyes wide.

"Marie," Longarm said. "Fetch me my hat and sixgun."

She nodded quickly and bent to pick up his Colt, then disappeared back through the ranks of silent men to get his hat. A moment later, as she gave him his Colt and hat, Longarm told her to move ahead of him out of the saloon. She scurried ahead of him out through the batwings as Longarm holstered his Colt and followed her from the saloon, the shotgun still in his hands. As the batwings flapped shut behind him, he heard the stampede of boots hurrying after him.

Longarm swung about and fired a blast into the air. Cries of sudden panic came from within the saloon. The stampede halted, then started up again, this time in the other direction. Longarm waited a moment longer, then discharged the second barrel.

The sound of the gunfire had brought a crowd, and as it surged around Longarm and Marie, the town marshal pushed his way through it. Longarm tossed the empty shotgun to the ground in front of the man.

"You'd be Big Bill Sanders, I reckon," said Longarm.

"That's right. And who in hell are you?"

"Deputy U.S. Marshal Long."

The man grinned. "Welcome to Antelope Junction, deputy."

Wearily, Longarm said, "That's all right, marshal. I've already met your welcoming committee."

Chapter 3

Big Bill Sanders laughed. "My welcoming committee? Not a bit of it, deputy. I was hurrying over to save you from the rascals in that place." He chuckled. "But it looks like you don't need any help."

Once Longarm saw the marshal, he recalled his conversation with Deegar and remembered where he had seen him before. On a dodger. The pen-and-ink drawing reproduced on it had done a good job of catching Big Bill's blunt, heavyset face and walrus mustache. "Where have I seen that face of yours before, Bill?"

"On many a post office wall, I'll bet," the fellow admitted with a laugh. "But I've served my time, deputy. And got myself a pardon to boot. This time I'm on your side."

It was then that Longarm recalled what he had been trying to remember. Along the border, about five years before, Big Bill Sanders was second only to Sam Bass in nortoriety. A botched bank job had finally brought Big Bill and his band of desperadoes to bay, which was why Longarm had stopped hearing so much of the man.

"Glad to have you on my side, then," said Longarm.

A pipestem of a man, dressed in black with a faded rose in his lapel, hurried up to the town marshal. The skin was

27

stretched so tightly over the man's face that it gave him an appropriately grisly appearance. He looked like an animated skeleton. "Marshal," he said, seeming to quiver with anxiety, "I understand there's a dead man in the Lucky Seven. The barkeep."

Big Bill looked with surprise at Longarm. "You shot Gus Wallow, did you?"

"Didn't have much choice in the matter."

Big Bill looked down at the shotgun Longarm had flung to the ground at his feet. "That's where you got that Greener, then. It must've taken some doing."

Longarm did not reply.

Big Bill turned to the undertaker. "All right, Tyler. Go tell Clint. He'll be paying for this funeral, not the town."

With a quick nod, the undertaker was off.

"Why don't we just mosey over to my office, deputy," Bill said, "and let your feathers settle a bit."

"Good idea."

Longarm turned then to the still very frightened Marie and suggested she go over to his hotel and get the key to his room from the clerk. She could stay in his room until he returned to the hotel, which wouldn't be long.

When he saw the look on her face, he took a deep breath and, moving closer to her, spoke softly and firmly. "Now don't go thinking you know what I want, Marie. It ain't that at all. I have some friends in Salt Lake City who would be willing to give you a home in return for some housework. And there's a fine young woman in the household who would be more than happy to befriend you."

Marie blushed, nodded dutifully, and headed back through the crowd toward the hotel. As Longarm watched Marie go, he winced at the whistles and catcalls that followed her down the street.

He turned to Big Bill Sanders. "Lead the way, marshal."

The crowd gave way as the two big men shouldered through it. The town marshal's office was next to the barbershop a few stores down from the Lucky Seven. There was a small jail in back. Big Bill hauled a chair out of a corner and set it down beside his desk for Longarm. Longarm thanked the man and sat down. As Big Bill settled in his swivel chair, he lifted a bottle of whiskey and two glasses out of a bottom drawer.

He poured without a word to Longarm, shoved the drink

28

toward him, downed his own whiskey in one gulp, then leaned back in his swivel chair, his shrewd eyes fixed on Longarm, who finished his drink and wiped his mouth gratefully.

"Now then," said Big Bill, "what can I do for you, deputy?"

"I'm looking for a federal peace officer, Pete Baker. He was last seen riding in this direction from Salt Lake City."

"Alone?"

"No, as a matter of fact. There was a Pinkerton with him. One Charles Halwell."

"About when was this?"

"Two weeks ago, at least."

Big Bill frowned. "I wasn't in town then, I'm afraid. There was a shooting near Deer Wells. A crazed farmer killed his hired hand. I ended up trailing the son of a bitch to Elko, Nevada. Just got back a week ago. I was gone almost a month."

"You went pretty far for a town marshal, didn't you?"

He smiled. "Nothing I like better than to shake the dust of this town, deputy. You stay here awhile, you'll see what I mean. And then again, I had a bone to pick with that son of a bitch anyway. Had a habit of beating up on his wife and kids and then coming in here and tearing up the cathouses. A real mean bastard. It did my heart good to find him at the other end of my sixgun." He smiled happily at the recollection.

"You brought him in?"

"I did like hell. He resisted arrest, and I shot him down. I put two bullets in him just to be sure. Like I said, deputy, it was a real pleasure. And besides, I saved this town the price of a rope."

"Nice of you."

"You don't approve."

Longarm shrugged noncommittally. "So you heard nothing about the federal marshal or the Pinkerton."

"Well, as I understand it, there was a shooting—in the Lucky Seven, as a matter of fact. Two drifters—Weed Leeper and Smiley Blunt—blew themselves up in a card game. That was the only excitement, apart from one of Clint Halloway's girls trying to kill herself with a bottle of laudanum."

Longarm crossed his long legs and leaned back carefully in the wooden chair. "You say Smiley Blunt is dead?"

"Yup. Him and his partner. They're planted right now in boot hill."

"It was Smiley Blunt that Deputy Baker was after."

"That so?"

Longarm nodded.

"Well, then. It looks like your federal marshal got here too late and went back empty-handed."

"You ain't heard the rest of it. The Pinkerton was after Blunt's partner, Weed Leeper."

"So he went back too."

"I don't like it, Bill. It smells. You're right. If those two gunslicks were dead when Baker and Halwell arrived in town, they would have returned. But the point is, they haven't. The federal marshal hasn't been heard from since he headed for Antelope Junction."

"What about the Pinkerton?"

"Don't know. I have yet to hear so much as a peep from their office. And so far, neither has my chief in Denver."

"What do you want to do, then?"

"I think I would like to visit boot hill."

Big Bill shrugged and heaved himself out of his chair. Placing the bottle of whiskey back in his bottom drawer, he swept his hat up off the desk and said, "All right, let's go."

Earlier, when Marie had left Longarm and headed for the hotel, she became aware of Pinky, standing in the alley beside the Lucky Seven, calling harshly to her.

Terrified at what Pinky would do if he got his hands on her, she pretended she did not hear him and kept going. Only when she reached the hotel and mounted the porch in front of it, did she dare to look back. There was still a crowd in front of the saloon, but Pinky had vanished from the alley beside the saloon.

Breathing a sigh of relief, she entered the hotel and approached the desk. Only when she reached it did she realize the clerk was not behind it. She looked around the small lobby and saw him peering out through the window at the milling crowd in front of the Lucky Seven.

Clearing her throat, she gained the young man's attention. With some reluctance he left the window and moved around behind the desk, adjusting his green eyeshade as he did so. Frowning, he peered at her inquisitively. Marie knew what he was thinking. He knew Marie, and he knew that she and the other girls who worked for Clint Holloway had their own cribs above the saloon. So what was Marie doing in here?

Marie cleared her dry throat, a sense of hopelessness falling over her. "Mr. Long sent me," she said. "He told me to get his key and wait for him in his room."

The clerk's eyes narrowed. "I . . . don't know if I can allow that, Miss Marie," he said hesitantly.

"It's not for what you think," Marie blurted desperately. "Mr. Long is going to . . . take me away from here. He has a job for me in Salt Lake City. He thought I would be safer waiting for him in his room."

The clerk indicated the window with a swift nod of his head. "You have anything to do with that excitement over there?"

Mustering what courage she had left, Marie said icily, "I don't think that's any of your business."

The clerk nodded quickly. She had told him what he wanted to know. He reached back for the key to Mr. Long's room and handed it to her. For the first time he smiled at her. It was a dirty, suggestive smile. "You sure this fellow is on the square with you, Miss Marie? You're a mighty pretty girl, you know."

Snatching the key from the clerk, Marie swept past the desk and headed for the stairs. Once she reached the second floor, she glanced at the number tab on the key and hurried down the hallway to room twelve. Letting herself in, she closed the door hurriedly behind her and, shivering slightly, sat down on the edge of the bed to await Longarm's return.

After a while her nervousness faded and she began looking around her at the small, mean room. Still, it was a private room, she reminded herself, and that was a lot more than she had. Then she recalled Longarm's promise to her in the street. A job as a housekeeper in Salt Lake City! It would be just the thing. A dream come true. She tried not to hug herself with delight. It was hard to believe she could be this lucky. And then she recalled that ugly remark the clerk downstairs had made. It had cut pretty close to the bone. Suppose this Mr. Long was just lying to her. Suppose, like all the others, what he really wanted was . . .

She shuddered in consternation at the direction her thoughts were taking and forced herself to examine the room more closely, as if this might keep her thoughts more securely tethered. She saw the man had dumped his saddle in the corner. It looked as if he had used the pitcher of water to wash himself when he came in; both the pitcher and the pewter washbasin were disturbed. For some reason this thought comforted her. She had a reassuring image of the man taking the time to clean off his face and hands before leaving the room to visit the saloon. Not many men she knew took the time to clean themselves—ever. His carpetbag was on top of the dresser. It might contain money or valuables, she realized. Yet he had sent her alone to his room to wait for him, trusting her completely. She took a deep breath. She would certainly not go near that bag. Under no circumstances would she give this man a chance to distrust her.

Feeling a little more confident now, she got to her feet and went to look out the window. All she could see was the roof of the back porch and the littered alley that ran parallel to Main Street. The outhouses looked so dilapidated and filthy, she thought she could smell them all the way from where she was standing. Two horses, their tails swishing constantly at flies, were tied to the porch railing. She could not see the neck of either horse.

There was a quick, sharp knock on the door. She turned, her heart leaping in her breast like a frightened animal. "Yes?" she called, starting for the door eagerly. "Is that you, Mr. Long?"

But it was the clerk who answered. "Got a message for you, Marie."

She pulled open the door.

The clerk was not alone. Standing behind him were Weed and Pinky. It was Weed who pushed the clerk aside and strode into the room. Marie was forced to jump back in order not to be struck by Weed's heavy shoulder as he pushed past her. Pinky followed Weed, but not before he had passed a coin to the clerk. Bitterly, Marie backed up as far as the bed and sat down upon it as Pinky closed the door and turned to face her.

His face looked terrible. Mr. Long had beaten the man unmercifully. One of Pinky's eyes were swollen shut, and his nose was not only swollen, but one of the nostrils looked grotesquely enlarged because of the bloody scab that filled it. For a moment, Marie thought Pinky was pouting, but it was not that at all; it was simply that his lower lip was puffed out so far.

Weed rocked on his heels as he looked down on her. Pinky swept past Weed and slapped Marie hard, on both cheeks. Holding her hand up to her flaming face, she cried, "Please,

32

Pinky! I did what you said. I offered to take him up to my crib. But he didn't want to go."

"So you drank with him instead and told him your miserable story," Pinky said, his words sounding clumsy and slurred as he tried to talk through his ruined lips. "You didn't find out a thing, did you? All you did was ask for a job—a chance to get out of here. Is that it?"

"Maybe—"

He slapped her again, this time so forcefully that Marie was flung down upon the bed. Tears now welled from her eyes and she began to cry miserably. She knew this would happen. There was no way she could escape. Mr. Long had only made matters worse for her.

"There's no maybe about it," said Weed, stepping closer to her and looking down without emotion at her cringing form. "You are working for Clint Holloway. He paid your father good money. Got the son of a bitch a train ticket to California. I admit Holloway didn't get much for his money, but dammit, you ain't runnin' out on Holloway and the rest of us now."

"What did you tell him about us?" Pinky demanded.

"Nothing," Marie protested desperately. "I didn't tell him nothing."

"What did you find out?" Weed demanded. "Who's he after? We know he's a lawman."

"He didn't tell me that."

Pinky shook his head in disgust. "If I know you, it was you did all the talking. You told him your tale of woe and didn't let him get a word in edgewise. Ain't that right?"

"If you'd let us alone awhile longer, maybe I could have gotten him to tell me."

"There wasn't no time for that. I didn't want him and Big Bill to come in and break up our party. That's why I moved in when I did."

Weed chuckled. "Maybe you moved in, Pinky, but that big son of a bitch sure as hell moved you out fast enough. I never saw you handled that easy in my life."

Pinky turned sullenly on Weed. "You could have helped out some."

"Sure, I could have. But it wasn't my play. This was going to be your operation. You said you could handle him easy. Remember?"

Baffled, seething, Pinky looked down at Marie. He looked

as if he were about to strike her in his frustration. Marie cringed involuntarily. Weed moved past Pinky and sat down on the bed. Resting his hand on her hip, he smiled down at her. "Pinky ain't the man for you, Marie, looks like. But Smiley and me—we'd sure know how to treat you right. You wouldn't have to go off to Salt Lake City with this lawman then. How's that sound, Marie?"

Marie looked fearfully up at Weed. She was glad he was not with his friend, that awful Smiley. But he and Pinky made a mean enough team. It didn't matter that Weed had shaved off that scraggly beard; it only made him look worse. The skin that had been protected from the sun and wind by his beard now looked sickly and pale—almost maggoty, as though he had a disease or something.

"But you said Mr. Holloway owned me."

"That's all right, Marie," Weed said, moving his hand up her waist and resting it boldly on one of her breasts. "Mr. Holloway's a good friend of mine." He chuckled again, and the sound of it made her shiver. "He understands the way a man like me needs a woman."

"Hey, wait a minute," protested Pinky. "Marie's *my* girl."

Without looking up at Pinky, Weed leaned close to Marie, his eyes narrowing. "That right, Marie? Is this here sorry excuse your man?"

Oh God, Marie thought. She hated them both. All of them! She couldn't let their filthy hands take her body! "No," she said, with a courage that astounded her. "I don't need either of you men to take care of me. I can take care of myself. You tell Mr. Holloway I'll stay here and work for him, but I don't want you to touch me, Weed—or you either, Pinky!"

Weed leaned back, smiled, then slapped her a stinging, ear-ringing blow.

"Looks like we're both going to have to give you a lesson, Marie. You don't talk to us like that."

He grabbed the neck of her dress and ripped it down the length of her body, exposing her breasts. The sound of the cheap cloth tearing filled the room. Marie opened her mouth to scream as Pinky reached under her chemise and grabbed her bloomers, but Weed's big, powerful hand choked off her scream as he flung her onto her back, then flopped heavily, clumsily onto her.

Marie stopped trying to scream then. She knew it was useless. Instead she began to cry. She sobbed softly, steadily, as if her heart had broken—as indeed it had. She could not help but contrast the soaring hope she had felt a few minutes before with the sordid, ugly reality of what she was enduring now. And it filled her with a sense of utter desolation.

"Stop crying," Weed panted as he labored over her, his stench almost smothering her. "Stop crying, damn you!"

But she couldn't stop. And when the slapping and then the punching began, she drifted off into merciful unconsciousness, still sobbing uncontrollably.

The two freshest graves were those belonging to Weed Leeper and Smiley Blunt, Longarm noticed. Already the undertaker's helper was digging a fresh grave alongside them.

Longarm stopped in front of Weed Leeper's grave. The only marker was a rough plank, with the name burnt into the wood by a hot poker. Longarm was surprised to see so many fresh wooden markers, with the names of the dead burnt on them in the same fashion. It looked to him as if the population of this particular boot hill was growing at a startling rate.

Another thing. He had never before seen a graveyard, even a potter's field such as this one, with so few given names on the markers. Most of the dead were identified by the rough and ready nicknames bestowed on them by their friends and fellow ruffians. Leaving Leeper's grave, Longarm walked over the rocky ground between the already weathering plank markers, reading the names of this sad cemetery's luckless inhabitants.

The Elko Kid. No-Nose McBride. Gimpy Winslow. Studs O'Hanlon. Dutch Dorfman. Abruptly, Longarm pulled up to peer more closely at one of the markers. *Lem "Cutthroat" Flynn* had been neatly burned into the plank, and under it the legend, "He called Bill Smith a liar."

Longarm: straightened and turned to Big Bill. "Were you here when this jasper was planted?"

"Nope. That was before I got here," Bill responded, as he peered down at the marker. "It was when that other marshal got shot up so bad. I didn't get called in until later. But I heard about this shootout. Lem Flynn here took a few bad ones with him, as I heard it."

Longarm shrugged. "Well, I don't know who this Bill Smith is, but he's done me and the State of Colorado a favor. My chief's been after us to get a line on Flynn for the past year."

35

"Looks like you can cross him off then, deputy."

"That's the way it looks, all right." Longarm glanced about him at the sad rows of weathered planks and the meager inscriptions on most. "In fact," he went on, "I think I recognize more than a few outlaws and confidence men we've been looking for for the past couple of years. The Elko Kid back there, for instance. Him and Lem Flynn had just plumb dropped out of sight. Now I can tell the chief where they dropped to."

Longarm snugged his hat down more securely and took out a couple of cheroots. "Let's get out of here," he said, handing one of the smokes to the marshal. "I've seen entirely too many of these godforsaken places."

The trouble was, Longarm reflected as he lit his and the marshal's cheroots, he was still no closer to finding Pete Baker and that Pinkerton. Best thing for now, he concluded, would be to bring Marie back to Salt Lake City with him, get her settled, then check back with Vail.

Maybe Baker and that Pinkerton had finally showed up.

It was the look of almost pure terror on the clerk's face when Longarm entered the lobby that warned him. The clerk managed a stiff, mechanical nod when Longarm asked him if Marie was waiting upstairs in his room. Longarm took the key from the clerk, flipped it once, casually, then mounted the steps to the second floor.

The door to his room was closed tightly, he noticed as he strode heavily past it and down to the end of the hallway. He turned the corner, held up for a moment, then turned back around and approached his door with the speed and silence of a big cat. He leaned his right ear against the door.

He heard nothing. If Marie was in there, he should be hearing an occasional sigh as she waited impatiently. Perhaps the rustle of her dress as she crossed her legs. Or the tap of her shoes as she paced. If she was at the window looking out, the sound of her at the window should have come to him, the whisper of a curtain being drawn back, perhaps.

But there was no sound at all.

He did not think she was asleep. He did not feel it was at all likely that a girl who had seen the violence and had felt the terror that Marie had experienced less than an hour before would enter the room of a relatively strange man and promptly lie down on his bed and go to sleep.

And so he waited. . . .

A board creaked on the other side of the door. "Shit," said a heavy voice, inches from Longarm's ear. "I could have swore that was him coming up them stairs. Maybe we ought to tell that clerk to give us a sign when he comes in."

"How the hell would he do that?" asked a second man, apparently standing across the room, near the window. Longarm recognized Pinky's voice immediately. "You want him to run up the stairs screaming out a warning? A fat lot of good that would do. I say we get the hell out of here while we can. I don't think I can take looking down at her much longer. Can't I at least close her eyes?"

"Go ahead, close 'em, if that'll make you feel any better. And you can hightail it out that window if you've a mind."

"I'd be afraid you'd fill my ass with lead."

The man near the door chuckled. "I might at that."

Longarm closed his eyes and rocked back on his heels. What Pinky had said about Marie filled him with a baffling mixture of outrage and futility. Only with some difficulty did he prevent himself from howling out his fury and kicking the door in. He took a deep breath, then moved silently away from the door and back down the stairs.

The clerk was craning his head so he could see up the stairwell. As Longarm descended the stairs, he leaned down and thrust the cavernous bore of his Model T Colt into the clerk's face and placed a forefinger up to his lips. Longarm thought the little man was going to collapse, but the fellow managed to grab hold of the edge of his desk as he shrank back.

Longarm grabbed the clerk's shirtfront and yanked him close, then thrust the barrel of his sixgun up under his chin. With cruel pressure he forced the fellow's head back.

"I want you to call Pinky down here!" Longarm whispered hoarsely. "But don't you give him any warning, you hear?"

The clerk nodded quickly, desperately, as much as he could with his head bent back. Longarm released the man, then waggled the Colt at him to get him over to the stairwell. Shaking visibly in terror, the clerk went to the foot of the stairs and called up the stairwell in a shrill, quavering voice, "Pinky! Hey, Pinky! Come . . . come down here. Please!"

There was the sound of a door being opened and a man swearing. Longarm flung the clerk to one side and raised his

37

Colt. Pinky appeared at the head of the stairs, a Remington .44 dangling carelessly from his right hand.

"Freeze, Pinky," Longarm told him softly.

The man's battered chin dropped in astonishment as he pulled up.

"Now call that partner of yours out too," Longarm directed.

Instead, Pinky ducked to one side, firing from his hip as he did so. But Longarm had seen the look in the man's eyes an instant before he made his move, and was already pumping lead up the stairwell. Longarm's burst took Pinky squarely in the chest, hammering him back and out of sight. Longarm started to race up the stairs, then flung himself flat as the second man appeared at the head of the stairs, firing wildly down at him. Hugging the stairs, Longarm rested his Colt on the lip of a stair above him. He waited a moment, then gave a prolonged groan. The firing above him ceased. Longarm waited and was surprised to hear—from behind him—another man groaning as well.

The second man's head, then his shoulders, appeared as he looked cautiously down the stairwell. Longarm nudged the barrel less than an inch and fired. The fellow spun back out of the way. Certain he had winged the fellow, Longarm leaped to his feet and raced the rest of the way up the stairs. He caught sight of the man darting into his room. As Longarm leaped over Pinky's sprawled body, the second man flung a shot at him from the open doorway. The slug took out a piece of the balustrade. Longarm ducked behind a wall.

The sound of a window crashing sent him racing down the hallway. He ducked into his room and was just in time to hear his quarry's heavy boots on the roof below the shattered window. When Longarm reached the window, he saw the second man leaping down beside his mount. Resting his revolver on the horse's neck, the fellow fired coolly up at Longarm.

The glass still left in the pane above Longarm's head shattered, and he ducked back. When he looked again, the man had mounted up and was kicking his horse into a gallop. Longarm fired after him, but without effect. In a moment the horse and rider had disappeared.

Longarm turned then to look down at Marie. Her cheekbone was still bruised from the beating Pinky had administered earlier that day, her face streaked from the tears that had come when they had raped her, and now she lay on her back, her torn dress flung from her, her bloomers ripped and pushed aside, her terrified eyes frozen wide—as she contemplated the onrushing horror of her meaningless death.

No wonder Pinky had wanted to close those eyes.

Chapter 4

When Longarm moved down the stairs to meet the town marshal who had been drawn to the hotel by the gunfire, he looked beyond those who were pushing into the lobby below him and saw the clerk crumpled up on the floor, the crowd already encircling him. Instantly, Longarm realized that it had been the clerk he had heard groaning behind him. Only the clerk's agony had been real, not faked, as a stray shot cut him down.

"What the hell's goin' on, deputy?" Bill asked as he came to a halt on the stairs beside Longarm.

"Marie is dead. Pinky and someone else killed her. Raped her first, by the look of it."

"Did you get them?"

"Pinky's behind me on the landing, dead. The other one got away."

"Who was it?"

"Beats the shit out of me. I never laid eyes on the son of a bitch before. I won't soon forget his face, though. He was sure as hell an unclean-looking hombre. But I got a hunch the clerk knew who he was."

"We'd better ask him quick, then," said Bill, turning and hurrying back down the stairs with Longarm.

Pushing through the crowd, Longarm saw at a glance that Bill was right: the clerk was not going to last much longer. The town marshal turned to a little man fanning himself vig-

41

orously with his bowler hat, and told him to fetch Doc Gibbs, pronto. The fellow clapped his bowler hat back on and bolted from the hotel.

Longarm went down on one knee beside the clerk. The fellow's eyes were open. His shirtfront had become a heavy shield of fresh blood, and Longarm could see the hole that had been punched in his chest just above the solar plexus. It was amazing that the man was still alive. His breath came in quick, shallow bursts. Cold sweat stood out on his pale, narrow forehead.

"Can you hear me?" Longarm asked, leaning close.

The clerk barely nodded.

"Who was that other one with Pinky?"

The man gasped and tried to answer. The attempt caused him to wince painfully. He began to cough violently. Longarm reached out and held him steadily. The man's coughing gradually subsided, but there were tears of pain in the clerk's eyes when he looked back at Longarm.

"Did you let them into my room?" Longarm asked the clerk.

The clerk nodded. "Marie was . . . Pinky's girl. He told me . . . to keep an eye on her."

"I reckon they must have paid you pretty good, didn't they?"

The clerk didn't answer that. He just closed his eyes. Longarm leaned closer. "Marie is dead. They killed her. Now tell me, who was that other man you let up into that room with Pinky?"

The clerk opened his eyes and turned his head slightly to look at Longarm. A thin trickle of blood was coming from the corner of his mouth, and his skin was the color of an old newspaper. "It was . . ." He began to cough.

Longarm leaned still closer. "Tell me! Who was he? Tell me now. You don't have much more time," he told the clerk brutally.

"We . . . we . . ."

The clerk's eyes closed. His head lolled loosely. A bone-deep shudder traversed the man's entire frame as he gave up his ghost—fitful, pitiful spirit that it was.

Longarm stood up, shaking his head in frustration, and saw the undertaker pushing through the crowd toward him. The man's gaunt face was alight with the prospect of more business.

Behind him came a well-dressed fellow who appeared to have some standing in the community. As he entered the lobby and shouldered his way through the crowd toward Longarm, the men hastily gave way before him. He was almost as tall as Longarm, and his shoulders had impressive breadth. There did not appear to be an ounce of wasted flesh on his powerful frame, yet his face had the look about it of an indoor man, a prosperous banker, perhaps. His fleshy face was a bit flushed, his eyes a pale blue.

Big Bill spoke up as soon as the man appeared. "Good day to you, Mr. Holloway," the town marshal said deferentially. "We got more bodies, looks like. Jimmy, here, is dead, and so is Marie. She's upstairs."

The newcomer glanced distastefully down at the clerk, then peered with narrowed eyes up the stairs. "Who killed the girl?"

"Pinky was one of them. He's up there on the landing. He's dead too. This gent beside me killed him."

The fellow frowned, then glanced incredulously at the town marshal. "You say Pinky did all this?"

"He wasn't alone. There was another one with him. He got away."

Longarm spoke up then. "The two men raped Marie and killed her in my room. They were after me, it looks like, and killed Marie while they were waiting for me."

"And who might you be?"

"Deputy U.S. Marshal Long. And who are you?"

The man smiled abruptly and stuck out a massive hand. "I am Clinton Holloway, owner of the Lucky Seven and this here hotel."

The fellow with the bowler hat returned with Doc Gibbs, who brushed past the three of them to inspect the corpse. The doctor was a bald-headed fellow with a pot belly. He did not impress Longarm much. His pants were greasy, his shirt filthy, and he stank of cheap whiskey. He dropped beside the clerk and opened his black bag. It did not take him long to look up at Holloway and say, "Hell, there's nothing I can do for him. He's dead."

"And there's two others upstairs. Certify 'em as dead, doc," said Holloway calmly, "and help Tyler get them the hell out of here. I'd like that done as soon as possible."

The doctor nodded and stood up, wiping his bald dome with a dirty handkerchief. Tyler, the mortician, leaned over the clerk's body, inspecting it closely. The undertaker was evidently measuring the young man for a coffin. It would be a small one.

Holloway turned abruptly to Longarm. "I suggest you and

I go to my office, deputy. If I am not mistaken, you are the man responsible for the excitement in my saloon earlier today—and for the fact that I must now journey to Salt Lake City in search of a new bartender." He spoke without malice, a slight smile on his face.

"I suspicion that's me, all right. If that office of yours has any Maryland rye, I might take you up on that suggestion."

"Marshal," said Holloway to Big Bill, "why don't you tend to things here? I'll see you later—at your office."

Big Bill nodded quickly.

"Follow me, deputy," Holloway said, shouldering his way ahead of Longarm through the crowd. "I have plenty of Maryland rye."

Longarm followed the man from the hotel, not at all reluctant to leave what had become a charnel house, and more than a little curious about this hearty gent who was so important a man in this mean little pimple of a tank town.

Holloway's office and living quarters were on the second floor of the building that housed the Lucky Seven. The owner of the saloon did not take Longarm into his office, but into the gleaming, well-furnished living room of his suite. Longarm was impressed by the opulence Holloway's suite displayed—impressed and surprised to find such evidence of prosperity in such a dusty, woebegone town. And then he reminded himself that selling booze to gunslicks had never been a losing proposition.

Longarm made himself comfortable in a deep upholstered chair while Holloway poured the Maryland rye he had promised. Handing the lawman his drink, Holloway sat down across from Longarm, his own drink in his hand.

"Deputy," he said, "I am not going to charge you or the government for the damage done to my saloon this afternoon, but I must protest your action in dispatching my barkeep. He was a fine, tough customer who kept order in what has become, over the past few months, a most unruly mob of patrons."

Longarm sipped his drink. "That's good of you, Holloway," he replied laconically. "But I'm not a bit sorry about that barkeep. He was about to kill me. And I ain't so sure he wasn't part of a conspiracy. He was certainly damned anxious to use that Greener of his."

"If I know Gus Wallow, he was simply doing his job—

44

attempting to stop the destruction of my place of business. There are no brawls allowed in my saloon, deputy."

"There's better ways of stopping them than cutting your patrons down with a sawed-off shotgun."

Holloway sighed. "Perhaps you are right. But now I find myself without a man I can trust behind that bar. I just don't know what I'm going to do without the man."

"You'll have to find another."

Holloway leaned back in his seat and regarded Longarm shrewdly. "Would you consider taking the job?"

"I already have one."

"I am sure it does not pay nearly as much as I would be able to pay you, deputy. I am serious. There has been a growing spate of violence in this town. I need a man of your impressive qualifications to take over. I confess I am at my wits' end in trying to combat it."

"The population of boot hill is growing some, is it?"

"Indeed it is."

"Seems to me, from the names I recognized on those markers, the result has been a net gain for civilization."

Holloway laughed ruefully. "I suppose you could say that. But some fine men have been gunned down along with the scum. I wish you would reconsider my offer."

Longarm shook his head.

"Why are you here, deputy?"

"I'm looking for two lawmen. They were last seen heading for this place. They were after a couple of men who are now sleeping in boot hill."

"These two lawmen—they have names?"

"Deputy U.S. Marshal Pete Baker and a Pinkerton, Charles Halwell."

"Never heard of them."

Longarm nodded. "They might have discovered that the two men they were after were already dead and started back to Salt Lake City on their mounts, then run into trouble somewhere out there in the flats, though I admit that seems unlikely. Those two lawmen had plenty of experience."

"What do you intend to do?"

"I was going to go back to Salt Lake City on the next train, to check and see if they've shown up. The deputy marshal, anyway. But I think now I'll take after that son of a bitch that killed one of your girls."

"Marie?"

"Yes, the girl you purchased for the grand total of fifty dollars."

"A princely sum, you must admit, for a girl with her meager endowments."

"She was just a young girl—a luckless human being, Holloway. You bought and sold her like she was a side of beef."

"She was worth a hell of a lot less, I assure you. I did her a favor. Her stepfather was a brute. She was better off without him. And so was I. He was a troublemaker whenever he entered my saloon. Last I heard, he was on his way to California. Good riddance." He smiled coldly at Longarm then. "I must say, it is difficult to think much of a man who would spend his time seeking the killer of a two-bit whore. Was she the best you could do, deputy?"

Longarm did not allow himself to get too exercised at the deliberate insult. He smiled. "And I don't think much of any man who would buy girls to stock his cathouse. A pimp is what I would call him, and I guess a pimp is what he is."

Longarm put his empty glass down on the table by his chair and stood up. Holloway stood up also, his ruddy face having darkened slightly, his blue eyes narrowed in anger. "And I take it that's your final word on my job offer, deputy."

"You heard me right, Holloway. Thanks for the drink."

"I hope you won't mind my giving some advice."

"Depends on the advice, Holloway."

Holloway smiled coldly. "You don't have to take it. What I am suggesting, deputy, is that you forget trying to avenge the death of that foolish little slut and return to Salt Lake City. More than likely, you'll find that the deputy and the Pinkerton have already shown up, safe and sound."

"Thanks for the advice, Holloway," Longarm said, clapping his hat back on and striding to the door. "Like you said, I don't have to take it."

Holloway heaved himself to his feet and started for the door to show Longarm out.

Longarm held up his hand. "I'll let myself out, Holloway," he said, pulling the door open and striding from the suite.

Smiley Blunt wiped the blood from his chin and grinned down at the woman on his bed. He had a cut lip, but she had a mouse growing under her left eye. The battle had been short but exciting. He had enjoyed it immensely. There was no pleasure

46

at all in taking a woman who wanted him. There never had been. Hell, there must be something wrong with any woman who would spread her legs for the likes of him. No, sir, not that kind for him. Give him a tigress anytime, someone who hated him preferably. It made it all the sweeter when he finally subdued her and turned her own body—her own filthy lust— against her.

Tracy reached for a bedsheet to cover her nakedness. Her coal-black hair spilled down over the right side of her face and covered most of her shoulder, one thick curl just reaching the nipple of her right breast.

"You through with me now?" she asked, her voice heavy with loathing.

"For now, slut. For now. There ain't much left for me to do in this goddamn place but split you." He smiled. "Just stay put. I'm not going far."

He pulled on his britches and shrugged into his shirt, then ran his hand through his dark, oily hair and looked about the bare walls of the bedroom. Jesus, how he hated this place. Weed was crazy. This was the worst deal he had ever gotten himself mixed up in.

The sight of the jug beside the bed mollified him somewhat. He bent and swept it up, slung it over his shoulder, and poured the rotgut down his throat. He choked a little, straightened up, and wiped his mouth with the back of his hand.

"Want some?" he asked the girl.

"No."

"Then maybe you better get up and make me something to eat," he said, putting the jug back down on the floor under the bed. "I just decided I'm hungry."

"You just got through eating."

"Sure. But all that excitement gave me a big appetite. You heard me. Fix me something to eat." He smiled, his bright white teeth flashing in the dim, stifling room. "Or I'll send you back to Clint's cathouse."

"I think I'd prefer that."

"I know you would. You're a whore. That's all you are— all you ever will be."

With a sudden inarticulate snarl, the girl flung herself off the bed at Smiley, the bedsheet falling from her nakedness. Smiley jumped back, still smiling, caught her clawed hands with his own, then flung her brutally through the doorway and into the kitchen. Slamming into the kitchen table, she almost fell to the floor, but hung onto the table for support and regained her balance.

"Some eggs," he told her. "Scramble me some eggs. And some fries. Don't forget the fries."

Beaten, the girl flung her hair out of her eyes, then reached for a ragged robe slung over the back of a chair and put it on. Without a backward glance at Smiley, she padded on bare feet over to the stove.

Entering the kitchen himself, Smiley strolled to the door and pushed it open.

At once he froze, then reached into the corner for his rifle. Moving back out of the doorway, he said, "Who the hell is that?"

The girl was in the act of poking some kindling into the stove. She turned to look out the open doorway. From where she was standing, she obviously could not see whoever it was that had attracted Smiley's attention. She left the stove and moved closer to the door, peering out cautiously. Then she saw the rider on the ridge.

"How do I know?" She said, shrugging.

"It better not be another one of your brothers."

"It isn't," she said, a sudden note of fear in her voice. "I'm sure of it."

"Then who the hell is it? I don't like his looks."

"Just a rider," the girl said hopefully. "Why not invite him in for supper?"

"So you can go to work on him?" He smiled at her. "You won't get away from me that easy."

"No," she said wearily, turning back to the stove. "I guess not."

"Hey! Here he comes. The son of a bitch is real nosy, looks like." Smiley smiled and cocked the Winchester. "I'll bet I could pick him off before he reaches the gate."

"You ain't just goin' to shoot him, are you?"

"Sure. What the hell? I don't know him. It ain't the town marshal or Clint. So why not? I'm getting bored, shut up out here with you. You want to bet I can't hit him? Hurry up. He's getting closer."

As he spoke he moved cautiously into a corner of the open doorway, leveling his rifle on the oncoming rider. The moonshine he had just consumed raised hell with his aim, he noticed. He chuckled and decided he would wait until the rider got a little closer, until he entered the compound, maybe.

He was so intent on his victim that he did not notice the girl approaching him from behind, a large kitchen knife in her hand.

A few minutes before Smiley Blunt spotted Longarm on the ridge, Longarm had been pondering Clinton Holloway's advice. It seemed to him that Holloway was not anxious to see Longarm go after the man who had killed Marie. But why? What reason could the owner of the Lucky Seven have for wanting to protect Marie's murderer?

It was a day later, and the sight of the ranch huddled below him in the shadow of a low, barren hill had caused Longarm to rein in his mount and peer through narrow, sun-weary eyes at the sad spectacle below him. The mean, poverty-stricken sight caused him to forget all about Clint Holloway. This ranch was obviously not owned by Mormons. The main ranch building was a single-story cabin attached by a veranda to a low bunkhouse. There were two barns, one larger than the other. Much of the fencing, especially that around the corrals, was in disrepair, and the roof of the smaller barn had a gaping hole in it.

Rhode Island Reds were clucking and pecking in the front yard; horses and some cattle were visible in the distance as slow-moving dots among the burnt-out brush and mesquite that covered the gently rolling landscape. It seemed pretty clear to Longarm that the present owner would soon be ready to sell out and move on to California. If, that is, he even bothered to put this sorry homestead up for sale.

Longarm nudged his mount on over the crest of the ridge. Parched after his long ride, he was craving a cup of coffee and hoping that the woman of the place might have a fresh pot on the stove. And he would count it a welcome bonus if the man of the place could help him pick up once again the trail of that pale-faced son of a bitch who had killed Marie. He was going in the right direction, he knew. A New England peddler had been stopped, beaten cruelly, and robbed the day before by a fellow who fitted perfectly the description of Marie's murderer. From the site of the holdup, Longarm had followed his quarry's trail until he reached hardpan a few miles east of here, where he had lost it.

The closer Longarm got to the ranch, the more desperate the place appeared. There was no doors on the barns. The windows of the bunkhouse had almost all been poked out. As he rode into the compound, a pig emerged from behind the ranch house. It was as lean as a greyhound. For a moment it glared through baleful eyes at Longarm, then spun about on its spindly legs and disappeared.

His eyes still watching the pig, he caught the glint of sunlight on metal out of the corner of his right eye. He flung himself out of his saddle just as the rifle barked. He was a split second too late. A slug tore into the fleshy part of his left shoulder, the searing impact enough to fling him backward as he flew through the air. He came down hard on the small of his back and had trouble regaining his breath.

His horse bolted. Momentarily paralyzed, Longarm found himself unable to reach for his Colt or the derringer as the fellow who had shot him emerged from the black rectangle of his doorway and started across the hard-packed front yard toward him, his rifle leveled. There was a bright smile on his swarthy face—and a woman dressed in a torn robe and little else followed stealthily after him, a mean-looking kitchen knife in her hand.

At last Longarm found he could manage to suck air into his lungs. His senses cleared somewhat and he became aware of a wet warmth spreading from the shoulder wound and down his arm. There was no pain yet, just an ominous buzzing sensation. He made a feeble attempt to get up.

"Don't move, mister," the fellow with the rifle said. "Stay right where you are—nice and still."

Then he halted, smiled, and raised the rifle to his shoulder. It was difficult for Longarm to comprehend it, but this smiling, easygoing homesteader was now going to finish what he had botched a moment before.

Longarm did not wait. He rolled swiftly, twice, and came up on his belly with his Colt in his right hand. The homesteader fired. Dirt exploded in Longarm's face as he returned the homesteader's fire blindly, then rolled over again, this time lurching up onto one knee to get off a more accurate shot.

It was not needed.

A surprised look on his face, the homesteader dropped his rifle. As Longarm struggled up onto his feet, the fellow crumpled slowly forward to the ground. He thrust out both hands to cushion his fall and stayed on all fours for a moment, the look of incredulous surprise still on his face, the handle of a kitchen knife protruding from his back.

Then he sprawled forward into the dust.

Chapter 5

The girl looked across the dead man at Longarm. She smiled. It was a smile so filled with triumph and revealing a satisfaction so profound that Longarm was chilled to the marrow.

Longarm moistened his dry lips. He was aware of blood, heavy and warm, encasing his left arm. "I guess I owe you my life," he told the girl.

"That's right. You do. Who the hell are you, anyway?"

"Name's Custis Long. I'm a deputy U.S. marshal. I think I'm going to need some help."

"Oh, you're wounded."

"Yes. And I'm losing blood."

"Come inside, then. It's a pigsty, but at least you'll be out of this damn sun."

The girl turned without a single glance down at the corpse of the man she had just killed, and headed back to the ranch building. Longarm followed after her. Stepping inside the place, he found he agreed with the woman. It was a pigsty.

The girl spun about in front of the stove to watch him enter, hands on her hips, her eyes watching the wounded man warily. But Longarm was in no condition to complain of her attitude. Weak in the knees, a cold sweat breaking out on his forehead, he slumped gratefully into a straight-backed chair at the head of the deal table and started to pull off his frock coat to get at his wound. The woman saw him struggling with the coat, lost some of her wary belligerence, and moved to his side to help him.

In a few minutes Longarm's shoulder wound was exposed. The bullet was still inside, and it had torn up the muscle some. A steady gout of blood was oozing from the wound. He had to stop the flow of blood, he realized—but more importantly— he had to take out the bullet and then cauterize the wound. He glanced at the stove. The woman must have been in the act of building a fire in it when he rode up. Fresh tinder and firewood had been piled on top of the stove and one of the lids had been removed.

"Light the stove," he told the woman. "Then get that knife out of your husband's back and hold it in the flame. I'll want you to dig out this bullet, then singe the wound."

The woman stepped back, her face suddenly pale. "I . . . I don't think I could do that," she said. "And besides, don't call that son of a bitch my husband. He wasn't my husband."

"I don't care what he was to you," Longarm replied. "Get that fire started and do as I say."

"Or you'll what?" she demanded, stepping back, her eyes narrowing.

"Or I'll likely die on you. Then you'll have two bodies to bury—and to explain."

She looked at him for a long moment, then shrugged and turned her attention to the stove. As she built the fire, Longarm found a dirty sheet in the bedroom, ripped it into strips, and wound it around his shoulder, managing to cut somewhat the steady, persistent flow of blood. His head spinning from the exertion and loss of blood, he folded his coat and shirt under his head for a pillow and lay down on the bare mattress.

"I'm resting in here," he called to the woman. "Hurry up with that knife."

There was no answer. But he heard her footsteps as she left the cabin to get the knife she had buried in the man's back. He closed his eyes and waited for her to return. . . .

He awoke with sweat streaming from every pore in his body.

Sitting up so suddenly that the room rocked crazily about him, he found himself in the midst of an inferno. The wall in front of him, the one separating the bedroom from the kitchen, was a single sheet of flame. The smoke was so heavy that

Longarm could barely see through the open doorway. Nevertheless, he was able to glimpse what remained of his erstwhile assailant's corpse. It was burning like a log in a fireplace, an overturned can of kerosene on the blazing floor beside it.

Each inhalation was a knife driven into his lungs. His eyes burned in their sockets. He grabbed his coat and shirt and, putting his head down, flung himself through the bedroom window. He landed outside amid the wreckage of glass and sash. At once the room behind him erupted into flame in what felt like a small but powerful explosion. He was showered with sparks and flaming bits of debris. Scrambling to his feet, he staggered about fifty feet away from the cabin, then collapsed, exhausted. He turned to watch the cabin go up. It did not take long, the fierce heat causing an updraft that sucked great flaming shards of wood and shingles high into the sky.

He did not worry about the woman. She was gone, more than likely on Longarm's horse. It was she, he knew without the slightest doubt, who had set the cabin aflame. It was her way of disposing of the man she had knifed, and of the marshal who had witnessed the deed. The girl had not killed the man she was living with to save Longarm's life, as Longarm had thought at first. She had simply used Longarm's presence as a welcome diversion to do what she must have been planning for a long time. Longarm shuddered. The female of the species might not be more deadly than the male, but she sure as hell was a match for him.

Longarm heard the anxious whinnying of a horse and turned his gaze to the barn. A blazing ember had landed on the sagging roof, and even as he watched, the flames raced up to the peak. The frantic stamping of horses' hooves came loudly now. Lurching weakly to his feet, he hurried toward the barn. Besides the fact that he could not stand the screams of roasting animals, he needed a horse to get out of this place and after that woman.

The moon was up and Longarm had all he could do to remain in the saddle as his mount topped a rise, then carefully picked its way down the far slope. Saddling the horse, after he had gotten it out of the barn, had taken almost all of his remaining strength, but he knew that with the saddle, he stood at least a chance of staying mounted until he could find help. By the time the horse reached the flat, Longarm had become aware of a change in the temperature. It was as if crossing that ridge had taken him into another climate. He heard crickets chirping in tall grass off to his right, and there seemed to be an almost palpable moistness in the air. And then he was sure he could smell fresh, running water. The horse whinnied softly and increased its pace. It could smell the water too.

With some difficulty, Longarm managed to straighten himself in his saddle and peer off to his right at the moonlit landscape. At once he realized where he was. He had reached the edge of the Mormons' extensive irrigation complex, a strip of lush land more than two hundred miles long. The water-filled ditches gleamed in the moonlight, cross-hatching the night landscape into neat blocks and extending as far as Longarm could see—almost to the base of the mountains, from the peaks of which the meltwater came to fill the vast network of ditches.

Directly ahead of him, Longarm caught a faint gleam of light. Peering through the night, he thought it just might be a lamp burning in the window of a farmhouse. He hoped it was not some kind of night mirage, because by that time he was in trouble and knew it. Before he had topped the rise, the clumsy bandage he had wound around his shoulder had given way, and since that time he had felt the fresh, hot blood warming his left side as once again it pulsed freely from his wound.

He rode for what seemed an eternity. The moon appeared to have leaped suddenly higher in the night sky—and then, abruptly, he was within less than a mile of the farmhouse. It was, he realized dimly, the horse's doing—it was hungry and thirsty and had smelled both grain and water at the farmhouse. The horse began to lope, determined to get to that farmhouse without further delay.

Longarm tried to slow the horse down. Instead he pitched sideways out of the saddle. Dazed, he looked up at the night sky, the jeweled Milky Way swinging wildly across the heavens. He might as well be drunk, he thought. His senses reeled. He tried to keep the ground from dipping under him. He gave it up and closed his eyes. The earth was like a gently rocking cradle, lulling him into a delicious sleep.

Only he mustn't sleep. He had things to do, promises he had made to himself. There were two people he intended to bring in before that long sleep came: the murder of that beaten-down little prostitute, and that woman who had tried to roast him. He would track them both, and it didn't matter that neither of them had anything to do with the missing federal marshal or that Pinkerton. He was going to get both of them.

The grass under him was becoming slick with his blood. He tried to get up. His horse was now quietly cropping the moist grass beside him, its urgent need to continue on to the farm apparently satisfied by the fresh graze at its feet. Longarm reached out for the reins dangling almost within reach. The horse caught the movement and drew back quickly, jiggling its bit and snorting.

Longarm waited until the horse resumed cropping the grass, then reached quickly over and snatched the reins. Again the horse shied back, but Longarm hung on grimly. The horse quieted, its ears flat, its flanks quivering. Longarm pulled himself to his feet. Once upright, he leaned heavily on the horse.

He could see the light from the farm window less than half a mile farther on. Just a little ways to go. Still leaning heavily on the horse, he kept his right hand about the saddle horn, took a deep breath, and tried to remount. He lifted his left foot and somehow fumbled it into the stirrup. Then he tried to drag himself up into the saddle. He got about halfway before he slid back down.

He waited and rested a minute, then tried it again. The third time he made it and dragged his right foot over the cantle. Once secure in the saddle, he took a deep breath and urged his horse toward that tiny light still gleaming in the darkness ahead of him. He rode sagged over the saddle horn, clutching it with his right hand. The blood pulsing out of his shoulder was causing his entire left side to grow so heavy that he found himself wondering if its weight might pull him off the horse.

It didn't, and he kept on until he reached the front yard of the farmhouse. The horse pulled up abruptly. Longarm tried to dismount, but lost his balance. Snatching vainly at the saddle horn, he felt himself slipping. He slid down the horse's shoulder and leg and piled limply onto the ground.

Lying flat on his back, he heard the horse stamp its feet and blow nervously. Longarm tried to call out to the farmhouse, but little more than a groan escaped his lips. He was surprised at how dry his mouth had become. He reached out clumsily for the horse, but misjudged the distance and struck the animal on the snout. The horse spooked and, uttering a startled whinny, bolted back and spun away from Longarm, then headed around the farmhouse toward the enormous barn that loomed behind it.

As the thudding of the horse's hooves died, Longarm heard the farmhouse door open. A splash of yellow light flooded the yard, falling just short of his supine body. He heard footsteps in the grass by his head and closed his eyes wearily. It had become too much of an effort for him to keep them open any longer. As his senses reeled into darkness, he felt for a moment the sudden flood of light bathing his head as someone held a lantern just above him. . . .

Two gaunt women, their angular faces filled with concern, were bent over him. He looked swiftly around. He was in a bedroom, undressed and tucked between clean sheets. The two women must have undressed him, he realized. And bathed him as well. He felt clean.

But he was on fire. His lips had cracked from the fever. And his left shoulder was throbbing with a sick fierceness that gave him the impression something wild was alive in there, tearing at the muscles. That damn bullet was still inside him.

"Water . . ." he managed. "Someone's put the torch to me, looks like." He tried to smile at the two women.

The tallest one, the woman standing behind her companion, quickly poured water from a pitcher on the night table into a tall glass and handed the glass to Longarm. He reached out for it shakily, sweat breaking out on his forehead from the exertion, then realized he wasn't going to be able to handle it. At once the nearest woman reached behind him and pulled him to a sitting position, took the glass from the other one, and held it to Longarm's lips. Longarm gulped the water down gratefully, then lay back.

"I'm Emma," said the nearest one. She looked to be about thirty. She appeared to be a few years older than her companion and her face was a bit softer and rounder. She had hazel eyes, a rich dark pile of hair braided into a crown on top of her head, a strong, almost square chin, but a mouth that appeared quite flexible, as if it were always on the verge of expressing some impish remark.

"I'm Custis Long," he told them.

Emma smiled then, suddenly, dazzlingly. "Marge and I just knew you weren't going to die on us."

Longarm looked beyond Emma to Marge, and managed a

smile. "Did you now? That's right comfortin'. Trouble is, I might die if I don't get this blamed slug out of my shoulder."

"Oh dear," said Emma, her face instantly troubled. "The bullet is still inside, is it?"

"That's right."

Marge leaned closer, her longish face concerned. She had wide blue eyes and a sprinkling of freckles over her high cheekbones. "What shall we do?"

"Get a doctor."

"There's no one for miles."

"How far?"

"All the way to Salt Lake City."

"Then you girls will have to dig it out for me."

"Oh my!" said Marge, straightening suddenly, her hand flying up to her chin. "I don't think we could do that!"

Emma turned to Marge. "Yes," she said firmly, "we can. We have to do it. Besides, I saw my father do it once on a kitchen table. An old hunter turned up at our soddy with an Indian arrowhead in his back. I saw the whole thing," she finished grimly. "I even held the lantern for my father."

Emma turned back to Longarm. "You'll need to get very drunk, mister. That's so you won't feel the pain. But we don't have any hard liquor in the farmhouse. And there's none nearby. Our husband was a good and pious Mormon. He did not partake of intoxicants in any form."

"Where is he now?"

"Dead," said Marge.

"He was old when we married him," said Emma. "We kept him quite contented until he passed last month. There is nothing for any of us to lament—except the fact that we don't have any way for you to deaden the pain."

"It wouldn't be a good idea, anyway," Longarm said. "I'm going to have to help you."

"Help us?"

"Yes. The first thing we have to do is get me out onto that kitchen table. Then we'll see what tools you've got for digging."

They had to work in the light of two kerosene lanterns. Marge held one high over Longarm's back as Emma worked on him. She followed his directions well. First she cleaned out the wound with hot water and soap, scrubbing it thoroughly at

Longarm's insistence, until the flesh around the puncture was bleeding cleanly.

Then she took up the small paring knife that she had already sharpened, lifted the chimney off the second lantern, and passed the blade through the flame until it began to glow.

"It's ready," she said in a small voice.

Longarm rolled completely over onto his stomach, his head swimming by this time as the fever edged him toward a kind of drunkenness. "Go ahead," he told her softly. "Probe for the bullet just above the shoulder blade. I'll tell you where it is when you hit it. Dig it out then, with the knife."

She did not answer him, and Longarm waited a few seconds before he looked back at her.

"What's the matter?"

"I don't think I can do it, Mr. Long."

"Sure you can. You saw your father do the same thing."

"No I can't. It was so long ago."

"All right then. Put me back in bed and let me die."

Emma gasped.

"That's right, Emma. I'll die if you don't dig that bullet out. Even as it is, I got a pretty bad infection. And that's what usually kills. Take your choice. Dig it out of me or help me back to that bed."

She compressed her lips firmly. "But the pain," she said.

He smiled coldly at her. "Don't give it a thought. I won't cry out. I promise. I don't want you to get scared or to panic. Believe me, I won't make a peep."

Grimly, Emma nodded. Longarm turned back around and waited, his right hand securely gripping the edge of the table. After a moment's further hesitation, Emma's trembling hand began to run tentatively over the flesh above Longarm's shoulder blade, where the slug had come to rest. When she came to the spot, Longarm told her.

"Can you feel it?" he asked.

"Yes."

"Then dig it out."

He felt her hesitating once again, and cursed softly, bitterly.

"I can't!" she cried in a small, desperate voice. She was beginning to weep.

"It's a cherry stone in a piece of pie! Cut it out!" he ordered her.

The pressure of her left hand on his back increased. He felt something slicing into the flesh. The pain made his head swim, but he smiled. "That's fine," he managed. "Just fine. Now cut it out."

He wanted to tell her to hurry it up, but he knew that would unnerve her. The knife's cutting edge seemed to grow in size as she worked—as if she had really driven a red hot poker into his back, the heat from it spreading fire deep into his lungs. He wanted to cry out, to roar like an animal, but kept his teeth clenched instead.

"You're doing fine," he told her softly. "Just take your time and dig it out."

"All right," she said intently. "I think...I got it now. It's so hard to tell if that's it...."

By this time he was almost ready to tell her to stop digging, to pull the knife out, when he heard her sigh, and felt the blade being withdrawn.

"Here," she said, her voice unsteady but proud.

He turned his head. Between her bloody thumb and forefinger she held a blackened slug, mashed almost flat from the force with which it had slammed into his shoulder bone.

He was too weak to say anything. He just nodded and rested his head on his right forearm and took a deep, painful breath. He heard her drop the slug onto the floor, and a moment later she began to swab at the hole she had just dug in his back.

Longarm closed his eyes and passed out.

A few days later, Longarm was sitting in a rocking chair in the front yard, watching Emma work.

She had brought a large wooden tub out to the water pump and was now busy scrubbing his clothes. She was using a washboard and the same huge bar of yellow soap she had used to clean his wound. She had explained to him earlier that she had not washed his clothes before because they were not certain he was going to live.

It gave him a great deal of comfort, therefore, to watch Emma scrubbing away in the bright early-morning light. Despite the heat, she worked with her head covered with a bonnet and a thick apron tied neatly about the front of her dress. She appealed to him. He liked her laughter, the way she moved, the touch of her hand on his body when she helped him dress. But he wished she would loosen her hair and let it fall down past her shoulders. From the look of it, when unpinned it might very likely stretch all the way down to her thighs.

Longarm grinned to himself. He must be getting better, he realized. And no wonder. These two women knew how to take care of a man. As soon as his fever had broken, they had begun to feed him almost continually. Rich, thick broths at first, then solid food. Pastries hot from their oven, steaks, massive baked potatoes with great dabs of butter melting in their steaming midst. He was rapidly regaining what weight he had lost.

And that was not all he was regaining, he told himself, a wry smile breaking the somber cast of his features as he realized how much he wanted a woman. Still, it was unseemly that he should allow his thoughts to go in this direction. He stirred uneasily and looked away from Emma's robust body as it bent rhythmically over the tub. He would have to remain a gentleman with these two fine Mormon women. After all, they had saved his life.

He felt a light hand on his shoulder, turned, and found himself looking up into Marge's smiling face. "You must taste the dumplings I am making," she told him.

He started to protest, then shrugged, stood up, and followed her back toward the house. She was not as heavily clothed as Emma, he noticed. Her figure was slimmer than Emma's, and as he watched her movements as she preceded him into the house, he felt himself becoming almost unmanageable. There was no way out of it, he concluded unhappily. He had been with these two long enough. It was time he rode out.

The dumplings were delicious. And as soon as he tasted them and confirmed this fact, she set an apple cobbler down before him. He looked at it, then up at her.

"I couldn't," he told her gently.

"But . . . I want you to have it. You look so peaked. And you were so awfully sick."

"I ain't sick any longer, thanks to you and Emma."

She smiled, pleased. "Just have a little piece then. And there's some fresh coffee on the stove."

"That's not what I want," Longarm heard himself say, his voice sounding strangely distant in his ears. As he spoke, he reached out both arms to her. "It's you I want."

"Oh my!" she said.

"Now," he told her, his voice sounding unnaturally harsh to him.

With a delighted cry, she melted forward into his arms. He kissed her on the lips and then kissed a patch of flour that dusted her chin. "Mmm," she said, pulling him gently out of his chair and leading him toward the bedroom. "We were wondering how long it would take for us to get you back . . . to yourself." She laughed softly, seductively. "Emma was beginning to lose hope."

He laughed then. "You mean . . . you and Emma . . ."

"Of course. What do you think? Our husband has been dead for more than a month now. And all this while we have been favored with the sight of your fine manhood. Our husband was almost seventy-four when he passed on. He did his best for us, but I am sure that even in his prime he was no match for you."

She pulled him gently toward the bed and began to undress him casually, a chore both of them had shared during the past week. The clothes he was wearing had once belonged to their dead husband, and fitted Longarm so loosely they were off in a minute. He lay back, naked, and watched Marge pull her dress up over her head. Both she and Emma did not wear corsets, he knew. Marge stepped eagerly out of her chemise and bloomers and flung herself onto the bed beside Longarm.

As they embraced, Longarm glanced toward the bedroom doorway. Emma was standing in it, undressing hurriedly. . . .

It was night. Marge was in the kitchen, humming softly to herself as she set about fixing what was going to be a very late supper.

Marge was done now, it seemed, and it was Emma's turn.

She had been quite willing to share him with Marge earlier, but as she had told them both at the time, she wanted Longarm all to herself later, when Marge had had her fill. Now, laughing softly, delightedly, she rolled Longarm gently over onto his back. To Longarm's pleased surprise, he was still more than able to oblige her. He wondered what in tarnation these two had been slipping into his food.

Emma had done as Longarm requested and unpinned her hair. As she mounted him swiftly and then lowered herself onto his erection, the hair hung down in thick coils about his head and shoulders, like a perfumed tent.

She leaned back, way back, closing herself even more firmly about his erection. He reached up and fondled her breasts. She moaned softly and began to rotate. He began thrusting. Her movements became more agitated, fiercer. She was a different woman from the Emma who had joined Marge in caressing him earlier. Indeed, her violent writhing almost threatened to dismast him. But there was no rhythm to it, no control. It was distracting Longarm, and he did not see how it could help her achieve an orgasm, since it was entirely too random.

He reached up and grabbed her hips firmly, slowing somewhat her wild bucking. She gasped in a fury and tried to push his hands away, but he persisted, thrusting up rhythmically and pulling down upon her with all the strength he could manage, considering his still-weak left arm. He continued his relentless upward thrusting, pulling her down onto him with an uncompromising brutality that matched each upward lunge of his own. At last he felt himself building to his climax. Abruptly, Emma moaned loudly and stopped trying to fight him. She was now in perfect synchronization with his movements. Her moans became outright cries, then shrieks.

"Yes! Yes!" she called out suddenly. "Oh yes! It's happening!" she shouted triumphantly.

In that instant the two came as one. Longarm, still driving upward, felt himself exploding within her as her entire body shuddered in unison with his. She wrenched herself back in an ecstatic series of orgasms, and kept climaxing until at last she fell forward upon his chest, her arms flung about him, sobbing softly.

But as Longarm tried to wrap his own arms around Emma, his face was covered with two warm, heavy breasts, as Marge flung herself down beside him in bed.

"Oh, you darling," she cried. "You did it for her. She came! Our husband could never do it for us! Please, do it for me too now!"

"You mean . . . ?"

"No I haven't. Not yet. Almost, but not really. Please, Mr. Long! Please!"

He started to tell them they didn't need to be so formal as to call him "Mr. Long," but the words got lost somehow as Emma pulled herself lazily back off his chest, her lips moving down his chest to his navel. "Help her too," she said. And then Longarm felt her warm, moist lips nibbling their way down to his spent erection. Her hot breath engulfed him, then her lips. An almost painful flame of desire lanced through his groin. Despite himself, he was still alive down there. Emma was seeing to that. He realized suddenly what these two women had had to do to keep that old husband of theirs erect. Longarm was in the hands of experts.

As his urgency mounted, he asked Marge, "What about those dumplings you been trying to fix all afternoon?"

"Here," she cried, thrusting a large nipple into his mouth. "Eat this instead."

With a happy growl, he closed his mouth about the nipple and rolled savagely over onto Marge and impaled her. *The hell with those dumplings*, he told himself gleefully, as Emma clambered on top of his back and hung on for the ride.

Two mornings later, Emma stirred in Longarm's arms, then sat up, waking him as well. Marge was standing in the bedroom doorway.

"Lem Hanks is riding up," she cried, her eyes shining.

At once, Emma leaped from the bed and began to pull on her bloomers. "I must look a sight!" she cried nervously. "Oh, do hold his attention while I fix my hair, Emma. Maybe you could meet him outside."

"Of course," Emma said, turning and hurrying from the room.

Longarm sat up in the bed, propping himself on his elbows. "Who's this fellow, Lem Hanks?"

"He owns the next farm," Emma explained happily, as she finished buttoning up her dress. "His wife died two summers ago and he's been courting Marge. But she told him last week not to come back here until he agreed to take us both. There was no way we were going to be separated over a man."

"Oh."

"Well," she cried triumphantly. "He's back. So that means he's going to take us both!" She began stroking her hair rapidly with her brush, her eyes shining eagerly as she looked into the mirror.

"How are you going to explain me?" Longarm asked.

"Don't need to. Neither of us is promised to anyone. We live alone. We can do with whoever we want. He knows that, and he better not ask any questions, either."

Finished with her hair, she stood up, took one last look at herself in the mirror, and darted from the room. Longarm watched her go, feeling just a little abandoned. He was so famished he could eat the wallpaper off the walls. Did the arrival of Lem Hanks mean Longarm was going to go unfed?

Still, Longarm told himself, he really should be relieved. It was about time he got back up into a saddle and headed for

Salt Lake City. He needed to send a telegram to Billy Vail so he could find out for sure if that federal deputy had turned up yet. If he had, Longarm's business in this wild country was at an end. He had long since lost the trail of that no-account who had killed Marie. And that woman who had tried to barbecue him was probably halfway to California by now, anyway. Besides, Longarm told himself philosophically, he might as well let bygones be bygones. After all, even if that woman hadn't meant to, she had prevented that crazy homesteader from killing him.

Feeling as light as a feather, he swung his feet off the bed. His mended clothes had long since dried and been folded neatly on the chair in the corner. He remembered Emma doing it the day before while he made furious love to Marge. Each time Emma had entered the room, she had reached over and grabbed Longarm playfully. She was a very grateful woman.

He sighed as he stood up and buttoned his shirt. He was going to miss these two insatiable Mormon women, but the more he thought on it, the more desperate did he believe Lem Hanks' position to be. Longarm was just moving through, but this poor innocent was going to bed down permanently with Emma and Marge. Perhaps Longarm should make some attempt to warn the man, let him know what he was getting into. These two females might just wear him down to a nubbin. They might even kill him. Longarm hadn't heard of any able-bodied males dying from it, but there was always a first time.

As he strapped on his cross-draw rig, he heard the two women outside the cabin laughing together with Lem Hanks, and caught also Lem's booming laughter in return.

Aw, what the hell, Longarm thought as he reached for his hat, he might as well let the poor son of a bitch find out for himself.

There sure as hell were worse ways to die.

Chapter 6

As Longarm rode toward Antelope Junction later that same day, he found himself more than a little depressed by the arid nature of the land, once he left behind him that incredible green miracle wrought by the Mormons' irrigation.

For this reason he found it difficult to understand that homestead he had fled in such a hurry earlier, and the two more he passed as he rode toward Antelope Junction. He stopped at one of them to water his horse and was given the water sullenly, even suspiciously, by a fellow who looked more like a prisoner serving time than a man intent on developing his new spread. What few cattle Longarm had noticed, riding up to the ranch, were built more like antelope than beef cows. And the reason for this was obvious to Longarm, if not to the fledging rancher. The sagebrush and cheat grass the man's cattle were being forced to feed on was more suitable for sheep and rabbits than for cattle being fattened for market.

Marge and Emma had spoken of these new homesteaders, or rather had passed on to Longarm what their husband's opinion of them had been. That venerable Mormon had pronounced them all mad—or worse, interlopers who eventually hoped to tap into the Mormons' irrigation system, an eventually he would fight—as would all the other Mormons on the strip.

Within a few miles of Antelope Junction, Longarm came upon a grizzled old prospector dragging an unhappy donkey behind him as he pushed himself doggedly over the sun-blasted landscape. The man appeared to be in some discomfort as he dragged his left leg behind him, though he was tough enough to keep on going without a whimper. At Longarm's appearance the prospector tightened up a bit warily, but continued on, staring bleakly ahead of him, seemingly determined not to acknowledge Longarm's presence. In fact he appeared hopeful that Longarm would ignore him and ride on by.

Instead, Longarm deliberately rode close enough to be able to inspect more closely the dark stain covering the man's calf. When he had satisfied himself that the prospector had been wounded—and recently—he reined up and dismounted. Resignedly, the prospector hauled up also.

"Howdy," the man said carefully, tying the mule's reins to a stunted juniper. "If it's water you're after, I'm plumb out." As he spoke, he limped painfully back to the burro's load and made a show of adjusting the handle of a spade he was carrying.

"I have all the water I need, and then some, oldtimer," replied Longarm, as he lifted his canteen down from his saddle horn. "Would you care to wet your whistle?"

The old man brightened considerably, relaxed his grip on the handle, and nodded. "Well now, that's real neighborly of you. My mouth's as dry as a sidewinder's belly at high noon."

Longarm walked over to the prospector and handed the canteen to him. The old man restrained his eagerness with some difficulty as he took the canvas-covered flask, unscrewed the cap, and tipped it up. He took a very healthy couple of swallows, then eased up slightly. Handing it back to Longarm at last, he wiped his mouth with the back of his hand and grinned gratefully at the tall lawman.

"Much obliged, mister. Had my canteen shot out of my hand back there a ways."

"And your leg shot out from under you, by the looks of it. Indians or Mormons?"

"Neither. A damned inhospitable granger. Guards his water like it was gold. I ain't blamin' him none. In this here wasteland that's just about what water is, but that don't give a man the right to shoot at a fellow human what needs water."

Longarm stuck out his hand. "Name's Custis Long. I'm a deputy U.S. marshal. You got a place of refuge near here?"

"Pike's the name, deputy. And I'm right glad to meet you. Sure, I got me a little cabin in them hills over yonder. But it looks like I'd better be moving on soon. I ain't a welcome sight to these damn fools settlin' in this basin, and there sure as hell ain't any gold, 'ceptin' maybe fool's gold."

"You need any help in making it to your digs?"

"That blamed round went clear through my leg. I cleaned the wound out with the last of the whiskey I had on me. It bled some and hurts like a rotten tooth, but I'll make it. Thanks."

"You want to volunteer the name of that jasper that shot at you?"

"Blamed if I know what his name was. A newcomer to this flat, he is—and the sorriest excuse for a granger I ever saw. They must be emptying out all the ratholes back East."

"Where's this new rancher's spread?"

The prospector turned and pointed to the horizon north of Antelope Junction. "I'd say it's ten miles or so in a straight line from here."

"What's the son of a bitch look like?"

"Like something a grizzly pawed a while, then threw back. He's got a pretty mean scar around his neck and a mighty unpleasant-looking walleye."

Longarm nodded grimly. "Well, it sure as hell don't look like I'll have any trouble recognizing the son of a bitch if I run into him. I tell you what, if I do, I'll be sure to say hello to him for you."

The old man smiled, revealing only a few teeth. Longarm figured the man was close to fifty-five, maybe older. But he was nut-brown and as sturdy as a rock, nevertheless. He would most likely make it to his cabin without too much difficulty now, despite the wound in his leg.

"Well, say, I'd sure take some pleasure in that, deputy," the prospector said. "Yes I would. Even more if I could be on hand to see it."

Longarm handed Pike his canteen. "Here. Keep this. You'll need it in this country. I'll reach Antelope Junction soon enough, and then I'll be getting on a train for Salt Lake City."

"Much obliged," Pike said, taking the canteen.

Longarm swung onto his mount and settled back in his saddle to watch as the old man took a quick swig from the canteen, packed it away among the rest of his valuables atop the donkey, then moved off. When the prospector had gone a ways, he turned and waved to Longarm, as if to tell the lawman that he was all right now, that he wouldn't need any more help.

Longarm returned the wave, nudged the flanks of his mount, and headed once more for Antelope Junction. As he rode, he promised himself he would keep an eye out for that walleyed galoot that had treated Pike so poorly. But first things first. It was important that he wire Vail, just to make damned sure that that deputy hadn't turned up.

Longarm read the unusually long and expensive telegram from Vail a second time, then crumpled it up and flung it into the street.

According to Vail, Pete Baker was still missing, and the Washington office—not to mention Vail—was still pretty damned hot about it. Where was their operative, they wanted to know, and why was Longarm having such a difficult time tracking the man? Did Longarm want Vail to send Wallace?

Longarm looked grimly about him at the depressingly wide streets of Salt Lake City, and decided he needed a drink. He knew he could return to Quincy Boggs' palatial home and plunder to his heart's content the hidden wall bar in Quincy's library, but he was reluctant to go back at the moment. It was early in the afternoon and Quincy would still be away on business, leaving Audrey alone—and more than willing to entertain Longarm. So far she had been a welcome delight, but he was in need of a little less excitement.

What he really needed was a chance to do some thinking, to ponder his situation in some detail. If Pete Baker and that Pinkerton had not turned up, Vail was right: Longarm's mission was far from accomplished. But right now it appeared to be a damnably difficult mission Vail had given him; as far as Longarm could make out, the ground might just as well have opened up and swallowed the two officers.

Longarm shook his head in weary befuddlement, and started across the network of tracks toward a community that consisted mainly of crowded, weatherbeaten tenements—the only red-light district the Mormon community allowed in their tightly governed city.

Longarm was familiar with the area. And as he gained the sidewalk on the far side of the railyard, he remembered his last visit to this side of the tracks—the Utah House in particular, an establishment catering to several sorts of vices. His visit had been informative, despite some chancy gunplay.

The Utah House was gone now, he saw, undoubtedly as a result of the fearsome ruckus his presence—along with that of Amos Barker, member of the fearsome Avenging Angels—had brought down upon the sporting house. It had been replaced by a new establishment called—ironically, Longarm had no doubt—the Mormon's Rest.

Curious to see what changes had been made, Longarm mounted the front steps and pushed through the double door. He was greeted at once by a young black boy, resplendent in satin breeches and waistcoat. The silver buckle on his shoes gleamed brightly, almost as brightly as his teeth when he smiled and held out his hand for Longarm's hat.

Longarm returned the boy's smile, handed him his hat, and moved on past him into a large room, along the far wall of which stretched a magnificent mahogany bar. A long, single-piece mirror had been placed behind the bar. Above it had been hung the lush pink representation of Lady Godiva. She was, of course, stark naked, had long golden tresses strategically draped over her fullsome figure—and rode an equally robust white horse.

At this time of day, the Mormon's Rest was quiet. Longarm purchased a bottle of Maryland rye from the silent but impressively built barkeep, took it with him to a table in a corner, and slumped down. Dark maroon curtains separated the bar from another room farther in. From it came the click of rolling dice, and occasionally, as patrons passed from the gambling room into the bar, Longarm caught a fleeting glimpse of the green felt of gaming tables, glowing in the soft gaslight.

He poured himself a drink and sipped it, aware each time he used his left arm of the violence done to his shoulder by that maniacal homesteader. Audrey had changed the bandage that morning, making a swift and efficient job of it. After that, of course, she had insisted on his repaying her, a chore he had performed with gratitude. His thoughts went from Audrey to that homesteader's woman. If the homesteader had been a maniac, what would that make his wife? He shuddered slightly and gently massaged the still tender shoulder reflectively.

It wasn't only the homesteader and his wife that bothered him. Evidently the entire basin was being taken over by eastern grangers, each one more vicious and unfriendly than the one before. Not that he could blame them. This basin they were trying to build into productive ranches or farmland was a harsh, cruel, unforgiving land. Only the incredible energy and disciplined zeal of the Latter-Day Saints had been able to make anything of it, and they were not about to share their hard-won bounty with Gentiles. "Let the godless infidels build their own irrigation systems" was obviously their sentiment.

And that was not very damn likely. What Longarm had seen of these new settlers did not inspire much confidence. It was a miracle of sorts that they had even been able to build, let alone manage, ranch buildings and corrals. Their cattle seemed to be running as loose and as free as the stunted deer and rabbits that inhabited the place, with as little meat on their bones as those creatures of the wild. No wonder these Eastern tenderfoots took potshots at riders and old prospectors, and seemed unwilling even to share what little ground water they were able to capture. The thing was, Longarm could not see how these ranchers could survive unless they could bring in a lot more water. Even more important, he couldn't see why they would want to bother.

And then he recalled the prospector's bitter words: *They must be emptying out all the ratholes back East.*

But were they?

As Longarm thought back on the few hombres he had encountered in the basin, he realized how little resemblance they bore to genuine Eastern tenderfoots. Like most of those hardcases that crowded into that little pesthole, Antelope Junction, they assembled the worst and most vicious flotsom washed up by this harsh and lawless land. Most men who lived and prospered in the West now had come from the East originally, except for those few of Spanish descent who drifted east from California or migrated from Mexico. So these men building on their homesteads in the basin more likely came from the East, as well. But they did not strike Longarm as recent arrivals. They had been peering through alkali dust and drinking brackish water for a long time before settling in this grim basin. Of that he was almost certain.

So again, he found himself asking why. What was the attraction?

He sighed suddenly, weary at last of all this fruitless speculation. He needed facts—information, perhaps, on these Gentiles who were now settling in the basin in defiance of all good sense. A visit to the Bureau of Land Management would seem to be in order. It could not hurt to check out the homestead claims, at least. If they were indeed emptying out ratholes back East, it might help to find out which holes.

He got to his feet, pleased that he had settled finally on some line of action, and brought his bottle of rye back to the bar. He was turning away from the bar on his way out when a large, hefty individual pushed himself into the room, obviously intent on going through it to the gambling room in the back. Longarm recognized the man at once as Clinton Holloway.

Both men caught sight of each other at the same time. Longarm was about to greet the man courteously, but when he saw the startled look on Holloway's face, the words died in his throat. Holloway looked as if he had suddenly suffered a stroke.

Or just seen a ghost.

"Anything wrong, Holloway?" Longarm inquired.

"Why, deputy! What a pleasant surprise. Of course there's nothing wrong!" Though Holloway was obviously flustered at Longarm's blunt question, his recovery was swift. He smiled at Longarm with sudden warmth. "I was just surprised to see you in here. Last I knew, you were heading out after that no-good son of a bitch who murdered Marie."

"That's where I was heading, all right."

"Any luck?"

Longarm shook his head and started past Holloway.

But Holloway took Longarm's arm and steered him back toward the table he had just vacated. "Now just hold up, deputy," he protested. "There's no sense in you running off like that. Why not sit down and have a drink with me? I tell you, this Mormon town is enough to make a strong man weep."

"How so?" Longarm asked as he sat back down.

Slumping wearily into his seat, Holloway beckoned to the bartender, then turned to answer Longarm's query. "If you're not a Mormon, you're nothing in this city. I'm just a Gentile to these so-called Saints, and that means I get short shrift. It is very annoying." He winked suddenly and indicated with a nod the barkeep who was on his way over to their table. "Take a good look at this barkeep, deputy."

Longarm glanced up as the barkeep approached, a bottle

71

and two glasses in his powerful grasp. He looked tough and battle-scarred. He had broken his nose more than once. Setting the bottle and glasses down before them, the barkeep looked at Holloway. "I'll be through here tomorrow, Mr. Holloway. I gave my notice this afternoon."

"Excellent, Ned. We can take the afternoon train to Antelope Junction tomorrow. I'll see to your ticket."

"Thanks, Mr. Holloway."

"Thank you, Ned."

As the barkeep left them, Holloway picked up the bottle and poured their drinks. He favored an expensive Scotch that was not entirely to Longarm's taste, but the lawman had no intention of making an issue of it as he nodded his thanks to Holloway and drew his drink toward him.

"That's my new barkeep, Deputy," Holloway announced. "What do you think of him?"

"He's big enough."

"And tough enough, from what I hear."

"You better warn him about the danger of pointing sawed-off shotguns at federal deputies, though."

Holloway nodded ironically, saluted Longarm with his glass, and downed his drink. Longarm did likewise, watching Holloway closely. He wondered why the owner of the Lucky Seven had been so all-fired anxious to drag him over to this table. It couldn't have been to introduce him to his new barkeep. And why had Holloway been so startled at the sight of Longarm a moment ago?

"So," Holloway began, shifting somewhat nervously under Longarm's cool appraisal. "How did you do in your search for Marie's killer?"

"Not too good," Longarm admitted, absently massaging his sore left shoulder.

Holloway's eyes narrowed in apparent concern. "I see you've got a tender shoulder there. Any connection between that and the man you were tracking?"

"Not that I know of," Longarm replied.

"A fall from your horse, perhaps."

"I don't fall off horses, Holloway."

The big man shrugged. "You don't have to tell me if you don't want to, deputy. I was just showing concern. It's obvious you've got a bandage around your shoulder. Makes your coat ride high."

Longarm found Holloway's interest in his wounded shoulder

more than a little significant. "A crazy homesteader shot me," he said.

"A crazy homesteader?"

"That's right. I was riding into his yard to make some inquiries, and before I could get close enough to hail the ranch, he shot at me. Then he came out of the ranch to finish me off. He would have too, if his wife hadn't followed out after the loony bastard—and stabbed him."

"Stabbed him?"

"With a kitchen knife. In the back." Longarm noted with interest the sudden pallor that fell over Holloway's ruddy face. "After that," Longarm continued, carefully noting Holloway's reaction, "this sweet young granger's wife attempted to burn me while I slept. She doused kerosene over her husband and the rest of the ranch house, then set him and the place afire. I was lucky to escape with my life."

"My God, Longarm!" Holloway seemed genuinely appalled.

"Some woman, wouldn't you say?"

"It's hard to believe."

"Believe me or not, as you please."

"It's not that I don't believe you," Holloway explained, taking out his handkerchief and beginning to mop his brow. "It's just that . . . what you say sounds so bizarre. To think that a man's own wife could do such a thing! But why did her husband fire on you in the first place? Did the woman ever explain that?"

"I didn't have time to ask her. She did say one thing, however, something I found a mite strange."

"And what was that?"

"She denied the son of a bitch that shot me was her husband."

Holloway sat back quickly and poured himself another drink. He seemed shaken considerably by Longarm's tale. It was almost as if what he was hearing from Longarm contradicted something he thought he knew to be the truth. And that Longarm found very interesting.

"You seem all shook up, Holloway," Longarm commented. "You didn't happen to know these two homesteaders, did you?"

"Me?"

"Yes, you. Maybe they came into town on occasion for supplies."

"Describe the woman."

Longarm described her—and what little he remembered of her husband. Listening carefully with a frown on his face, Holloway shook his head finally. "I don't recall her or her husband. But there's a whole mess of these grangers and their wives moving in to settle this land, so there's no reason why I would."

Longarm leaned back in his chair. "Reckon not."

Holloway poured himself another drink and sipped it slowly. Then he folded his handkerchief carefully and put it back in his pocket. He had calmed himself down and was making a good show of looking casual. Clearing his throat, he smiled across the table at Longarm. "Where are you headed now, deputy?"

Longarm shrugged. "Guess I'll poke around some more. That federal deputy and the Pinkerton ain't turned up yet, so I still got a job to do."

Holloway nodded and finished his drink. Slapping the empty glass down on the table, he got to his feet and held out his hand to Longarm. "Good luck to you, deputy," he said as he shook Longarm's hand warmly. "I'm certainly glad you survived your recent adventures intact."

"Thanks. And where are you off to?"

"I have a dinner engagement not too long from now, with a very lovely woman." He smiled broadly, his bluff assurance returning. "She thinks she is the equal of any man, and I intend to show her differently. A real challenge, Longarm—and a formidable beauty."

"Well, good luck to you, then."

"By the way, deputy, at which hotel are you staying? We might be able to get together later this evening for a drink."

"I'm staying with Quincy Boggs."

"Boggs? Isn't he a member of the First Council of Seventy?"

"That he is."

"You move in exalted circles. Perhaps I might prevail on your good offices in the future. Having someone like Quincy Boggs on my side might prove advantageous."

"It would, I suppose—as long as whatever you have in mind is legitimate."

"But of course," Holloway said, his eyes suddenly wary. "What else could I have in mind?"

"In that case, I'd be glad to introduce you."

"I'd appreciate that, deputy," Holloway said. He nodded

74

briskly, turned, and strode from the place. And that was odd, Longarm reflected. He was almost certain that when Holloway entered earlier, he had been bent on going into the gaming room on the other side of the maroon drapes.

His meeting with Longarm seemed to have changed his mind.

Chapter 7

Longarm was correct. Holloway's sudden, unexpected meeting with Longarm had changed his mind. All thought of gambling away the afternoon before he met with Laraine Grover had vanished the instant he clapped eyes on the tall lawman.

Now, as he strode angrily down the street, what he felt was quite close to a wild, ungovernable fury. Two of his hirelings had lied to him. He did not like that. It was dangerous. Only incredible good luck had brought him into contact with the deputy U.S. marshal this afternoon, and with it an awareness of his danger.

Arriving at the entrance to a dingy hotel, Holloway entered the small lobby and moved swiftly up the narrow stairs and down an unlighted corridor. He paused momentarily before a door, knocked briefly, then pushed his way in.

Weed Leeper—the clean-shaven Weed, who had reverted to his real name, Mike Snefflin—was lying fully clothed on the mussed bed, reading something by Ned Buntline. He came alert when he saw the look on Holloway's face, and sat up.

Holloway slammed the door shut behind him. "Where's Tracy? Where's that lying bitch?"

Weed frowned. "Beats the shit out of me. She's been gone since morning. What's wrong?"

"I just had a drink with that deputy U.S. marshal—Custis Long."

Weed sat up on the bed. "You *what*? He's dead! Tracy killed him."

Holloway smiled thinly. "Very good. You almost convinced me."

"What the hell is that supposed to mean?"

"You knew that Tracy was lying—that she was the one who killed Smiley."

"*She* killed Smiley?"

"That's right."

Holloway looked closely at Weed. The man's pale, mottled face had screwed into a sly wonderment. He appeared to be truly surprised at this news. He scratched his head. "I guess that ain't so hard to believe, at that," he said. "How'd she do it?"

"With a kitchen knife. In the back."

Weed nodded, a small smile lighting his face. He shook his head. "I guess she just got tired of him beatin' on her. I warned the poor son of a bitch about that. Tracy's got a fierce temper, she purely has."

The door behind them opened. Tracy walked in, saw the two of them, and frowned. She was dressed in a long, pale dress with crimson lace at her throat. Her lustrous black hair was gathered in a tight bun under her pink, wide-brimmed hat. The parasol she was carrying was somewhat frayed around the edges, but all in all, she looked quite smart for a streetwalker. Holloway had no doubt that that was what she had been doing. She had never made any secret of the fact that she regarded the average Mormon as easy pickings for a woman of her talents.

Almost as if she could read Holloway's mind, she looked quickly away from the man's face and busied herself closing her parasol.

"How was business?" Weed asked.

By way of an answer, she dropped her purse on the bed beside him. "Good enough to get us out of this fleatrap," she snapped, glancing poisonously at Holloway as she did so.

"I just met the man that you say killed Smiley," Holloway told her.

She spun on him, her face suddenly pale. Quickly she glanced toward Weed, frowning. "What the hell's he mean? What are you two up to?"

78

"It's what you're up to that matters now," replied Holloway. "I just got the whole story from Deputy Long. You killed Smiley. Stabbed him in the back, then set fire to the ranch, after dousing Smiley with kerosene. You left both the deputy marshal and Smiley to burn. Smiley burned, all right. But the marshal escaped."

The tip of her pink tongue snaked out to moisten her suddenly dry lips. "Shit," she said softly, almost delicately. "I never thought that big son of a bitch was going to wake up again. He was hurt bad. Smiley shot him in the shoulder and he was bleeding like a stuck pig."

"Well, he did wake up. And now he's on the prowl once more, sniffing around, trying to put this all together."

"Let me take care of him," said Weed.

"No, dammit! Taking care of that other deputy and the Pinkerton is what brought this one prowling. And there's more where he came from! Don't you have any sense?"

"I'm as smart as you are, you son of a bitch," said Weed softly.

Holloway felt the menace of Weed's words slicing like a knife into his gut. He took a deep breath and held his temper. Like the others, Weed would get his comeuppance, but all in good time. All in good time.

"I'm sending you both back to that burnt-out homestead. I've arranged it so the claim is in your name. I need that property. Fix up the buildings and there'll be a sizable bonus in it—for both of you."

"I want to stay here," Tracy said.

"You'll do as I say, or I'll turn you in to the deputy marshal."

"You son of a bitch."

Holloway slapped her. She spun all the way around, reached out for the brass bedstead, and missed. Rubbing her cheeks, she looked up at him from the floor, tears of rage streaming from her eyes. "You wouldn't dare hit Weed," she taunted him. "You're another Smiley."

"You'll do as I say. You don't have to like it. Just do it. I'm paying you well."

"I hate it out there!"

"It won't be for long."

"A *day* is too long."

Holloway turned to Weed. "Take her with you. She's your wife now. Mr. and Mrs. Michael Snefflin. Just don't turn your back on her."

"This deputy," Weed said, his eyes narrowing. "He's still looking for me, ain't he? For the killing of that little bitch, Marie."

"Yes he is. He is a man who does not soon forget such things, I imagine."

"Is he staying at your hotel? Is that where you met him?"

"No. He's staying with a friend in Salt Lake City. A very influential friend, I might add. Quincy Boggs. That's why I want you to steer clear of him for now. His murder would bring down upon us not only more deputy marshals from Washington, but also these damn Mormons. So far, they've left us pretty much alone. And that's how I want things to remain. Is that clear, Weed?"

"I'll need some money," Weed said by way of reply. "That cabin was burnt to the ground."

Reluctantly, Holloway reached for his silver pouch. He knew Weed had him over a barrel for the moment and was accordingly gouging him. But he did not see that he had any alternative. He had to get these two away from Salt Lake City before that confounded lawman stumbled upon them and apprehended them. If that were to happen, he had no confidence at all that Weed and Tracy would remain silent.

"Take what you need, Weed," Holloway said. "Just don't be greedy."

"Don't worry," said Weed, grinning up at the man. "I'm not going to make the goose that lays all these golden eggs unhappy—just a mite poorer is all."

A moment later, after retrieving the pouch from Weed, he glanced at his pocket watch. He had just enough time to meet Laraine, he realized. With a single, withering glance at Tracy—who had pulled herself back up onto her feet by this time—he turned and left the room.

The bespectacled clerk waiting on Longarm in the Bureau of Land Management seemed somewhat nervous, but Longarm figured this was due to the way he towered over the little man and the fact that he had introduced himself as a deputy U.S. marshal. The clerk's name was Fred Tillot, and he favored the petty bureaucrat's inevitable green eyeshade. He seemed genuinely anxious to please, however, as he scurried about, producing the huge ledgers in answer to Longarm's queries.

At last the clerk cleared his throat and readjusted his eye

shade. "Maybe if you told me what it was you were looking for, deputy, I might be able to find what you want."

Longarm looked down at the man. "Tillot, if I knew what I was looking for, I'd tell you, sure enough. But maybe I could ask you a question. Do you have any idea why so many damn fool Easterners are trying to homestead on this basin land?"

"Why, deputy, I been wondering on that since I first come out West, and that's a fact. I've seen the damn fools come out here and dig up the land and turn good pasture or farmland into gullied washouts, then move on to plunder more land. I long since stopped asking myself why. Besides, it's working. The government wants the West settled, and that's exactly what it's getting. It doesn't matter by who or how, just so we get live bodies on this here land so we can claim it for Uncle Sam."

Longarm was somewhat amused by the clerk's extended response to his question. He nodded sagely to what the man had said before asking, "Are you sure there were no rumors of gold—or silver—somewhere out there on that basin land?"

"None that I know of."

"Maybe someone has tapped a deep artesian well—or maybe the Mormons have decided to expand their irrigation system to include the entire basin."

"Sure haven't heard of anything like that. Neither one seems very likely. No, sir. Not a bit of it."

"Then you have no idea at all why these Easterners are flocking in here."

"Didn't say that."

"So what's your guess?"

"Never underestimate the obstinacy of an ass."

Longarm nodded. "Guess maybe that's the answer, all right." He pointed down to the ledger and the deed entry the clerk had just brought to him. Longarm was pretty sure this was the same section that insane homesteader and his wife had staked out. "You remember anything about this couple? Walter and Tracy Hannon?"

The clerk adjusted his glasses and peered closely down at the scrawled signatures. He seemed to come alive at once. "Well, sir," he said, "I don't recollect much about the mister, but his missus sure made an impression on me."

"Can you describe her?"

"Sure can. Coal-black hair. Nice heft to her, and she carried herself like she knowed it. High cheekbones, cat's eyes."

Longarm nodded. That was the girl, all right.

"I could tell that husband of hers didn't much appreciate her. Seemed like he was always yellin' at her. Imagine he might have slapped her around some now and then. But he'd best watch it, I'm thinking. She was a real spitfire. I could tell that from the look in her eyes."

"It won't do any good to warn her husband now."

"How's that, deputy?"

"She killed him."

The man gasped. "Surely you jest!"

"I'm not making any jokes, Tillot. She damn near fried me at the same time."

Shaken, the clerk looked down again at the ledger and shook his head.

"I want you to keep an eye on this deed," Longarm told him. "I want to know if anyone reclaims this section. I want to know if no one reclaims it. You got that?"

The clerk nodded. "All right, deputy. I'll do that."

"Are you the only one who works here?"

"I have an assistant. He's not here today."

"Tell him the same thing. I'll be in directly to check this out."

Again the clerk nodded.

Longarm started from the office. As he pulled open the door, he glanced back and saw the clerk still staring down at his ledger. The man was obviously remembering what Longarm had told him about Tracy Hannon. Good. The clerk would not soon forget the circumstances surrounding any claims on that deed. It wasn't much, and he still didn't know what he was looking for, but it was something.

When he left the Land Management office, Longarm didn't have far to go; he simply crossed the hall to the office of the local geological survey. Once he was through the frosted-glass door, he found his way blocked by a high counter, behind which stood a tall, very beautiful woman, despite an obvious attempt on her part not to appear so.

Her dark red hair was kept in a severe, tight bun on the back of her head; her hazel eyes took Longarm in coolly, appraising him seemingly without emotion. She wore no face powder or rouge, and across her lean, shiny-clean cheekbones, he saw a sprinkling of freckles. She was dressed in a bottle-green dress with lace at her throat and wrists. Her waist was incredibly slim, the swell of her bust somewhat unnerving.

"Yes?" she asked, putting down the file she had been about to lock away, and turning to approach the counter.

Longarm introduced himself and showed her his badge. She told him her name was Laraine Grover.

"What crime have I committed, Deputy?"

"None." He smiled. "None I know of anyway."

"That's a relief," she said. Her eyes were disconcertingly cool. She seemed determined not to be impressed by Longarm. "How can I help you?"

"You can tell me if the survey has revealed any interesting deposits of minerals—gold, silver, copper—out on that basin to the west of Antelope Junction."

Her thin, finely traced eyebrows went up a notch. "On that basin?" She smiled. "Alkali, marshal, and plenty of salt. That's all, I assure you. Are you thinking of prospecting?"

"As a matter of fact, Miss Grover, I did meet a prospector out there. But he didn't seem to be having any luck."

"I wouldn't think so. You'd be doing the man a kindness if you told him to forget his fruitless quest. There are no fortunes to be made in that basin, I assure you."

"Would you mind if I looked over your survey map?"

She went over to the gate, pulled it back for him, and stepped aside as Longarm walked through. "Follow me, marshal. You may see for yourself."

He followed behind her splendid figure as she led him into a back room featuring a single large window that looked out over the courtyard. Sunshine poured into the room and over a large table, upon which a large map of the entire basin, including portions of the Great Salt Lake Desert, had been tacked. Leaning over the map, Longarm noted a faint scattering of symbols indicating the locations of various mineral deposits. There were indications of traces of gold and some silver, even iron and copper—but all at such low concentrations that there was no doubt in his mind that the woman was correct.

Turning to her, he smiled. "You're right. Not that I doubted you."

"You had no reason to Marshal Long," she said, returning his smile coldly. "I am a fully trained and qualified geologist."

"That so?"

"I graduated from Yale four years ago. Geology has been my hobby since I was a little girl."

Longarm was aware that she expected him to be surprised at this, so he did not fail her. "Isn't that a mite unusual for a little girl?"

"Perhaps," she said, a little defiantly, her lovely chin jutting out slightly. "I suppose you are one of those who feel the only proper roles for women are as housewife and mothers. Perhaps you do not feel we should even be allowed to vote."

Logarm grinned at her. "Why, sure, ma'am, if that's really what women want."

"You are very condescending, marshal. You don't really believe men and women should be equal before the law—as they are before God."

"Why, ma'am, I believe a woman is equal to any man— and can more than likely do as well at most things."

"Do you, now?" It was clear she did not believe him.

"Of course I do. I figure it's all up to the woman, though. I just don't figure you women should always blame us whenever you get tired of washing diapers and men's underpants. Near as I can figure, a woman who knows her mind is free enough to do what she wants—and usually will. The rest of the women will be content to hide behind their skirts."

Longarm had spoken indelicately to get her reaction, and was not disappointed. At his mention of men's undergarments, her face had gone crimson. She was determined not to be sidetracked, however. She pulled herself up to her full height, which brought her lovely hazel eyes almost on a level with his. "That is not very fair, marshal—accusing women of cowardice, of hiding behind their skirts."

"I wouldn't say they're cowards, ma'am—just sensible. Besides, most women will find their men right alongside them, behind the same skirts."

She laughed, despite herself.

"I must say, for a lawman you talk with a good deal of sense."

"Now who's being condescending, ma'am?"

Again she blushed. "Forgive me, marshal. You are right, of course."

"My friends call me Longarm."

"And mine call me Laraine," she said, turning and leading him back out of the room and into the outer office.

"Maybe we could continue this discussion at dinner, Laraine," Longarm said, as he snugged his hat down securely and pushed himself through the gate.

"Thank you, Longarm. I am sure I would enjoy that. But unfortunately I have another engagement for this evening."

"Well now, there are several more evenings in this week, if I'm not mistaken."

She laughed, but before she could reply, the door opened and Clint Holloway stepped into the office.

"My word, deputy!" the man exclaimed. "Are you by any chance following me?"

"You're the one keeps walking in on *me*," Longarm replied.

"Certainly you remember my telling you I had an important dinner engagement this evening. Well, this is the lady."

Longarm looked at Laraine Grover and grinned. "Now that you mention it, I do remember. And you are right. She is a most formidable beauty."

Longarm touched the brim of his hat to Laraine Grover, who was blushing once again, and moved past Holloway out of the office. He had not taken too many steps down the hallway, however, before he pulled up suddenly, a frown on his face.

Was it coincidence alone that had brought Clinton Holloway and Longarm together in the office of a lovely woman geologist?

Longarm paid the hackie; as the driver cracked his whip and pulled his horse around in the dark, narrow street, the lawman took out a cheroot. He had some difficulty lighting up in the sudden night breeze that had sprung up. Then, puffing contentedly, he started up the walk to the entrance to Quincy Boggs' residence. He wondered suddenly if it would not be a good idea for him to take Boggs and Audrey out to dinner as payment for their hospitality and warmth—Audrey's especially—not that it could ever really be enough to repay either of them.

As he approached the doorway, a woman appeared from the shadows beside it. He paused, astonished. He recognized the woman. Tracy Hannon. And in her hand she held a small revolver. Before he could react, he heard quick footsteps behind him and felt the muzzle of a revolver being thrust brutally into his back.

"Don't go reachin' for nothin, deputy," a man's voice told him. "Just turn around nice and quiet-like and head back down this walk." To emphasize his words, the man dug the muzzle still deeper into the small of Longarm's back.

Longarm turned about and moved ahead of the man back to the street. Once they reached the sidewalk, the man pushed him roughly to his right and Longarm caught sight of a carriage pulled up under a tree farther down the street. He started to turn about to get a glimpse of the man behind him, but the jasper shoved his gun barrel into Longarm's back with such force that Longarm was sent stumbling and almost lost his footing.

The girl had darted ahead of them in the darkness and was inside the closed carriage, holding the door open for them. As Longarm ducked his head to enter the carriage, she reached out to pull him in. He started to say something to her—but the man getting in behind him brought the barrel of his gun crashing down upon Longarm's skull.

He was unconscious before he sprawled forward into the woman's lap.

Chapter 8

With a curse, Longarm turned and yanked on the chain. It had caught on a beam. Grimly, he yanked on the chain again. This time it broke loose with such suddenness that he was flung awkwardly back. He sat down heavily in the midst of the charred rubble.

Tracy's laughter came from behind him. He picked himself up and turned to face her. "If you'd take off these damn manacles, I could get this job done in less time."

"Sure you could. But I like to see such a big man in chains. It gives me all kinds of ideas."

Tracy was still in the same pale dress she had been wearing when she and her new husband had shanghaied Longarm four days earlier. It was filthy now, and there were at least two long rents in the skirt. Because of the heat, she wore nothing under it, and Longarm could see portions of her bare thigh as she moved. Her unpinned hair spilled down loosely about her shoulders. Her face and neck were dirty, and pieces of straw were sticking out of her hair. She was a mess. But Longarm had no doubt that he looked considerably worse.

Since arriving at the burnt-out homestead, the three of them had been sleeping and living in the barn; and because of his chains, Longarm had been unable to wash.

The woman had come out to check on his progress. Her confederate, a man who called himself Mike Snefflin—the same one, Longarm realized now, who had raped and murdered Marie—had left yesterday for Antelope Junction to get supplies and building materials. The two of them had argued for most of the previous morning about Mike's trip into Antelope Junction. Tracy had wanted to go along, but Mike had insisted she stay behind to keep an eye on Longarm. Tracy had tried to get him to chain Longarm to a barnpole, leaving water and some food close behind him. But to Longarm's considerable relief, Mike had prevailed. Longarm still had more than enough work to do, Mike insisted.

And Mike had not been talking idly, Longarm realized gloomily as he glanced about him. Only the fireplace and chimney were still intact. The roof and most of the walls had collapsed inward on the fire Tracy had set, helping to extinguish it, it appeared—but not before the damage to the ranch building had been almost total. Since he had been brought to this place, Longarm had been shoveling out charred shingles and other debris. Now he had the five massive roofbeams to drag out into the yard.

"You ain't done much this morning," Tracy said. "What's the matter with you? A big man like you should have got that all cleared out by now."

"Lend me a hand, why don't you?" said Longarm.

"Sure."

She turned and walked back across the blistering yard to the barn, the bottle of whiskey held loosely in her hand. She tipped the bottle up to her lips a moment before disappearing into the barn's cool, shadowy interior. With another curse, Longarm bent to get a firmer grip on the beam he had been in the act of dragging out into the yard when his chain had tripped him up.

Using his head this time, he wrapped the long chain about the end of the beam, flung the chain back over his shoulder, and bending well forward, he began to drag the beam out. He was almost to the yard when his left boot broke through a rotted floorboard, flinging him forward. The beam dug him viciously in the rear as he went down.

Wearily, cursing silently, he picked himself up carefully and pulled his left foot out of the hole in the floorboard.

When he had regained consciousness four days earlier, he

had found himself slung over the pommel of a saddle, Mike Snefflin grinning down at him. The sun, as Longarm recalled, was a fearsome eye that had been boring a hole in the back of his neck. When he tried to get loose, he found that the heavy chain that still encumbered him had been wrapped about his long body several times, making any movement of his limbs virtually impossible.

The first thing he had asked for had been water. He might as well have asked for the moon.

"There ain't no water for you, you big son of a bitch," Snefflin had laughed, a mean smile on his curiously raw face.

Longarm had realized then how futile any argument with this man would be; and during the rest of that miserable ride, he had had to endure the excruciating agony of knowing that resting only inches from his burning cheek was Snefflin's canvas-covered canteen. Longarm could smell the moisture seeping through the canvas. In his fevered imagination he could feel the metallic neck of the canteen resting on his lips and taste the cool water running past it into his parched mouth.

But there had been no water until he reached the burnt-out homestead. Snefflin had dumped him unceremoniously in the barn, then locked Longarm's shackles to one of the barn's two main support beams, after which he had ridden away in the direction of Antelope Junction, to return late the next day with Tracy astride an unhappy nag that appeared all but ready to give out.

The horse had since wandered off to die in the scrub, and that was what Longarm had felt like doing more than once. What kept him silently diligent, despite the lack of water and decent nourishment, was the hope of eventually settling accounts with these two. This desire was what kept him going. He knew that one or the other of them would make a mistake before long. It was not in the nature of these two to do anything well or with consistency.

Already Tracy, taking out her disappointment at not being able to ride back to Antelope Junction with Snefflin, was well on her way to becoming very, very drunk. Thinking of this gave Longarm a new burst of energy. Free of the treacherous floorboard, he dragged the beam out of the blackened shell and well into the yard.

Straightening up wearily, he saw Tracy coming toward him. He was disappointed to see how steadily she walked. At the rate she had been drinking Snefflin's whiskey, she should have been barely able to walk. He thought with some irony, then, of his conversation with Laraine Grover. Hadn't he told her that a woman was equal to a man in some things? Yes he had. And the way this Tracy could carry her liquor was sure as hell a case in point.

She pulled up in front of him, her once-provocative beauty almost completely obliterated by her slatternly appearance. The only clean things about her were the whites of her wide, half-mad eyes. She flung her stringy hair out of her eyes suddenly and leaned close to him.

"Like something to drink, would you?" she demanded, her face twisted into an unlovely leer.

"I would," Longarm admitted.

She straightened triumphantly and with such violence that for a moment Longarm thought she was going to fall over backward. She was not entirely sober, it appeared. "You'll have to earn it then," she told him.

He pointed mildly to the beam he had just dragged from the ranch house. "Isn't that enough for you?"

"No," she said. "That's not enough."

Longarm's shackles were locked securely about both wrists. The chains were exceedingly heavy, and at least a couple of yards in length. It was as if he had two heavy coils of jump rope attached to his hands. The best way he had found to proceed was to gather up the heavy links and carry them about with him. He had considered the possibility of running off with them, since his legs remained unshackled, but it would have been an impossible task in this miserable country, carrying such weight with little or no water available and no way to secure any game. In fact, Longarm was pretty certain that neither of them would have minded if he had attempted such a foolhardy move. They knew—as he did—what the odds of his escaping would be.

But Longarm was also aware of what a weapon his heavy jump rope could be—under the right circumstances.

Now, with Tracy so close, he found himself considering a move. This was the best opportunity he had yet been given; and with Snefflin gone, his chance of success was better than even. Carefully he closed his fingers about the heavy links resting against his palm.

"If that's not enough," he told her. "What do I have to do?

I haven't had anything to drink for at least an hour."

"Oh, that's too bad," she said. "But I'll let you have all you want—if you do what I say."

Longarm frowned. "What is it you want?"

She turned abruptly and strode away from him, back toward the barn. "Follow me," she told him. "And hurry up. It's too damn hot out here." She glanced provocatively back at him over her shoulder. "We can talk in here—where it's cool."

Longarm groaned inwardly. That single glance had told him precisely what Tracy had in mind.

She stopped in front of the barn and turned impatiently. "Hurry up," she said. "Unless you'd rather fry out here in this damn sun. There's a whole barrel of spring water in here."

With a resigned shrug, Longarm followed after her.

The barn's cool interior was a welcome relief, the pungent smell of the hay almost intoxicating. And then he spied the water barrel against the wall, a long-handled dipper hanging on a nail beside it. He hurried toward the barrel, plunged the dipper deep into the water, and quenched his thirst slowly, carefully, allowing the icy water to trickle down his chin and across his bare chest.

With the heavy links scratching at his neck, he finished up by pouring a dipper full of water over his steaming head. Then he replaced the dipper and turned to face Tracy.

She had stepped out of her dress and was watching him hungrily, the bottle still in her fist. The bottle was all she was wearing.

"Come here," she said. "Show me how much you appreciate my kindness."

"Is that what I have to do to earn that drink?"

"Yes."

"I've already had the drink. You should have made me wait."

"You refuse?"

Longarm nodded.

She blinked uncomprehendingly. "You don't want me?"

"It ain't that," he lied. "I'm too tired. I'm not in the mood, you might say. A man has to have . . . certain conditions, if you know what I mean."

She smiled. "Oh, is that all?"

Longarm nodded. "I'm right pleased you understand, Tracy."

She laughed—a low, seductive chuckle that caused the hair on the back of his neck to prickle. "I know how to take care of that," she told him, taking a step toward him. "You'd be surprised at the old men I have been able to get to rise to the occasion."

Longarm shrugged, tightened his hands once again about the chain links, and started toward her. She was, it appeared, going to make it easy for him. But she halted a good three feet from him.

"Look at me," she said. "This is all yours. Not many men get to see a woman naked—stark naked. I've seen some men go wild at the sight. One old miner broke down and cried. Damned if he didn't. Ain't you goin' to show your appreciation at such a sight?"

"Like I said, Tracy, I'm having a little trouble getting into the mood."

"Follow me," she told him, walking to his right and coming to a halt in front of an empty stall.

He saw that she had already placed fresh hay in it. As he approached it, she stepped out of his way and pointed to a beam that was nailed to the side of the stall.

"Loop that chain of yours over that beam," she told him. "Then lie face down in that hay."

Frowning, he said, "What the hell you got in mind, Tracy?"

She reached behind her and pulled a bullwhip out of a corner. "Never you mind what I got in mind. You'll find that out soon enough. Now do as I say, damm it."

Grabbing his chain, he hefted it a moment, gauging the distance between them. Tracy's eyes gleamed, and a tight smile creased her sweat-streaked face. She took a single step back and brought up the whip. "Don't do it, deputy. I'll cut that big, dumb, handsome face of yours to ribbons with this whip."

Longarm looped the chain over the beam and then lay carefully down in the hay. At once, Tracy knelt beside him. She took both his wrists and yanked them down the length of his body. "I want these two hands of yours behind your back," she told him, grunting from the exertion.

"All right, dammit. Let me," Longarm told her.

He drew up his knees and passed the loop of the chain under her feet, then straightened so that he was lying facedown in the hay with his manacled wrists resting on his buttocks.

"That's fine," Tracy said. "Now roll over, you great big handsome son of a bitch."

Longarm rolled over.

She was on her knees beside him, the bottle once again in her fist. She tipped the bottle up and drank greedily, then flung the near-empty bottle away. Longarm heard it shatter against a stall. A wild smile on her face, she leaned over him so that the hard, thrusting nipples of her breasts were inches from his face.

"Take them," she said huskily. "Take them nipples and suck them, deputy. Like a babe sucks at his ma's tits. Do it, damn you."

He did the best he could, seeing that he had only one mouth and she had two oversized nipples. She got so excited and leaned on him so heavily he thought for a moment he was going to smother under the overwhelming fullness of her breasts. The rank absurdity of such an eventuality acted as a prod. Heaving mightily, he swung his face away from her and tried to bring his manacled hands out from under him.

She pulled back and slapped him smartly on his right cheek; the force of it caused his eyes to sting. "Be good," she told him. "Keep those hands of yours behind you, you hear?"

"Well, dammit, woman. Give me a chance to breathe, less'n you've got a hankering to screw a dead man."

"I ain't tried that yet, deputy. But maybe I will, and maybe you'll be my first one." Then her face softened and she bent and kissed him on the lips, impudently, her tongue thrusting hungrily, provokingly into his mouth. He had an urge to clamp down viciously and chop the hot, wriggling thing in two. As she kissed, her hand unbuttoned his fly, reached in, and fumbled eagerly with his cock. After a moment she stopped kissing him and sat back, distinctly annoyed.

His cock was no bigger than when she started on him.

"I told you," he said laconically. "A man has to have certain conditons."

She took a deep, exasperated breath. "You sound like a girl, for Christ's sake."

Longarm smiled. "I think I got a headache."

"No you ain't," she told him grimly. "But you will, if you don't get in the mood pretty damn soon."

"You get me frightened, and I'm just liable to shrivel right up to nothing."

"I know what's the matter," she told him, after studying the situation for a moment. It was like she was a small kid that had been puzzling over a problem in arithmetic. At once she finished unbuttoning his fly. Swiftly she peeled his britches down, and after that his underwear. Yanking off his boots in a fury of impatience, she pulled his clothes off and flung them away.

Before he could pull away she flung her mouth down upon him, swallowing his defenseless penis. He felt his manhood shriveling away from her frantic lips, growing even smaller. With an angry cry, she grabbed his balls in both her hands and began to squeeze. At once Longarm came to attention. With an unhappy but not altogether unwilling sigh, he let her have her way with him.

"Ah!" she cried triumphantly a few moments later, just as he felt it building in him and his hips began to tremble. She pulled her educated mouth away from his erection and flung herself on top of him. For a terrible moment he was afraid her angle was too sharp, that she was going to break the damn thing off. He had heard of such awful accidents. In some cases, it was rumored, the man spent the rest of his miserable life with a bent cock, looking for a woman with a similar problem.

And then she had him inside her and he could feel her contracting around him, tightening on his erection like an angry fist.

"Oh, damn you!" she cried, flinging her head back. "I knew you had the biggest one of all. I could tell by those big hands of yours!"

He could feel the tip of his cock pressing against something hard deep within her, and knew he had touched bottom. He suddenly wished he could use his hands. He wanted to grab her bony hips and grind her down still harder upon him. After holding back all that while, he now found himself almost as wild as the woman atop him.

But Tracy didn't need his help. She was moving wildly yet carefully, with amazing vigor, as she leaned over him, swinging her still-erect nipples across his face. "Take them!" she shouted fiercely. "Take them, damn you!"

Obediently he snapped at one of her enormous nipples and closed his mouth about it. He tried to hurt her, to swing it wildly, like a puppy worrying a length of jerky. But it only made her wilder. She began flinging her head back and forth, the wild black spray of her hair at times blocking out her straining features.

With a sudden, keening cry, she came—and continued to come. He came as well, his loins seeming to explode under her. Again he wished he had the use of his hands, and for the first time he realized how stiff they were getting, manacled together and forced to support the weight of both of them.

He tried to pull away.

"Don't!" she told him. "Don't you move an inch. Just let it soak inside me. If you get out, it'll be like pullin' the plug. Besides, you're still nice and hard. Mmm! There certainly is a lot of you."

Longarm wondered where he had heard that one before, and blinked unhappily up at her. "You goin' to let me get on top of you?"

"Wouldn't be safe," she said, smiling and tightening the muscles of her vagina around his cock. He almost cried out.

"Then get to it," he told her. "My arms are getting mighty sore, trussed up behind this way."

"We'll just stay like we are," she told him. "If you knew how many times I've been on the bottom during this short lifetime, you'd understand my wanting to turn the tables now. I must say, it's brought back all my old enthusiasm—somethin' I'd thought wasn't never going to return."

She leaned forward and kissed him hard on the mouth, her lips prying his aside. In spite of himself, he began to react a second time. She wrapped her legs around under his buttocks, then pulled his torso up and forward a little to give his arms some relief—and all the while her pulsing, thrusting pelvis was working on him, building him to another climax.

Her lips still on his, she came again—and again. She was coiled about him, battened to him like some huge, unholy leech as she climaxed almost continuously. At last, with a suddering groan, she rolled off and lay beside him, her eyes closed, her face slack. The liquor hadn't gotten to her, but his cock sure as hell had.

He scrambled to his feet, bent swiftly, and skipped over his chains. Then he lifted his shackles from around the post. Her eyes opening suddenly, she saw what he was doing and rolled swiftly out of the stall, snatching up her bullwhip as she moved.

She was on her feet, crouched like a cat, her pendulous, gleaming breasts swinging. The bullwhip whistled through the air, its tips coiling about Longarm's shoulder with a stinging whack that exploded in the dust-laden air of the barn with the force of a gunshot.

Wincing from the cruel lash, Longarm flung his chains up, intercepting the lash as Tracy drew it back again. The tip of the whip became entangled in one of the chain's links. She tugged frantically, but Longarm swiftly grabbed the chain and yanked, ripping the whip from Tracy's hands.

With a furious, angry cry of rage, Tracy darted for the corner of the barn where she and Mike slept. And where their guns were cached. Longarm grabbed the handle of the whip, coiled it expertly, then sent it snapping after her, despite the weight of his shackles. The whip coiled about one of her ankles. She sprawled facedown, her naked form sliding across the straw-strewn floor. He could not have been surprised to learn that she'd picked up a few splinters along the way.

He raced closer, and when she tried to get up, he snaked the whip at her again, this time catching her about the waist. She shrieked in pain and tried to crawl away from him.

"That's the way, deputy! Go to it! Give the bitch a lesson!"

Longarm spun to see Snefflin standing in the barn doorway, his big Colt out and leveled on him.

"She was after you, was she? I'll bet she got what she wanted, too! Now it's her turn to pay, eh?"

Longarm was momentarily confused. If Snefflin was serious, it meant he would allow him to punish Tracy. For now, that is. But what would Snefflin do to Longarm afterward, when Tracy demanded that Longarm be punished? Tracy was his confederate and ally. Snefflin could not allow himself to become totally estranged from her.

"Go ahead," said Snefflin. "What's the matter? You were doing fine there."

"I think she's had enough."

"Do you now?"

"Yes."

"Well, I don't. There's a bottle of my whiskey over there, broken. She's been into my private stock, she has, and I told her about that."

Longarm straightened. "All right, then. Here. Take this whip and finish the job yourself."

Snefflin hesitated, then holstered his Colt and started into the barn. Longarm heard Tracy curse, but paid it no mind. Behind Snefflin, and moving fast for an old man, was the wounded prospector Longarm had met more than a week before. In his hand he held an ancient but well-kept Walker Colt.

Pike had been watching the burnt-out homestead for most of the morning. At first he could hardly believe what he was seeing—that fine gentlemen of a U.S. deputy in chains and being forced to clean out that burnt shell of a ranch house.

Then he saw the woman and the way she was acting. He left his mule behind and crept closer when he saw her come after the deputy and invite him into the barn. There was no doubt in Pike's mind what the she-devil was up to, or that the poor, worn-out deputy was going to have to find some inspiration of a sort to satisfy her.

He was still outside the barn, moving closer, when he heard the sound of thrashing inside, after which came the sharp crack of the whip, followed a moment later by the woman's cry of anger and outrage. He was about to rush the barn when he heard behind him the sound of approaching hoofbeats. He ducked down behind an abandoned farm wagon and waited.

But he was waiting no longer. It was obvious now that this deputy had just about turned the tables on that she-devil when this newcomer with the drawn sixgun showed up to set matters right.

He heard the taunting words of this fellow, therefore, with some confusion as he straightened up and started to move as softly as possible along the edge of the barn toward the open doorway. The newcomer was telling the deputy to go on whipping the woman. He sure as hell was angry about something.

Of course. After all, he had just come upon his woman fooling with the deputy, hadn't he? But now the deputy was right smack in the middle. Pike knew he had to do something, and he was glad he was on hand to do it.

There wasn't any gold in this blasted hellhole, and a little action like this was bound to liven things up some. Hell, he might even get a glimpse of a naked woman. Been a long time since his eyes had clapped onto a sight as good as that.

He reached the doorway a moment after the fellow with the gun stepped into the barn, and saw the deputy, the chains still on him and the whip in his hand, about to give the whip to the new arrival. Then his eyes saw the woman coiled up on the floor before them. Pike almost swallowed his chaw of tobacco. She was plumb naked, as naked as a turkey at pluckin' time!

The heavy Colt in his hand wavered.

The girl screamed a warning to the newcomer, and pointed at Pike. Pike saw the man whirl and draw his sixgun in one practiced, fluid motion. On shit, he thought. I bought it this time!

The gun in the newcomer's hand spat fire. Before Pike could bring up his own gun, he felt something heavy, like a fist, strike him just above his sagging belt buckle, knocking him back and to the ground. He had already cocked the Walker and it exploded as his elbow struck the floor of the barn.

He saw the deputy leap forward then and fling his manacles over the head of the gunslick, dragging him back violently. The sixgun dropped from the fellow's hand. The deputy flung the newcomer from him and snatched up his gun. Pike smiled, leaned back, and closed his eyes.

It was going to be all right. All right...

Longarm hesitated momentarily. He had seen where the bullet had taken the old prospector, and wanted to go to his side. Then he heard Snefflin scrambling through the hay and slamming out through the barn's side door. A second later came the dim thunder of hooves as Snefflin fled.

Longarm hurried to the prospector's side. The man's eyes were closed, but he was smiling.

Longarm turned his attention back to Tracy. "Get me the keys to these chains and unlock me. Now!"

Tracy scrambled to her feet and disappeared inside the grain room. Longarm looked back at the prospector. His eyes had opened. Longarm put his arm under the old man's head and lifted it.

"How you feeling, Pike?"

"I got a bad hit down there, I'm thinking. Feels like somethin' mighty heavy's growin' in there."

"You're gutshot, Pike. I'm sorry. You shouldn't have dealt in on this hand. You didn't owe me anything."

"It's dry out there and it looked cool in here. Besides," the man said weakly, managing a faint, lascivious grin, "I done seen me a naked woman. Maybe that was worth it."

"She's a whore, Pike."

"She's a woman too."

Longarm frowned and inspected the man's wound a little more closely. The hole was not so large, and the flow from it was not too great, but the color of the blood was bad. And it smelled even worse.

"Deputy!" Pike cried weakly, attempting to lift his arm to point.

Longarm spun. In the shadows beside the door to the grain room, Tracy was standing with a gun in her hand. It was pointed at him.

"Drop it, Tracy," he told her. "You're too mad to shoot straight, and you know it."

In reply, she fired at Longarm. The slug whispered a warning to Longarm's soul as it whipped past his cheekbone. That was a pretty good shot for a woman. Longarm aimed and fired in one single movement. Tracy slammed back against the wall, then sagged brokenly to the floor of the barn.

Longarm looked back at Pike to thank him. He didn't need to. The man was lucky, after all.

He was dead.

Chapter 9

Tracy had rolled over onto her stomach and was groaning slightly. Longarm bent and pulled her over gently. His bullet had entered her left side, just above her flaring pelvic bone, and smashed its way out the other side. It had obviously done a lot of damage as it plowed through her, but the wound did not appear to be fatal, unless it became septic. Blood seeped steadily from the wound, covering her naked flank; bits of straw and hay were mixed in with it.

"You've killed me, you bastard," Tracy told him through tight lips.

"No I didn't. Not if we stop the bleeding and get the wound cleaned up."

"How we goin' to do that? I'm dead, I tell you. And you killed me."

Longarm picked up the gun she had dropped. It was his own .44. He stood up and looked down at her. "All right," he said. "You're right. I've killed you."

He turned and went into the grain room. The two had fixed it up some. There was a straw-filled mattress along one wall, and a crude bunkhouse woodstove in front of the window. A rusted coffeepot sat on the stove. In one corner his frock coat, vest, shirt, and hat had been flung down, along with his gunbelt.

In another corner stood a rainbarrel. He walked over to it. The barrel was half-filled with scummy water. That would have to do, he realized.

Then he looked about for the key to his manacles. They had used it once during his captivity to free him so that he could wash, so he knew the key was not too securely hidden. In a monent he spotted it, hung on a nail just inside the door.

He hurried over to it, unlocked his wrist shackles, and flung the chains from him. Then he stretched luxuriously.

"Deputy!" Tracy called. "Please. Don't let me die!"

Longarm stepped through the doorway. "Changed your mind, did you?"

"Yes. Oh yes! That old man. I can smell him!"

Longarm glanced at the shriveled figure lying in the sun at the barn's entrance. He had voided himself noisily when the bullet took him. The barn was filling with the stench of an old man's bowels.

"That's the smell of death, Tracy," Longarm told her.

"I know. I know," she moaned. "I don't want to die!"

Longarm flung his weapon over onto his pile of gear in the corner, left the doorway, and carried Tracy into the room and placed her as gently as he could on the filthy straw mattress. He told her to lie still and then busied himself heating water in the coffeepot and tearing a chemise of hers into strips.

When the water was boiling, he dropped the torn strips of her chemise into it, then began cleaning out her wound. She cried out and cursed him, and at first the blood flow increased, to her trembling dismay. But at last, when Longarm was fairly certain he had only clean, fresh blood oozing from the wounds, he wrapped freshly boiled strips of cloth about her waist, succeeding finally in stanching the flow of blood.

"You saw what I did," he told her. "You'll have to do the same thing. Boil fresh dressings before putting them on the wound."

"Them hot rags burn. They burn like hell."

Longarm shrugged. "All I wanted from you was the key. You didn't have to go for my gun."

"Damn you, deputy."

He smiled thinly. "Tell me where Snefflin has stashed his whiskey and I'll bring you some. You can use the whiskey if you don't want to use boiling water."

She brightened somewhat. "That loose board behind the rainbarrel," she told him. "Inside a wooden box. Bring me a fresh bottle and take one for yourself, if you've a mind."

He brought her a bottle. She pulled the cork and tipped the bottle up, gulping it down like it was water. He had not secured a bottle for himself. When she had finished her drink, he hunkered down beside her.

"Feel better?"

"Not now. But I will."

"Tracy, I want to know what's going on around here. What are you and this Mike Snefflin doing out here? You're not homesteading this section. You're holding it for someone else. Who?"

"You think I'd tell *you*?" she said. "The man who near killed me?"

"I did something else not long before."

"Hell, I was the one did that." She smiled maliciously. "I raped you, you big, stupid son of a bitch."

"You won't tell me, then."

"That's right. I'd rather burn in hell than tell you anything."

"What about Snefflin? He ran off and left you."

She took another prodigious gulp from her bottle, then glared in fury at him. "He's all talk, that one. The famous Weed Leeper!" She spat. "Get after him if you want, but don't corner him. Like all rats, he's dangerous in a corner."

Longarm leaned closer to her. "Weep Leeper? Is that what you called him?"

"That's the son of a bitch's name, all right. Snefflin's the name he was born with, back East. But Weed's the name he used since he came West—and before he shaved off that awful beard of his."

"That fellow you killed—your husband. Was that Smiley Blunt?"

She tipped up the bottle end emptied it some more. "Sure!" she told him recklessly, her face flushed now, her breath coming in rapid exhalations. She was drinking herself into a stupor and was already close to losing consciousness. "But that miserable son of a bitch wasn't my husband. You think I'd marry a bastard like that—or Weed? Smiley and Weed. What a pair they was!" She shook her head blearily and reached once more for the bottle she had slammed down on the floor beside the bed. "Weed shouldn't'a killed Marie. She was a little weepy dishrag, but she didn't know no better. It wasn't right." Lifting the bottle once more to her lips, she drained it.

Longarm stood up and looked down at her. The bottle dropped from her fingers. She stared blearily up at him.

"I feel fine now, deputy. Jush fine."

"That's good, Tracy."

"You find that no-good rat, Weed. Hear?"

"I'll do that. Then I'll come back for you."

"You make him tell you what's goin' on. He'll scream like a stuck pig when you corner him."

"Where do you think he went, Tracy? Back to Antelope Junction?"

"No." She closed her eyes. "The . . . Elko Kid, more'n likely." She hiccupped loudly and began to snore.

Longarm picked up Weed Leeper's fresh tracks along about sundown. The tracks made a straight line through a narrow gully and were still heading, without guile or attempt at concealment, toward a low lift of mountains, purple in the gathering dusk.

After burying Pike, Longarm had found the grassy depression where the old prospector had left his mule; but at sight of Longarm the mule had turned tail and bolted. For better than an hour, Longarm chased it in a futile attempt to bring the animal to bay. At last, wondering if perhaps it was the clinging stench of Pike's dead body that was spooking the mule, Longarm gave it up as a bad job and pushed on afoot after Weed, through the blistering afternoon.

Weed's trail had just about played out when Longarm came across fresh tracks. Glad for the shade, he entered the gully into which they led, and found fresh water oozing through cracks in one sheer wall of rock. He held the neck of his canteen under a rock shelf and waited patiently for the steadily dripping water to fill his canteen. It was icy cold and clean of alkali or sulfur. He hated to leave the spot, but made himself push on through the gully, coming out at last with the sun beneath the horizon and Weed Leeper's trail disappearing ahead of him in the gloom, but still heading on a beeline toward the low mountains ahead—and a cleft that was only now visible.

It was pitch dark when Longarm reached the low ridge of mountains and followed Weed's tracks into the canyon opening before him. In the smooth sand carpeting the canyon floor, Weed's tracks stood out clearly in the bright moonlight shed by a moon that hung like a ghostly lamp over Longarm's right shoulder. About a mile into the canyon, Longarm came to an impressive open spot resembling a vast amphitheater. It was at least a mile across. Pines clothed the distant slopes, and in among them, Longarm caught the bright gleam of a kerosene lamp.

He had found Weed's destination—a ranch building in among the trees, where the allegedly dead Elko Kid would give the equally dead Weed Leeper comfort and refuge.

Keeping to the slopes, Longarm started for the tiny pinprick of light winking at him from deep within the distant pines.

The Elko Kid was furious. He had just entered his cabin a few minutes before and been informed by Lem "Cutthroat" Flynn that as a result of Weed Leeper's bungling, Longarm was on the loose.

Lem "Cutthroat" Flynn was a tall, lean Texan known not only for the livid scar coiled like a snake about his throat, but for the equally scabrous look of his left walleye. Lem was reclining on the Kid's cot, a near-empty bottle of whiskey in his hand, as he glanced up at the unhappy Weed Leeper and the Kid.

"Now what's the matter with you two?" Weed wanted to know, looking from one face to the other. "What's so special about this deputy?"

The Elko Kid took a deep breath. He looked as if he wanted to throw himself on Weed Leeper and was holding himself back only with the greatest of difficulty. The Kid was a man in his thirties, but small and frail of build, with a pale, beardless face and blue eyes that peered out at the world in a perpetually sullen, wary squint. There was about him the thin-boned look of an adolescent, but the poisonous glint in his eyes warned any onlooker that the Kid was not a pale youngster to be treated lightly.

He was now standing in the center of the room, staring down incredulously at Weed Leeper. Both his hands were thrust into the pockets of his filthy duster, his black, floppy hat pulled down over his pale forehead.

"Do you know who that deputy is, you damn fool?"

"His name is Long," Weed replied.

"That's right. Long. Custis Long. Maybe you heard of him? His friends call him Longarm, you stupid son of a bitch!"

"Longarm?"

"That's right. He's out of Denver, and I've spent too many years looking over my shoulder 'cause I knew that big son of a bitch was on my tail. Why the hell did you think I was willin' to hole up here for that asshole Holloway?"

"Same reason as me. To get the law off your back."

"Hell, mine's a better reason than yours. Longarm is more than the law. He's a goddamn spook. And now, you stupid son of a bitch, you've led him right right to me!"

"You call me a son of a bitch one more time, Kid, and I'll kill you."

"Son of a bitch!"

Weed blanched. He wanted to draw. Oh, how he wanted to throw down on this puking kid, but he saw the man's eyes and noted once again the black-edged holes punched in his duster. The Kid never bothered to draw; he just fired both guns through them two holes. He probably had a gun in each hand right now.

"Aw, shit, Kid, you got no call to treat me like this. I didn't know nothing about this big galoot, 'cept he did sure as hell make mincemeat out of Pinky back at the saloon in Antelope Junction."

"Was it Holloway told you to kidnap him?" Lem Flynn asked, sitting up on the cot and peering unnervingly at Weed with his one terrible walleye.

Weed swallowed. "No. It was Tracy's idea—and mine. I think she had a hankerin' after him, and we didn't want to have to clean out that cabin by ourselves."

"Beautiful. So you kidnapped Longarm to do it for you. It is really a wonder to me you have managed to live so goddamn long, Weed."

"Hell! He was as meek as a kitten while he cleaned out that homestead."

"And how'd you manage that?" the Kid asked.

Weed smiled proudly. "I got me some manacles, heavy ones. We made him wear them chains everywhere, even while he was working. He got so tired, he didn't have no strength to cause any trouble."

"But he had strength enough to chase you away, didn't he?"

106

"It was that damn woman—and a fool prospector. He just appeared out of nowwhere, and the next thing I knew that chain was around my neck and I lost my gun."

"Sounds like Longarm, all right." The Elko Kid shook his head and looked with exasperation at Lem Flynn, his partner.

The big Texan got up from the cot and stretched. "I better get back to my spread," he said. "With Longarm loose and about, I'm thinking maybe I'd better get my gear ready and say goodbye to this here territory."

"Holloway wouldn't like that," said Weed.

"Shit on Holloway. I'm thinkin' of my neck. That fool's got more money than brains anyway. What the hell's he want with all this scrubland?"

"What's it matter? It's been a good deal for us."

"Not anymore," insisted Flynn. "Not if Longarm's onto him—and I'm thinking he is by this time, or pretty damn close. If you left him with that woman of yours, she's probably told him a bellyful."

"Hell, she don't know any more than I do."

"She knows enough."

Lem clapped his hat on and glanced at the Kid. "I'm leaving now. You want to pull out of this?"

"Yeah. Maybe that ain't such a bad idea. I'll meet you in Antelope Junction this Friday, and see who else we can get. But first we better study on it awhile. And wait to see which way Longarm moves. It might be the only one he'll go after is Holloway. That way we'll still be in the clear."

"I say we hit Holloway, then move out."

"That's a thought," agreed the Kid.

"Hey," said Weed, "how about letting me in on some of this action?"

The Kid glanced contemptuously at Weed for a long moment, then shrugged. "Sure. But only after you grow back that beard. You don't look human without hair on your face. Lem and I ain't ridin' with anyone looks like that."

Lem laughed loudly as he pushed the door open and stepped out into the night.

The moment he was gone, the Kid turned on his unwelcome guest. "You better ride out of here too, Weed. Now. I don't want you bringing Longarm to this place."

"He don't even have a horse."

107

"I don't care what you say. I ain't comfortable, knowing that big son of a bitch is out there somewhere, looking for you. How long you been waiting here with Lem?"

"I got here a little after the noon hour."

"You been here too long. Get on your horse."

"But what'll I tell Holloway?"

The Kid smiled, and suddenly his face was as old as death. "I don't care, Weed. But you better not mention what Lem and me was jawin' about here, or I'll find you faster than that deputy and kill you. Slow."

Weed swallowed. "Hell, you know me better than that, Kid. Besides, if you're goin' to clean out Holloway, I want in." Weed licked suddenly dry lips. "Why would I want to tell him anything?"

The Kid looked at Weed for a long moment. Weed could tell that the Kid was trying to figure whether he could trust him. Then, abruptly, the Kid shrugged. "Maybe you better stay here, Weed. Hell, if that lawman followed you, we can handle him. There won't be no trick to that. Right?"

"Sure," Weed said, trying to fix a smile on his face. He knew suddenly that he had said too much, that his implied threat had alerted the Kid, who no longer trusted him. Weed could stay, all right. But now he was a prisoner of the Kid's. "That's real white of you, Kid. Thanks."

At that moment the door opened and three men pushed into the ranch house, taking off their hats and stamping their feet the way men do after a long ride. These were the Kid's hands. They had joined him after Holloway had fixed it so he could stake a claim to this isolated ranch. The Kid had not bothered to tell Holloway until after they had joined him.

They knew Weed, and when the Kid told him Weed was going to bunk with them for a while, and then told them about Longarm, the three looked at Weed with eyes devoid of any warmth. They too knew about Longarm, it seemed—and realized what Weed's foolhardiness might have done to what had been an ideal hideaway.

Longarm was resting above the ranch house in the pines when he heard the one rider move off and the other three ride in. He waited until things quieted down inside the long cabin, then slipped down the slope, climbed through a corral fence, and moved up to the ranch house and peered in through one of the windows.

He saw the Elko Kid, Weed Leeper, and three others.

As he peered in through the window at the Elko Kid, he wondered if the Kid ever took off that damn duster. It was mentioned in every description Longarm had ever read of him; yet here he was, obviously attempting to build a new identity, and still wearing it.

Longarm knew enough about the Elko Kid to realize that taking him in alone would be difficult enough—like trying to carry a wildcat in a potato sack. But taking him along with Weed and those other three gunslicks who had just ridden in was out of the question. There were just too many of them. He would have to go back for Big Bill Sanders and gather up a posse.

He slipped away from the ranch house, heading for the barn. As soon as the lights winked out and its occupants went to sleep, he intended to borrow a mount and ride out of this canyon, back to Antelope Junction.

And when he got there, before he gathered up his posse, he figured it might be a good idea for him to poke around a bit and find out what in blazes was going on around here. Perhaps when he brought the wounded Tracy back to Antelope Junction, she might be a little more willing to talk. She just might tell him why the Elko Kid and Weed Leeper were not buried in boot hill, and maybe she'd know whose bodies were in those coffins instead.

And then he thought of Pete Baker and that Pinkerton, and realized he wouldn't have to ask Tracy after all.

Chapter 10

Longarm rode into Antelope Junction on his borrowed horse a little after midnight and prodded awake the Antelope House's desk clerk to secure a room. He left the hotel late the next morning, intent on hiring a buggy and riding out to see Tracy. He had left her with more than enough to drink and plenty of food on hand, but he did not like the thought of her alone out there, wounded as she was.

But first things first. He badly needed a bath and a good meal. He found a barbershop and enjoyed a steaming hot bath in a huge iron tub in back, and climbed out of it feeling ten pounds lighter. After his shave, he did not complain at all when the barber charged him an outrageous fifty cents. Feeling as fresh as a daisy and just about as lightheaded, he tipped the barber a dime and started across the street to Ma's Vittles, a small restaurant next to a general store. He had visions of eggs and fries and slabs of homemade bread dancing in his head as he crossed the street; otherwise he would have seen Holloway and Laraine Grover leaving the general store long before they saw him.

"Well, well, deputy!" Holloway cried, as he came to a halt on the sidewalk before the restaurant, his hand outstretched. "Our paths cross once again, it seems."

Longarm pulled up in some astonishment—not so much at

111

running into Clint Holloway, but at seeing Laraine Grover on his arm in this godforsaken tank town.

Touching his hatbrim, he bowed slightly to her. "A pleasure to meet you again, ma'am."

"What on earth happened to you?" she asked, glancing at his soiled pants and unpressed jacket. His shirt, Longarm knew, was filthy as well. He had planned on visiting a tailor just as soon as he got something into the aching pit just under his ribcage.

"Ran into some very unpleasant people," Longarm drawled. "A crazy woman and a dead man. They wanted me to help them clear away a burnt-out ranch. But I managed to weasel out of it."

Laraine gasped at his words. "Why, Longarm, surely you must be joking!"

"Wish I was, ma'am."

"What was that you said?" Holloway inquired, frowning and leaning closer, his pasty face suddenly paler. "A dead man and a crazy woman? A burnt-out ranch? Laraine is right. Surely you jest!"

"Never mind," Longarm told them. "Nothing to worry yourselves about. Now, if you'll excuse me, I'll hustle in here and get me some breakfast. It's been a long time since I've had a decent meal."

"Why, of course," Laraine said, laughing lightly. "We wouldn't want to keep you from your nourishment, Longarm."

He said goodbye to them and hurried on into the restaurant, aware as he did so that his deliberate attempt to get a reaction from Holloway had worked. Twice now, the owner of the Lucky Seven had been caught off balance by Longarm, and this time Longarm was pretty certain he knew why. The Lucky Seven was a nice cover, but that was probably all it was. Holloway had other irons in the fire. He was mixed up in this crazy business somewhere, and what his role was, precisely, Longarm would make it his business to find out soon enough. With that vow, he sat down at a corner table and at once waved at an oversized waitress.

She saw the stark need in his face, it seemed, and hurried over with a breakfast menu.

An hour or so later, Longarm entered Big Bill Sanders' office. Bill looked up from his cluttered desk, a welcome smile on his face.

"Howdy, Longarm," the town marshal said, putting down the dodger he had been looking over. "You bringing in that son of a bitch who shot Marie?"

"You mean Mike Snefflin?"

"That's right. He's the bastard done it. I made some inquiries after you left. He was in that room with Pinky."

Longarm took off his hat and sat down in the chair by the town marshal's desk. "We'll bring him in together, Bill, soon's I get a few matters taken care of—only his name is Weed Leeper."

Big Bill was in the act of placing a bottle of whiskey and two glasses down on his desk. He glanced up at Longarm through suddenly narrow eyes. "What was that, Longarm?"

"I said the man who calls himself Mike Snefflin is Weed Leeper, with his beard shaved off. Right now he's at the Elko Kid's ranch."

"You must have been grazing on some locoweed. Them two is as dead as doornails. Weed Leeper and the Elko Kid are sleeping out there in boot hill."

"No they're not."

Big Bill poured them their drinks, then pushed a glass toward Longarm. "Maybe you'd like to explain that."

"I'm not sure I can right now. Take a ride with me to a burnt-out homestead. There's a wounded girl out there. Her name's Tracy."

"Tracy Randall?"

"If that's her last name. Every time I see her she's with a different man."

"She and Wally Harmon were homesteading a ranch out in the basin somewhere, last I heard."

"You mean her and Smiley Blunt."

Big Bill shook his head in confusion. "You better go a little slower, Longarm," he said wearily, tipping his drink up and finishing it. "What in blazes are all these dead men doing homesteading in the basin?"

"I'm taking it as slow as I can. But I figure Tracy might be willing to tell us what this is all about by now. She's the one told me that Mike Snefflin is Weed Leeper—and that he was heading for the Elko Kid's place. When I followed Weed and found him there with the Kid, I realized she knew what she was talking about—that it wasn't the whiskey talking."

"You say she's wounded?"

"I'll explain that while we ride. You coming with me?"

Big Bill grabbed his hat and stood up. "Wild horses couldn't keep me away from this one, Longarm. It sure as hell beats sortin' these fool dodgers. Let's go," he said, starting past Longarm.

Swiftly downing his drink, Longarm followed the big man out of the office.

"She's out here, Longarm," Big Bill called.

Longarm left the grain room and found Bill bent over a huddled form in a dark corner of the barn. He hurried over and looked down. Wrapped in a ratty army blanket, Tracy glared up at them both through eyes bright with fever. Her teeth were chattering violently.

"Let me take a look at that wound, Tracy," Longarm told her. "You don't look so good."

"Just get me some more of that whiskey, will you?" she pleaded softly, through clenched teeth. "I can't move so good. I got the shakes somethin' awful. And it hurts. My whole body is so damned sore."

"We can't see nothin' in here," said Big Bill. As he spoke he picked Tracy up and carried her out of the barn and set her down in the shade of a stunted cottonwood. Then he carefully wrapped her nakedness in the blanket. Tracy started to say something to Longarm, probably to remind him she wanted more whiskey, but she couldn't get the words out, as her teeth began chattering violently.

Longarm knelt by her side and inspected her wound. It looked clean enough. There was no swelling, no angry red swelling around either the entry or the exit hole. But her lips were cracked and her skin was on fire. She had something bad, and that was for damn sure.

He wrapped the bandage back around her waist and stood up. "We'll have to bring her in to Antelope Junction," he told Big Bill, "and let Doc Gibbs take a look at her."

"Fat lot of good that'll do her."

"Well, it's something. We can't just leave her here."

Longarm had rented a buggy, and the two men had ridden out to the homestead in it, with their horses following along behind. Still wrapped only in the army blanket, Tracy was propped up in the seat beside Longarm. Then, with Big Bill riding alongside, they rode back to Antelope Junction as fast as the buggy and Tracy's condition would allow.

It was close to sundown when they got into the town and summoned Doc Gibbs. The doctor had Tracy brought to his office and private quarters above the undertaker's parlor. Big Bill put the now-unconscious girl down on a cot in a corner of the office, then stood back.

The doctor flipped back the blanket and took off the bandage Longarm had fashioned. He did so without comment, then examined the wound. After a moment he straightened and turned to Longarm. "Looks clean enough. But she's septic. Must have a mighty fever. How long's she been like this?"

"Since we discovered her, at least. About three hours."

"Mmm," Doc Gibbs said, turning back to the girl and reaching into his black bag for his stethoscope.

"Doc," said Big Bill, "We was hoping to speak to her. She has some information we need. When do you think she'll be out of this?"

The doctor had noticed something. Ignoring the town marshal's question, he put aside his stethoscope and leaned close to Tracy's face, then reached his dirty fingers in past her cracked lips. To their amazement, he attempted to pry her mouth open. But he couldn't. Only then did the two men notice Tracy's rigidity, and how tightly her teeth were clenched.

The doctor gave up trying to pry open Tracy's jaws and stepped away from the cot. He studied her a moment longer, then turned to the two men. "You want to know when you'll be able to talk to her?"

"That's right," said Big Bill.

"When did this happen?"

Longarm spoke up. "You mean when was she wounded?"

"Yes."

"Yesterday morning sometime."

The little man frowned. "That recent, was it?"

Longarm nodded.

"And where was she when you found her just now—before you brought her in?"

"Where?"

"Yes," the fellow said impatiently. "Where? In her house, in the barn. Where?"

"The barn. The ranch house was burned down a little while ago. She and her partner'd been living in the barn."

The doctor nodded unhappily, then looked back at Tracy. The girl was moving about now, groaning softly. Her jaw

115

was no longer rigid, but she was trembling violently from head to foot in a series of sharp, convulsive movements. She started to cry out, but suddenly her mouth snapped shut again. She began to twist and moan. She was evidently in great pain.

"What's wroing with her, doc?" Big Bill asked. But Longarm did not need to ask; he knew what it was already.

"Lockjaw," the old sawbones said wearily, as he slowly wrapped the filthy blanket back around the shuddering girl. "And from the looks of it, she is not going to be talking to either of you gents, not ever. This came on her fast, real fast—so that means there isn't anything I can do."

"Lockjaw?" Big Bill repeated, his bushy eyebrows arching. "Jesus, doc, you sure?"

"Yes, goddammit, I'm sure. I've seen this enough times."

The man went over to his desk, picked up a bottle that was already open, and swallowed its contents in a few swift gulps. He slammed the empty bottle back down onto the desk, then looked with dull, unhappy eyes over at the girl as he brushed his mouth off with the back of his hand. It was a bottle of laudanum the man had just emptied, Longarm saw. Doc Gibbs was obviously addicted to the stuff.

"Take care of her, doctor," said Longarm. "We'll be back to check on her later."

"Who's going to pay me?" the little man demanded. "This is not going to be very pleasant, watching this girl die."

"I'll pay you," said Longarm.

"You'll pay?" The doctor found that difficult to believe. "Why?"

"Because I'm the one who shot her."

As the two lawmen descended the outside steps that led from the doctor's office, Big Bill asked Longarm, "What do we do now?"

"I want to talk to that undertaker of yours—that fellow with the rose in his lapel. I'm hoping he'll be able to fill in some details."

Big Bill shrugged and followed along behind Longarm as he entered the undertaker's parlor. It was a small, crowded room. The shades were drawn. The highly polished knobs and planes of expensive furniture gleamed like eyes in the dimness. Truman Tyler's thin wisp of a figure materialized from behind a draped doorway and glided toward them.

"Yes, gentlemen?"

"Tyler," Longarm began, "who the hell are you burying in boot hill?"

"I beg your pardon?"

"Who've you got buried under Weed Leeper's marker—and Smiley Blunt's?"

"Why, you've just answered your own question. Who else but those unworthy gentlemen you just mentioned?"

"Well, there's something wrong with your method of burial then, Tyler."

"I beg your pardon!"

"There must be. Weed Leeper is alive and well, and until a little while ago, so was Smiley Blunt. And pretty soon I'll be bringing the Elko Kid in—but this time for a burial that will stick."

"I am sure I don't know what you're talking about. You must be mad. I buried the Elko Kid myself."

"How do you know it was the Elko Kid?"

"Mr. Holloway said it was."

"He was the one who brought the body to you?"

"Yes."

"Did he bring all those famous murderers in for burial?"

"I don't know what you mean by that, but it was either him or one of his employees who summoned me over to the Lucky Seven after one of those terrible gunfights."

"And Holloway would pay for their burial."

"Yes, whenever there was not enough money in the dead man's pockets to defray my expenses. He is a very generous man."

Longarm nodded. "And you never questioned the names he gave you?"

"Why should I? What did I care who they were, so long as I was adequately recompensed for my attendance on these worthless folk."

Longarm took a deep breath. "Well, Tyler, I think we're going to have to dig up some of those coffins of yours and have a look inside."

The man took a half-step back. His skeletal figure seemed to waver in the dimness, like a column of rising smoke. "Surely," he hissed softly, "surely you do not mean that!"

"I mean it and you are going to help me."

Truman glanced at the town marshal. "Are you going to

117

allow this . . . this sacrilege, Bill? In all my years in the service of the bereaved, I have never heard of such . . . such an abomination."

"I think you better do what Mr. Long wants, Truman," Big Bill drawled. "It sure as hell ain't goin' to be very pleasant, but he's got his reasons."

"Well, certainly then, I have a right to know what those reasons are."

"Sure," said Longarm easily. "I'm looking for two men."

But that was obviously not enough for Truman Tyler. "Looking for two men! That's no explanation—unless it is dead men you are looking for."

"I am afraid you hit it right on the nose, Tyler. We'll be back later. You just make sure you're ready."

The undertaker swallowed unhappily. "And when might that be?"

"Tonight," said Longarm, a grim smile on his face. "It'll be a mite cooler then."

The undertaker took out a handkerchief and began to mop his pale brow. He had given up protesting, and was no doubt contemplating the grisly night's work ahead of him.

Back in Big Bill's office, Longarm told the marshal about the posse he wanted for the next day.

"Steer clear of any of those gunslicks in the Lucky Seven," he said, sipping his whiskey. "Get as many of those roustabouts who're working for the railroad as you can. I don't figure they're all that happy about this sudden infusion of bad blood into Antelope Junction."

"No they ain't, as a matter of fact," Big Bill said, slumping back in his chair and nudging his hat up off his forehead.

"When did all these gunslicks start drifting into this place?"

"Before I got here, Longarm. But not too long."

"About the same time that Holloway purchased the Lucky Seven?"

"Yeah. Now that you mention it, I guess it would be. He ain't been here all that much longer than I have."

"And who brought you in?"

"A committee of the townsmen, made up mostly of railroad workers and storeowners."

"How did Holloway take it?"

"Fine. He was on the committee and welcomed me to the town with a tab at his place."

"Real generous."

Big Bill smiled. "I thought so."

"When did he attempt to cash in that IOU, Bill?"

The town marshal smiled. "Just once. A customer worked over one of his girls pretty bad, and he wanted me to look the other way. He mentioned he might be able to sweeten my monthly paycheck and maybe extend my tab at his place to include the upstairs."

"But you didn't look the other way."

"Nope. I held the jasper until the girl came to me and told me it wasn't him. She could hardly walk at the time, and of course I knew she was lying—that she was being forced to say that so I couldn't hold the bastard for the grand jury. So I had to release him. But I told him that if he ever showed up in this town again, I'd beat his brains to mincemeat with the barrel of my sixgun. I guess he believed me, because he ain't showed up since."

"And your relations with Holloway since then?"

"Cool. Real cool."

Longarm got up. "I'm going to my hotel. You see who you can round up for that posse. But keep it quiet, real quiet. I don't wany anyone to know about this posse until we ride out."

"Better yet," Big Bill said, "why don't I tell the members of the posse to leave town separately, without a fuss. We can join up outside of town."

"Good idea, Bill. But that might not do much good unless you also tell them you'll beat to death the first one who lets the word get out there's a posse heading out of here."

Longarm was getting to his feet when a slight figure paused in the doorway behind him. Longarm turned to see a towheaded kid with bright blue eyes. They were gleaming with excitement.

"What is it, Tim?" Big Bill asked, getting to his feet.

"It's Doc Gibbs. He sent me to get you. Said you better hurry if you want to see that girl alive."

They hurried, but they were still not in time.

Doc Gibbs was at his desk, staring over at the cot where the dead girl lay. "It was not pleasant," the doctor told them. "She suffered a terrible death, a most terrible death. The speed with which this affliction took her was appalling. I have never seen the like. I tried to quiet her, but it was hopeless." He looked bleakly up at Longarm. "There was nothing I could do. Nothing."

"How much do I owe you?"

"Give me a couple of dollars."

"That all?"

"It'll buy me a bottle. That's what I need now."

"I'll send up Tyler," Longarm told the man as he handed the doctor two silver dollars.

The fellow took the money and nodded dully, then pushed himself erect, shrugged into his grimy frock coat, and disappeared out the door, leaving Longarm and Big Bill alone with Tracy's figure huddled under the army blanket.

"I think the doc's got a good idea," said Big Bill. "Maybe we should kill that bottle in my desk before you go back to your hotel room."

Longarm nodded gloomily. Truman Tyler had another body to plant in boot hill. And this time there'd be no doubt who it was, sleeping under the rocky slope. Maybe they could kill two birds with one stone and dig a fresh grave for Tracy at the same time that they dug up the others.

"Let's get out of here," Longarm said softly.

Chapter 11

Longarm was stretching out wearily on his bed, his head buzzing mildly from the whiskey he and Big Bill had just consumed, when there came a soft, hurried knock on the door. He sat up on the bed, the springs creaking loudly, and reached for the .44 he had just tucked under his pillow.

"Yes?" he called, moving swiftly to the side of the door.

"Longarm? It's me, Laraine Grover. I must speak to you."

Longarm let the Colt drop to his side and pulled the door open. Laraine ducked swiftly into the room. She was wearing the same dress she had been wearing that morning. It was slim-waisted, bottle-green in color, and extended in a tight, figure-hugging curve all the way to her ankles. There was white lace at her throat, wrists, and ankles. Her red hair she had piled into a pompadour. Despite the wilt that was inevitable after a long day in this dusty town, there was still a tantalizing coolness about her as she stood before Longarm and looked at him, her hazel eyes dancing. "I don't know what you must think of me," she told him, "coming to your room like this."

Longarm closed the door behind her and smiled slightly. "What will Clint Holloway think?"

"That's why I'm here."

"Because of what he'll think?"

"No. Because of what I think he's trying to do."

She looked over at a wicker lounge chair near the window. "Can I sit down?" she asked.

"Of course." Longarm waved his gun at the wicker chair.

"Thank you."

Longarm dropped his Colt in his cross-draw rig, then slipped back into his frock coat and sat down on the edge of the bed. "What's Clint Holloway trying to do, Laraine?"

"I wish I knew for sure, but it is something dishonest, I'm afraid."

"It is?"

"Yes," she said firmly. "I think he's trying to convince settlers to homestead in the basin—so he can buy it back from them later, dirt cheap."

"You mean after the poor simps get discouraged and find they can't grow anything but locoweed and alkali dust on those blistering flats."

"Yes."

"What's his motive, Laraine? What's he up to? Why does he want that land?"

"He thinks there's gold out there, Longarm."

"You know he thinks that for a fact, do you?"

"When I questioned him about it in Salt Lake City—I told him he was crazy—he dared me to come out with him and check what he had found. That's why I'm in this awful place now."

"And?"

"Nothing."

"I don't understand."

"I mean he has shown me nothing. No claims, no soil samples, nothing. And now I am a prisoner in this hotel. His prisoner."

"You didn't act like a prisoner when I bumped into you two this morning."

"I thought we were on our way out to check a claim he had purchased. He had just finished showing me a bag of gold he said came from the claim. I was almost convinced then that he was on to something. But then—after he saw you—he took me to my room in this hotel and warned me to stay until he got back."

122

"Did he tell you where he was going?"

"No he didn't. But he certainly seemed upset."

"You don't know why he was upset?"

"I am as confused as you are, believe me. Longarm, what did you mean when you said a dead man and a crazy woman tried to make you clean up a burnt-out ranch?"

"Just what I said."

"Please. I need to know. Clinton was most upset when he heard that. I am sure it had significance for him."

"I was hoping it would."

"Then tell me what you meant."

"It's a long story, Laraine, and I won't know for sure until later tonight."

"Later tonight?"

"I'm going to have to visit boot hill and dig up some graves."

She pulled back in her chair, her hand up to her mouth. "I don't think that's very funny, Longarm. I really don't."

"I don't think it's funny either," Longarm told her coldly. "I ain't exactly looking forward to it."

"Then, my God, why are you doing such a horrible thing?"

"I have met men who are supposed to be buried in boot hill. They're alive and still kicking, Laraine."

"That's ghoulish. You can't mean that. You don't look like the kind of a man who believes in ghosts."

"I don't, but there's a ranch house in a canyon not far from Antelope Junction. In that ranch I saw two men who are supposed to be buried in boot hill—Weed Leeper and the Elko Kid. As soon as I can get a posse together, I'm going out there. And this time, when those two land in boot hill, they'll stay there."

Laraine shuddered involuntarily. "Do you think Holloway could have anything to do with this?"

"He's mixed up in this ugly business somewhere. You say its gold he's after. I find that hard to believe. I saw those maps in your office, don't forget. He's after something, but it sure as hell ain't gold."

"Let's talk about something else," she said, her voice pleading, almost desperate. "Clinton has not been at all nice to me, cooping me up here in this miserable hotel all day. And now you say he's mixed up in some fearful business with dead men." She shuddered. "Let's talk about something else."

"Must I remind you, Laraine?" Longarm drawled. "It was you who knocked on my door a few minutes ago and started talking about Holloway."

"You don't have to remind me. What's the matter, Longarm? Are you angry with me for coming in here?"

"No, not angry, just a little curious."

"You don't trust me."

"Not entirely, Laraine, if you want the truth."

"Oh, please, Longarm. I've had a terrible day. Can't you be nice?"

Longarm shrugged. "I can be nice. What did you have in mine?"

She sighed and got to her feet and walked over to the bed. Coming to a halt just before him, she turned slowly. "Unbutton me," she told him.

He did as he was directed. As he worked, she unpinned her flaming hair and let it cascade down over her shoulders. It did not make his task any easier. At last the bottle-green dress sank to the floor in a rustle of expensive silk and corduroy.

"Now unlace this horrible corset, please."

His fingers felt clumsy as he worked at the laces, the heady perfume of her hair adding to his difficulty. Finally she was free of the encumbrance and turned back around to face him as the corset followed her dress to the floor. She was clad only in her bloomers and pale stockings, a short chemise over that. Swiftly she flicked the chemise over her head, revealing her firm, upthrust breasts in all their glory. "I'll let you finish the job," she told him, her voice husky, her hazel eyes smoky now with desire. "And please, for God's sake, hurry up."

"I'm still dressed," he told her, smiling.

"Details," she murmured impatiently, leaning over swiftly, her fingers unbuttoning his fly. He leaned back on the bed as she peeled off his britches, and shrugged out of his holster, placing his sixgun under the pillow. Then he reached down and stripped off her bloomers. With a sigh she rested her weight fully on him then, and ran her cool fingers up under his shirt. He unbuttoned it swiftly and peeled it back off his shoulders. It was a new shirt he had only recently purchased in the town's general store, but in his surprising eagerness to please this woman, he almost lost one of his buttons as he shrugged out of it.

124

"Mmm," she said, her lips circling the nipple of his right breast, her tongue flicking at the nipple.

He took her face between his two hands and pulled her lips up to his. She responded passionately, her mouth and tongue working with wicked abandon, the corona of her abundant hair covering him with its flaming mantle. As her lips and tongue worked him to a frenzy, he felt his erection suddenly engulfed by her silky moistness—and then, triumphant, she reared back and plunged herself down upon him with almost heedless abandon. He heard her gasp with delight as he felt himself swelling up inside her.

But this was not the way he wanted her. He pulled her down upon him, then scooted backward, farther up onto the bed, and rolled over onto her, sliding still farther into her with such fury that this time her gasp was involuntary. Her arms were like steel bands about his shoulders now, as she pulled his mouth down upon hers and began thrusting. He was caught up at once in the practiced abandon of her driving pelvis. His big hands found the firm cheeks of her buttocks. He lifted her hungrily up under him and drove into her still deeper.

A moment before the trembling in his flanks went out of control, she began to gasp, then cry out—small, tiny gasps at first, then long moans. At last, as he exploded deep within her, she reached her climax and let out one long, high-pitched scream that set the hair on the back of his neck prickling.

"Oh, I'm not through!" she cried anxiously, holding herself tight about his still-erect cock. "I'm not through! Stay in there!"

A very determined woman, she flung herself over onto him until she was once again astride him.

This time, Longarm let her have her way. She leaned far back. He took her hands in his. She began to work herself up and down upon him at a faster and faster rate until, to his own astonishment, he felt a second orgasm stirring deliciously to life deep within his loins. Again she began making her delighted sounds. He found himself being carried along now, infected by her contagious and thoroughly abandoned excitement. The ache in his loins increased. Suddenly he grabbed her hands with such force that he thought he would crush them, but she was not thinking of that now as she too climaxed— and climaxed again, each time signaling the event with high, excited cries of delight until, spent at last, she collapsed forward onto his body, her lips fastened upon his.

But she seemed angry about something. Her kissing was fierce, almost punitive in the way her teeth nipped at his tongue and lower lip. He was afraid she would soon be drawing blood. He pulled his mouth away from hers.

"What's the matter, Laraine? You unhappy about something?"

"Oh, you darling," she told him. "It's not you. It's all the other men, the ones who get their way, then roll over and go to sleep, just when a girl is ready to play. Do you know how furious that has always made me?"

"I can imagine."

"No you can't. It has never happened to you."

"One-shots, you mean."

"Yes. That's what I mean. They slam it in, have their pleasure, then pull out and roll over. It has always amazed me how little time it takes them to begin snoring. Pigs, all of them."

"Except me."

"Except you, Longarm. Oh, you are so aptly named, you know."

"I've been told that, yes."

"Don't be so smug. And come back here and do me again."

With an inward sigh, aware of the many unpleasant tasks that still lay before him, he took her back in his arms and matched her kiss for kiss.

Before long he had forgotten about graves and dead men rising to kill again—and Tracy Hannon, or Randall, or whatever, huddled lifeless under an army blanket in Doc Gibbs' office. . . .

It was pitch dark when Laraine let herself back into her room and lit the lantern sitting on her dresser. The man asleep on her bed stirred as the light awoke him. He rubbed his eyes and sat up.

Clint Holloway was still wearing his vest, but he'd loosened his tight collar and his belt. He had not bothered to pull off his boots, however, and the bedspread was soiled where his muddy heels had rested on it.

"Well?" he asked. "Took you long enough. What did you find out?"

"Not much."

126

"Did he believe your story about me thinking there might be gold out there on the flats?"

"No."

"What's he up to? How much does he know?"

"He'll know a lot more pretty soon. He's going to dig up boot hill, find out who's really buried there."

Holloway ran his fingers through his rumpled hair. "Jesus."

"And he said something about getting a posse together."

"A posse? What for?"

"Something about a ranch in a canyon. He thinks he can find Weed Leeper and the Elko Kid there."

For the first time Holloway smiled. "You did fine, honey. Just fine. I'll send someone to warn the Kid. He'll be waiting for Longarm and his posse to show up—and that'll be the end of his poking around. We'll plant the big son of a bitch right alongside that Pinkerton. And that fool of a town marshal with him, if he goes along. Two birds with one stone."

"And soon after, we'll have more deputies swarming in here to investigate," she responded, frowning. "Are you sure there isn't a better way?"

"No there isn't. Not if he wouldn't go for that story you told him. If he won't believe that, he'll just keep on digging until he comes up with the truth. Best thing is to let the Kid and the rest of his boys take care of him. By the time the government sends more deputies in here to find out what happened to him, we'll have the entire basin tied up. I'll tell the boys to lie low then, stay out of town and wait. It shouldn't take me too much longer to close this deal, now that I have your assays." He looked sharply at her. "Do you think he suspects you?"

She frowned. "I'm not sure whether he does or not. He said something before we . . . stopped talking. Then, later, when I left his room, he said he wanted me to stay in the hotel until he returned tomorrow, so he could take me safely back to Salt Lake City. He told me not to trust you as far as I could throw a piano. I kissed him and thanked him."

"Kissed him, did you? Was that all you two did?"

She smiled. "You wanted to know what he was up to, didn't you?"

"Yes. I wanted to know. Come here. Show me how you did it."

Laughing softly, she moved toward him, sat on his lap, and

began to unbutton his shirt. "Here's how," she said, pushing him gently back onto the bed, her lips closing about his.

The blade of Big Bill's spade struck one of the coffins. It echoed hollowly in the damp air. Longarm held the kerosene lantern higher as the undertaker began shoveling off the dirt remaining on the lid. The two gravediggers in the next grave had almost uncovered the second coffin. Longarm waited a moment longer, then jumped down into the grave beside Big Bill. Still holding the lantern, he reached down and tried to lift the coffin's lid. It was nailed shut.

"Sim! Over here," called Tyler to one of his gravediggers. "Bring the wrecking bar."

The little, overall-clad workman hopped over the ground between them, a small crowbar in his hand. In a moment there was the sound of a nail screeching as it was pried out of the green wood. The lid lifted slightly. At once the odor of corruption from within the pine box smote Longarm like a fist. Sim swore and dropped the wrecking bar. Uttering muffled cries, both Big Bill and Tyler scrambled out of the hole, Sim following after.

Grimly, Longarm stayed where he was and flung the lid all the way back. For a moment he had some difficulty keeping the contents of his stomach down as he held the lantern over the coffin and peered down into it. He saw a very old, very thin man, wasted in death, the bloodless, parchmentlike skin of his face looking like old, yellowed newspaper. He had the feeling that if he were to touch the dead man's face, it would dissolve instantly into dust.

This man was supposed to be Weed Leeper, but it was the face and body of a much older man; and as Longarm recalled his memorized description of Deputy U.S. Marshal Pete Baker, he knew that he was looking down at the earthly remains of that deputy. His head spinning somewhat as he tried not to inhale too deeply, he leaned over the coffin's edge and reached into the breast pocket of the deputy marshal's frock coat and pulled from it the dead man's wallet.

He put the lantern down then and climbed out of the hole, and with his back to the open casket, opened the wallet. Big Bill picked up the lantern and held it high as Longarm examined the wallet's contents. A deputy U.S. marshal's badge gleamed dully. Despite the lantern's feeble light, Longarm was able to read the name beneath it: Peter Donnelly Baker.

Longarm closed the wallet and pocketed it. Then he glanced over at the next coffin. He knew now what he would find in that grave, also. The Pinkerton. But there was no need to dig any further or reach for any more moldy wallets.

He had completed his mission—or most of it, at any rate. He had found Pete Baker—only Billy Vail wasn't going to be having that one more drink he had wanted to have with his old sidekick.

Chapter 12

Longarm leaned back in Big Bill's chair and inhaled slowly. But the cheroot's pungent smoke could not entirely banish the stench of death and corruption that still clung to him. Big Bill was finishing his second glass of whiskey. Truman Tyler had returned from boot hill with them, on Longarm's strong invitation, and was sitting unhappily on the marshal's cot, awaiting the interrogation he knew was coming.

Longarm cleared his throat and directed his baleful gaze at the cadaverous undertaker. "I don't understand it, Tyler," he drawled. "How could you plant those two and not know who you were planting?" Longarm took out Baker's wallet and waved it at the man. "You didn't even check Baker for identification, didn't even look through his wallet or the Pinkerton's, you were in that much of a hurry. Is that how it was, Tyler?"

"Yes," the man snapped unhappily, his sunken eyes gazing warily across the room at Longarm. "Two more dead gunmen. What did I care for the niceties? Holloway paid me well to bury them, so I buried them."

"You didn't question what he told you about these men. You took his word for everything. He was paying, so you just shrugged and set your gravediggers to work. Is that how it was, Tyler?"

"Yes. That's how it was."

Big Bill spoke up then. "How much did he pay, Tyler?"

"Enough."

"How much, damn you!"

"Fifty dollars."

"For each body you planted?"

"Yes."

"How many bodies in all, Tyler?"

The man's prominent Adam's apple bobbed nervously; Longarm saw tiny beads of sweat standing out on his forehead. "Eight."

Bill glanced at Longarm, eyebrows arching.

Longarm said, "Wasn't that a mite steep, Tyler? All that money to bury dead gunslicks? That didn't make you at all suspicious?"

"Sure, I wondered some. But if I didn't bury them, his boys would—and I wouldn't get a cent. Christ, the men were dead enough. They sure as hell needed burying, so I did what had to be done."

"And you were well paid for it."

"Yes."

"Why, Tyler? What's Holloway up to?"

"He runs the Lucky Seven. That's all I know."

"You mean you don't ask questions."

"I try not to. I see what happens to them that does."

"Is there gold out there in the basin, Tyler?"

"Gold?"

"You heard me."

"I'm sure I wouldn't know."

"Does Holloway think there's gold out there?"

The man moistened his dry lips with a single flick of his tongue. "I don't know what Holloway thinks."

"Well, maybe you'd better find out, Tyler. You're in this with him. Boot hill was planted by both of you. And before long a jury will have to decide which of you is the most culpable."

"But . . . but I was not involved in the deaths of those men. I did what had to be done. Someone had to bury them. That's my job in this town. I just buried them. I didn't kill anyone. I had nothing to do with that."

"You just buried the bodies."

"But that's *all* I did," the man cried. "You have to believe me. It's the truth!"

"I don't have to believe you, Tyler. And neither does a judge—or a jury." Longarm looked away from the undertaker. "You can go now, if you don't have anything more you want to tell me."

The man stood up slowly, his wraithlike figure swaying. "I . . . don't have anything I want to tell you now. Not right now, that is. I mean . . . I got to think on this some more."

"You do that, Tyler," said Big Bill, pouring himself another drink. "You go back to that small, dark parlor of yours and think."

Tyler fled the office. Longarm pushed his empty glass toward Big Bill, and sighed wearily as Bill filled it for him.

"What now?" Bill asked.

"I think we should start thinking about that posse for tomorrow."

"I've got some pretty good men in mind. I've already spoken to a few of them. Mostly railroad men, like you suggested, and men who were here before Holloway bought out the Lucky Seven."

"Good. How many in all?"

"I figured seven in all, including us."

"Should be enough for what I have in mind."

"And what's that?"

Longarm lifted his drink to his mouth and drank it down in one gulp, welcoming the warm splash it made when it struck his stomach. Slapping the empty shotglass down on the desk, he smiled at Big Bill and took up his cheroot. "Had a visit from a pretty lady not so long ago. Told her all about my plan to go after the Elko Kid. I figure she's probably gotten back to Holloway by now and told him all about it."

"Jesus!" Big Bill exploded, nearly choking on his drink. "The Kid and his boys will be waiting for us. We'll be riding into a trap."

"Not if we don't want to, Bill. We'll let them set the trap, but we'll be the ones who spring it."

"You sure we can do that?"

With a smile, Longarm leaned forward and began to describe his plan.

Cutthroat Flynn appeared on the slope well below the Kid's perch. The Kid called out to him. Cutthroat glanced up, saw the Kid, and waved.

The Kid reached over the ledge a moment later and hauled

Cutthroat up beside him. The lean gunman straightened and brushed off his Levi's, then turned to face the Kid, his walleye fixed malevolently on him. He pursed his fleshy lips and lifted his hooked nose warily. He reminded the Kid of a torn-up old eagle who still had enough fight left to ruffle his feathers some. The Kid frowned. He knew Lem was getting impatient, and he didn't much blame him. Since early that morning, Cutthroat had manned the canyon's far slope. He had taken his position without argument, but it was obvious he was now having second thoughts.

"What's eatin' on you, Lem?"

"How much longer we gonna squat up here, Kid?" Lem asked. "This damn sun is hot, and we're roastin' on these rocks like lizards that don't know no better."

The Kid looked back down the slope at the canyon far below. After he got Holloway's warning last night, he had called in his and Lem's men and placed them in the rocks above the mouth of the canyon. This was the only grail they could take into his ranch. Longarm and his posse would have to pass this way. Holloway's message had made it clear what the Kid was expected to do: wipe out every damn one of them and bury each man without a trace. A tall order, but it was one the Kid was grimly determined to carry out—so long as it meant ridding himself of Longarm for good.

"We'll stay here until the posse shows, Lem. We ain't got much choice."

Lem picked absently at the livid scar that circled his neck. "You think we can trust Holloway to know what he's talking about? Suppose Longarm has other ideas?"

The Kid shrugged. "We'll see. If the posse left this morning, they should get here pretty soon. But Longarm ain't no fool. He'll take his time and maybe send some outriders ahead. We got to keep an eye out for any tricks, that's all."

"I don't like this waiting up here, sweating like pigs on a spit. You say we ain't got no choice? I say we just ride into town and throw down on Longarm, then take care of Holloway."

"One thing at a time, Lem. One thing at a time. Right now we got Longarm to rope. That damn Weed led him here just like I thought, so we got to deal with him."

"And then?"

"Hell, if we finish up Longarm, we don't have to light out.

We can sit out here on our homesteads and let Holloway play his hand, then take what we want from his pot when he pulls it in."

"We still don't know what he's up to—why he wants this basin land. The more I think on it, the crazier that man looks to me."

"He knows what he's doin', I'm sure of it. We just got to be a little more patient and take care of this day's business."

"Maybe." Cutthroat looked back down the slope. The Kid was relieved to feel the walleye no longer peering at him. "Maybe. Anyway, one thing's for sure. I aim to finish Weed's beans before this day's over."

The Kid nodded and thrust his hands deep into his duster, a cold smile on his pale face. "When Longarm shows, maybe he'll do the job for us."

Cutthroat nodded and sighed wearily. "I'll go on back across and try and settle the boys down," he said.

"Remember what I said. Wait until all the posse is in the canyon. We can't let a one of them escape to tell his story. And wait for my signal."

The tall gunman grunted and turned his walleye on the Kid once again. "That rifle of yours better not miss."

The Kid's right hand left the pocket of his duster and plucked up a rifle leaning against a rock face. He hefted it with both hands and smiled. "Just wait for my shot. When Longarm peels off his horse, open up. The thing is, we got to get that son of a bitch first. That'll take the heart out of the posse for sure."

Cutthroat nodded without further comment and started back down the slope. Watching him go, the Kid took a deep breath. Cutthroat's walleye had a way of making a man think of graveyards and vultures. He was a fearsome enemy, but a loyal and steady ally when it came to flying lead and long night rides before the law. The thing was, Cutthroat hated to wait for things to happen. His pride was in *making* things happen.

Well, this time he would just have to wait.

It was an hour or so before sundown, and Longarm was nervous. It had taken him most of the afternoon to place his men. He and Big Bill and the rest of the posse had worked their way carefully over the slopes above the canyon, slowly, painstakingly picking out each of the Kid's men as they waited in the rocks below. What he was afraid of now was that he Kid would get discouraged and call off his men just when Longarm was ready to spring his surprise. That he had guessed Laraine's and Holloway's intentions so well was a source of some satisfaction to him; and he had felt a grim pleasure the first time he had pointed out to Big Bill the sunlight glinting on an outlaw's gunbarrel on the slope far below them.

He was waiting now for Big Bill to get in position on the other side of the canyon. Impatiently, Longarm stood up and peered across at the canyon's rim. But just as he got to his feet, he made out the town marshal's burly figure striding out from behind a juniper Longarm had pointed out to him earlier.

Longarm levered a fresh cartridge into his Winchester's firing chamber and gave Big Bill the signal to begin by waving his right arm once over his head; his left shoulder was still giving him some trouble. He saw Bill disappear back behind the juniper and assumed the man would soon be joining his two posse members as they moved with him down the slope.

Longarm turned and waved to the couple of posse members he had stationed well off to his left, and watched as they started down the slope. Once they were out of sight, he turned to the fellow who had elected to stay with him, and pointed to the slope below.

"Let's go, Biff. You take that fellow on the right. I'll take this one to the left just below him."

As lightly and silently as possible, the two men picked their way down the steep slope. After descending about thirty yards, Biff peeled off to Longarm's right and soon disappeared among the rocks. Longarm kept going. In a moment he saw a stooped figure, rifle in hand, move out from behind a clump of bristlecone, his attention riveted to the canyon floor below. Even from the back, the outlaw looked vaguely familiar.

Longarm kept going, his rifle tucked into his waist, his right forefinger coiled about the trigger. The closer he got, the more certain he became that he had seen this jasper before. And then his left foot sent a small avalanche of gravel down the slope ahead of him.

The gunman turned swiftly, his face lifted as he peered up the slope. Yes, Longarm had seen him before. He was the homesteader who had been so unpleasant when Longarm had asked for water for himself and his mount. Longarm smiled when he saw the startled look on the homesteader's face. In a panic, the man swung up his rifle. Longarm kept his own rifle at his hip and fired twice at the man, each slug catching him high in the chest and slamming him back against a rock face. The rifle in the homesteader's hand went off, the round ricocheting off a rock on the slope above Longarm. Dropping his rifle, the homesteader sagged to his knees.

Keeping his rifle at the ready, Longarm continued on down the slope as gunfire erupted suddenly on both sides of the canyon. The battle had been joined. He had almost reached the fellow he had just shot when he heard gunfire off to his right, just a little above him on the slope. The reports sounded alarmingly close. Longarm glanced over and saw one of the Kid's men scrambling toward him, a sixgun in his hand. Behind him raced a perspiring Biff. Neither man had yet seen Longarm, and Longarm realized he was in their line of fire.

As Longarm threw himself to the ground, Biff fired after the fleeing gunman. The bullet missed and plowed into the slope behind Longarm. The gunman ducked behind a boulder and got ready to return Biff's fire. Sitting up swiftly, Longarm levered a fresh cartridge into his firing chamber and snapped off a shot. He caught the gunman in the back, the round punching him into the boulder. The fellow collapsed, his sixgun clattering to the ground. Startled, Biff pulled up. Then he saw Longarm and hurried toward him.

"Hey!" Biff cried. "We got two of them."

Longarm reserved comment as he got slowly to his feet. Pointing to the man he had just shot, he said, "Maybe you'd better check him out. He might still give us trouble. I'm going to take a look at this one."

"Sure."

Longarm scrambled down the slope to the homesteader he had shot first. The man's hat was off, his long, dirty hair hanging down over his face as he sat with his back to the rock face, his head slumped forward, his arms wrapped about his chest. Longarm bent forward and reached out to grab the man's lank hair, intending to pull his head up to see if the man was conscious. The moment his fingers touched the greasy hair, the gunslick opened his arms.

A sixgun in the man's right hand exploded.

The detonation, so close to his head, stunned Longarm. Momentarily deafened, he felt the sting of the gunpowder as the slug whistled past his right cheekbone. His reaction was swift. Kicking out with his right boot, he caught the man's gunhand and sent the revolver spinning out of sight down the slope. With a desperate cry, the wounded man flung himself on Longarm. Longarm found himself being flung backward. The fellow's shirtfront was soaked with fresh blood, making it difficult for Longarm to get a firm grip on the man as he struggled to free himself from him.

He spun about and managed to break loose. Then he strode in closer and sent a sledging uppercut to the man's chin, driving him back toward the canyon, yawning wide behind him. Weak from loss of blood, the fellow made a feeble attempt to reach out for something to grab. He found nothing and dropped out of sight. Longarm hurried to the edge of the slope and saw the man falling through the air for a distance of thirty feet or more before he came to a sudden, jolting halt against the side of a projecting ledge. He lay on his back, as still as death, staring sightlessly back up the slope at Longarm.

Longarm turned around to see Biff hurrying toward him.

"You all right, Longarm?" the man cried.

"Just a little bloody is all. How's that jasper back there?"

"He's dead as a mackerel. Hey, I been thinking. That shot of mine earlier must have come pretty near to hittin' you."

"Too damn near," Longarm admitted. "Let's go. This isn't a surprise anymore. And the Kid is still down there somewhere, waiting for us."

The Kid was swearing bitterly as he scrambled down the steep slope and dropped to the canyon floor. The rocks behind him had come alive with members of Longarm's posse. The son of a bitch had known what the Kid had planned. Jesus! That Holloway was a fool. Somehow he had let Longarm know what was up. Cutthroat was right. The thing to do was to take what that pompous ass Holloway had, then light out. This whole deal had gone rotten.

He glanced toward the canyon's entrance and saw two members of Longarm's posse dropping to the canyon floor, guns drawn. One of them was Big Bill Sanders. Drawing his own gun, the Kid raced away from them, heading deeper into the canyon. His horse and those of his men were in the pines across from the ranch, a considerable distance to go on foot. He stumbled, finding it difficult going in his riding boots. A shot rang out behind him and a round ricocheted off the wall of rock beside him. He turned, snapped a shot at his pursuers, then struggled on through the darkening canyon. As he ran, he caught sight of Weed and Cutthroat racing ahead of him.

He called out to them, "Where's the others?"

"Tom and Slick got it first thing," Cutthroat called back. "I saw them go down."

"We been suckered!" Weed bleated.

The Kid increased his speed and overtook the pair. From behind him came the sound of more firing. Good! Not all of his men were out of action yet. They just might be able to hole up in the ranch house, then slip away as soon as it got dark.

Waco Brown dropped to the canyon floor ahead of them. He was obviously wounded, but managed to struggle to his feet as the Kid reached him. The Kid grabbed him by the arm.

"You hurt bad, Waco?" he asked.

"Naw. The slug just chewed out a piece of my ass." The man laughed hollowly. "It's more an embarrassment than a wound."

Cutthroat slapped Waco heartily on his back. "Keep going then. The horses ain't far."

A quarter of a mile farther on, as the four men left the canyon and entered the timber stand where they had left their mounts, two more of their men joined them. In a moment the six men—including the fellow with the shot-up ass—had mounted up and were spurring their horses furiously across the flat toward the ranch house in the pines.

Longarm emerged from the canyon in time to see the six horsemen disappear into the gathering dusk. There was no doubt as to where they were heading. Longarm was disappointed. Holed up in that ranch, the Kid would be able to hold off the posse without too much difficulty—and once it got dark they would sure as hell make a break for it.

So let them, he told himself. Even in the darkness they would be relatively easy to cut down. Longarm turned to meet Big Bill and Biff as they raced out of the canyon toward him.

Once inside the cabin, the Kid looked around at what was left of his forces, and swore bitterly. The two who had joined him just before they reached their horses were Will Turpin and Dutch Ansel. Will was a short, tough man—a brawler who liked nothing better than to mix it up on occasion—and it was no surprise to the Kid that Will had managed, somehow, to break away from that posse. Dutch Ansel was a sullen, glowering bully who looked as if he had already shit in his pants. The man was so scared, he stank.

"Dutch," the Kid said, "take a look outside. Let me know when you hear hoofbeats. I figure that posse will be surrounding this place soon."

"Jesus! Why me?"

"Because you're stinking up the place. Now get out there and hole up on the slope behind the barn so you can see anyone coming."

"But, Jesus! Suppose they see me!"

"Shoot back."

"It'll be pitch dark soon."

"Then you can come back in. Now get out there. As soon as you see anyone or hear anyone, you tell us. Hear?"

The man nodded miserably and turned. He hesitated at the door, his hand trembling as he reached for the doorknob.

"Damm it, Dutch," Cutthroat growled. "Get on out there!"

The man opened the door and slipped out.

The Kid went to the window and watched Dutch scurry across the yard toward the barn. A moment later he left the barn by the rear door, scooted up the slope to a small stand of juniper, and disappeared from sight. The Kid watched for a moment longer. Then, satisfied, he turned back to the others.

"All right. We got a lookout, which is all Dutch is good for now. Waco, how's that ass of yours?"

"Hurts like hell."

"Can you ride?"

"Not with this other hole in my ass. That ride across the flats just about did it for me."

"All right. You stay in here. When that posse closes in, you show them plenty of firepower. We're going to the barn to hole up. Soon's it's dark enough, we're going to ride out. I want to make that posse think we're still holed up in here. You go that?"

"But what about me?"

"You can't ride. As soon as you hear us ride out, give up."

"Jesus!"

"Well, you can keep on firing until they break in here and blast you, or you can let them burn you out. Take your choice."

The man nodded unhappily. "I'll give up."

The Kid nodded, then turned to the others. "Let's go. Give

Waco all the extra rounds you can spare, then head for the barn."

A moment later the four men dashed through the gathering darkness into the barn.

It was Biff, moving down from the pines above the ranch, who saw the movement in the clump of juniper above the barn. He hauled up too hastily and sat down, his boots digging up the slope and sending a small avalanche of rocks and loose dirt down ahead of him.

He caught the gleam of metal momentarily as a shadowy figure moved for a moment out of the cover of the junipers. Then a sixgun's blast lanced the darkness. The slug caught Biff squarely on his gunbelt, the force of it spinning him around. Furious, he turned back and poured fire down into the junipers. There came a cry of pain and outrage, and the next thing he saw was a dark figure tumbling down the slope, heading for the barn.

At once the Kid and his men opened up from the ranch. Biff inspected himself quickly and found no wound. The gunbelt had deflected the round. Elated at his reprieve, he got to his feet and charged eagerly down the slope after the son of a bitch who had fired on him.

That was when a wild rifle shot from the cabin caught Biff in the neck, just below his Adam's apple. The round punched all the way through, coming to rest against the inside of his spinal column, halfway down his back. Biff tried to call out as he felt his legs melting beneath him. But he no longer had a voice. Astonished, he reached up to his neck and felt his hand being splattered with a torrent of his own warm blood. Then he struck the soft ground, plowing into it facedown—the darkness following swiftly after the feel of the cool earth.

Longarm was in the pines at the foot of the slope, approaching the rear of the ranch house with Big Bill and the rest of the posse, when he saw Biff go down. He knew it was Biff, since he was the only man Longarm had sent around to that side of the barn. He swore unhappily and hoped the man was not hurt seriously.

Gunfire suddenly erupted from a window at the rear of the cabin, spraying the pines, cutting off branches, and sending prickly showers of pine needles down upon them. Longarm aimed at the powder flashes in the window and opened up himself. The gunfire ceased, only to begin again at another window. Big Bill and the others opened up then.

Longarm dashed from the pines and around to the side of the cabin, intending to cut off any escape from the front of the ranch house. With Biff out of action, there was no one to prevent the gang from piling out and making for the barn. He rounded the cabin just as a confused, very frightened outlaw pulled up in front of him, a smoking sixgun in his hand.

Longarm realized this was the one who had shot Biff. The .44 in Longarm's hand bucked twice, and the outlaw was flung backward into the shadows. When no fire erupted from the cabin in answer to his two shots, Longarm continued on around the corner of the ranch house and up onto the sagging front porch. Without slowing down, he lowered his shoulder and smashed through the door.

Once inside the cabin, Longarm flung himself to the floor. A dark figure lunged toward him from out of the shadows, holding a rifle. The rifle detonated, its round smashing into the floor beside Longarm's head. In the light from the muzzle flash, Longarm caught an instant picture of the outlaw's face and the disordered cabin. The outlaw firing at him was its only occupant!

Longarm continued to roll over the dark floor as the outlaw levered a fresh cartridge into his firing chamber and fired again. The slug snicked at the hem of Longarm's coat. Meanwhile, rounds from the posse outside were pouring into the cabin. A kerosene lamp suddenly exploded, sending tiny shards of glass and bright fingers of flame across the table it had been resting on. The outlaw was suddenly visible, bent over the table, searching the darkness for Longarm's scrambling figure. He was looking the wrong way. Crabbing swiftly to his right, Longarm brought up his sixgun and emptied it at the outlaw. The man dropped his rifle, clutched at the table, then sagged to the floor, pulling the flaming tabletop over onto him.

Still keeping low, Longarm ducked back out the door and raced around to the rear of the cabin.

"Hold your fire!" he called into the darkness. "There's no one left in there! The Kid's gone!"

As Big Bill and the rest of the posse broke cover and ran toward him, a sudden explosion of hooves came from the barn. Longarm turned and raced back around the ranch house—just in time to see the Kid and the rest of his men bent low over their mounts' necks as they galloped out of the compound. Only when Longarm tried to get off a shot at the fast-disappearing band of outlaws did he realize he had already emptied his gun.

Swearing bitterly, he dropped his empty Colt into its holster.

Chapter 13

Once through the canyon, the Kid pulled up. Will Turpin, riding alongside, pulled his mount around in irritation. Weed and Cutthroat caught up to them and reined in.

"What's wrong, Kid?" Cutthroat asked. "Why you stopping here?"

"I want someone to stay back in them rocks and slow up that son of a bitch Longarm. We'll need time to finish what we planned in Antelope Junction."

Cutthroat nodded, a grim smile barely lighting his features. He knew what the Kid had in mind.

The Kid looked at Weed Leeper. "Weed, ride on back there. Guard that canyon. Hold off Longarm and his posse for as long as you can, then join us in Antelope Junction."

Startled, Weed looked incredulously at the Kid. "Now hold it right there, Kid. I ain't layin' back for this Longarm. That man's poison, I know that now. I aim to put as much distance between me and him as this horse will allow."

The Kid shifted his weight slightly and thrust his right hand into the pocket of his duster. Two quick shots rang out, and the horse Weed was riding collapsed crookedly to the ground. Weed just managed to leap free of the thrashing animal.

"Finish him off, Weed," Cutthroat said. "I hate to see a horse suffer."

First panic, then fury registered on Weed's face. He clawed for his sixgun. But when he saw the smile on the Kid's face, he pulled himself together and, with deliberate care, withdrew the weapon he needed to finish the horse. "This ain't right, Kid. You shouldn't oughta do this to me."

"Why not, for Christ's sake? Look what the hell you did for us. You was the one brought Longarm out to your place, then led him to my ranch. He must've spotted me in the cabin. That's why he came for us. If you'd left Longarm sniffin' around in Salt Lake City, we wouldn't be in this fix. I ought to shoot you down alongside that animal."

"Finish him off," Cutthroat repeated impatiently, "or we'll finish both of you ourselves." As Cutthroat spoke, he drew his iron and leveled it on Weed.

The furious outlaw turned his weapon on the still-thrashing horse, held the muzzle close to its temple, and fired. The horse flopped heavily to the ground.

"Now go on back there and slow down that posse," said the Kid. "You show me you can do something right for a change, and maybe we'll let you ride with us again sometime."

"Only don't count on it," said Cutthroat.

"Damn you! It's suicide, and you know it. I won't have a chance."

"Well, you ain't got no chance with us, neither. This way, maybe you can shoot Longarm off his horse and keep the mount for yourself."

"Here," said Will Turpin, throwing Weed his rifle, and following it with an extra cartridge belt. "You'll need this, bucko."

Weed snatched up the rifle without thanking Turpin and stared wildly back up at the three. "Damn you! All three of you! I'll get even for this. Don't think I won't."

"That mouth of yours is gonna end this right here," said Cutthroat quietly, "if that's what you want."

"Get on back there," snapped the Kid. "I'm sick of lookin' at your face. All I want to see now is your ass. Move!"

Weed argued no more. He hustled around the dead horse and lit out for the canyon. In a moment the moonless night closed about his scurrying figure. The Kid pulled his horse around. He felt better already. He had never liked Weed Leeper. And if the man was as stupid as he appeared, he just might slow down Longarm some.

The three riders rode into Antelope Junction a little before midnight. Leaving their lathered horses at the tie rail in front of the Lucky Seven, they pushed through the saloon's batwings and strode up to the bar.

The new barkeep looked at them questioningly. "Yessir, gents. What'll it be?"

"Holloway. He upstairs?"

The man hesitated. The Kid saw his right hand drop below the counter. So did Turpin. The little man reached out and grabbed the barkeep by his string tie and yanked him close, twisting the string. The barkeep's eyes bulged.

"Leave that shotgun right where it is, bucko," Turpin said, smiling, "or I'll haul you over this bar and wipe the floor with you!"

The man nodded frantically. Turpin relaxed his hold somewhat, and at once the barkeep showed both hands, empty, above the counter.

Turpin let him go.

"Now once again," said the Kid, "where's Holloway?"

"Upstairs in his office."

The Kid nodded to Turpin and Cutthroat and led the way to the stairs. As he walked through the saloon he was greeted by smiling, unwashed faces. A few called out to Will Turpin. The three men waved back. Since most of the Lucky Seven's patrons were in on this deal with Holloway, the Kid felt no hesitation in turning his back on the barkeep Turpin had just manhandled.

The three mounted the stairs, and without bothering to knock, the Kid pushed his way into Holloway's office. The owner of the Lucky Seven was in the act of entering the office from his adjoining suite when the three men appeared. The look on his face betrayed only mild surprise. It was obvious he was under the impression that his warning had enabled the Kid to bushwhack Longarm's posse.

Until he saw the grim look on their faces.

Holloway frowned. "How did it go? Did you get my warning?"

"We got it," the Kid replied, pushing the door shut.

"Well, then? What happened?"

"Longarm knew we was waiting for him. We were the ones got the surprise."

"But how could he have known?"

"I don't care how he knew. You screwed it up somehow, Holloway, and that's enough for us. We're pulling out."

Cutthroat drew his Colt and pointed it casually at Holloway's generous midsection. The man was dressed in a fancy silk robe and was wearing slippers. His black silk socks were held up by garters. He was a real dude, all right. And if the Kid knew him the way he thought he did, Holloway had one of his own girls back there in his bedroom. He was testing out the merchandise.

Holloway gasped when he found himself staring into the bore of Cutthroat's weapon. He took a small step back. "Here! Put that cannon down, Lem! There's no need for that!"

"Where's your money, Holloway?" the Kid demanded. "I told you, we're lighting out. This deal's gone sour."

"I don't have any," the man bleated.

"Shit. Don't try that on us."

"Let me show you! I've sunk all the cash I have in this operation. How much do you think it takes to bankroll all you homesteaders? Look, don't take my word for it! Let me show you my safe!"

Cutthroat waggled his Colt at the man. "Go ahead. Show us."

Holloway darted swiftly for the wall behind his desk. He folded back a wall panel, revealing a safe about four feet high. At once he bent to the combination and spun the dial. Despite shaking hands, he had the door open in seconds. He got to his feet and stepped back.

"Go ahead," he told them. "Look in there. See what I got. Homestead deeds, that's all. I'm flat. All I got now is what I sunk into this saloon."

The Kid pawed through the safe, pulling out the deeds and anything else he could find. There was a small bag of coins in the back. Getting to his feet, he dumped the coins onto the desk.

He counted less than twenty dollars.

"How come, Holloway?" demanded the Kid. "The way you been throwing money around, I figured you were old Midas himself."

"Later, maybe. But not now."

148

"What's that supposed to mean?"

"It's like I told you. Before long, I'm going to have enough money to buy all those homesteads from you—with a handsome profit for each one of you."

"What the hell's on that land, Holloway?"

"I can't tell you."

"It ain't gold, is it? Or silver?"

"Not . . . exactly."

"I think you been chewin' on locoweed, Holloway."

"No matter," Holloway countered. "If you'll just stay with me a few weeks longer, you'll see that I'm not crazy."

The Kid took a deep breath. Damn. It was clear he wasn't going to get rich by robbing Holloway. Not tonight anyway. "Longarm's out there, Holloway. He's onto your scheme. There's no way we can stay in this crazy game of yours—not now."

"Yes you can. Kill Longarm and that town marshal. By the time anyone comes to investigate, I'll have completed this deal."

"Longarm's a hard man to kill," the Kid said.

"Longarm and Big Bill. You'll have to kill both of them. They'll be coming back here, won't they?"

"Yes. But we'd be smart to be long gone when they do."

Holloway took a deep breath. "I'm willing to forget all about you trying to rob me," he told them, his voice steadying. "I figure you got a right to look out for yourselves, with Longarm on your tail. But the thing is, we can still take Longarm. It's us against him."

Cutthroat looked at the Kid. "I don't like it. This whole thing's done collapsed, I tell you, Kid. I say we take what we can and clear out before that tall son of a bitch gets back here."

Turpin spoke up then. "No, Lem. I say we stay here and boil Longarm's innards. He got a buddy of mine in Texas some years ago. I know of the man. Sure, he's tough. But he puts his pants on one leg at a time and squats when he shits, like all the rest of us. I say we give it one more shot. Hell, if we leave now, we ride out broke, with our tails between our legs."

Cutthroat shrugged and looked at the Kid.

The Kid glanced warily at Holloway. "You say we stay and kill Longarm and the town marshal. How do you propose we do that?"

"As soon as he rides in, I'll go out to meet him. I'll bring him and Big Bill up here. I'm sure the two of them will be very anxious to hear my explanation of what is going on in this town."

"I see. And when he comes up here, we'll be waiting."

"Yes."

"This better go easier than that other bushwhack we planned."

"It will. There's only one thing we have to worry about."

"What's that?"

"Tyler. He's ready to spill his guts to Longarm. If he gets wind of this, he might warn the lawman. I'm sure he saw you three ride in here."

"I'll take care of him," said Cutthroat.

"The sooner the better."

"I told you, I'll take care of him," Cutthroat repeated. "He gives me the creepin' willies. I swear he's already dead, anyway."

"So we'll stay," said the Kid. "Here. Where we can keep an eye on you, Holloway."

Cutthroat holstered his weapon carefully, his eye on Holloway. "You heard the Kid. We'll hole up here. Maybe you can at least show us some hospitality."

The man brightened. "I can do better than that," he cried, rubbing his hands together. "There's two girls—new arrivals. You'll find them real anxious to please. Wait'll you see them."

The Kid felt his loins quicken. "Show us."

Holloway led the three men out of his office and down the hallway to a rear suite. It was the most expensive crib in the house, the Kid realized, and when Holloway opened the door for them, the Kid knew why.

The suite was decked out in red curtains and wall drapes. The walls had lush paintings of full-breasted women cavorting with animals in a manner that made his heart leap. There were mirrors over the huge bed, mirrors like those he had heard about in a New Orleans sporting house. Sitting on the bed were two dark Mexican girls. Dressed only in lacy shifts, they had shiny black hair combed out so long it reached all the way down to their waists. One of them, the Kid noticed, had green eyes.

"There's only two of them," said Turpin. "What about me?"

"These girls are very inventive," Holloway assured him. "They'll do fine. You'll see."

"Never mind," said Turpin. "This ain't my style. You two go on in there. I'll hang back and keep an eye out for Longarm." Then Turpin looked carefully at Holloway. "You ain't got any . . . boys, have you?"

Holloway paled. "You mean . . . ?"

"You know what I mean, bucko."

Holloway shrugged. "I'll see what I can do. Now that I think of it, there is one rather fair young lad working for me in the kitchen."

"That's fine," Turpin said. "See you, gents," he said to Cutthroat and the Kid.

As Turpin and Holloway moved back down the hallway, the Kid turned to Cutthroat. "Why don't you go visit the undertaker, Lem? I'll warm these two up for you."

Lem licked his lips as he gazed into the room at one of the girls. She was terrified of him, he could tell. Cutthroat liked that. It quickened his blood, the look of fear in a woman's eyes just before he took her.

"Yes," he told the Kid. "You do that." He smiled wolfishly. "I won't be long."

Laraine was waiting for Holloway when he returned to his office. She had been in the next room when the Kid and Cutthroat had entered, and had heard everything.

"You poor man," she said with mock pity. "You had been saving those two recent imports for yourself—without, of course, telling me."

Holloway took a handkerchief from his robe's pocket and mopped his brow. "Business before pleasure, my dear," he murmured, slumping into an easy chair. "Do you realize how close I came to having my head blown off by that walleyed son of a bitch? I almost pissed in my pants."

"I could smell you from the bedroom," Laraine said icily. She moved around to face Holloway, and leaned back against his desk. She was wearing a pink robe over her nightgown. "But I don't blame you. I hate that Kid—and his sidekick, Cutthroat, makes my skin crawl. You should be glad you're so low on funds."

"What about that, Laraine? You see how it is. I can't hold these . . . these animals at bay much longer. When is the head of that syndicate you've been telling me about going to reach Salt Lake City?"

"Early next week."

The man sighed. "For both our sakes, I hope you're right."

"I heard about Longarm."

"That son of a bitch is a hard man to kill. But maybe we won't have to kill him."

"You have a plan?"

"I have a plan."

She left the desk and moved close to him. "Good. Let's hope this one works better than the last one." She reached down and rested her cool hand against his fevered cheek.

Holloway shuddered. What he had in mind was tricky. It frightened him just to think of it, but he knew it was his only chance if he wanted to satisfy Longarm and get those two gunslicks off his back. And if it didn't go just the why he planned, it still might work out for him. He took a deep breath and got to his feet.

Laraine stepped back. She had expected an embrace when she moved closer to him.

"I've got to get dressed," he told her. "There's no telling when Longarm and the rest of that posse of his will ride in. I've got to be ready."

"Of course."

"You're not angry about those two girls?"

She laughed. "Why should I be—if you're not unhappy with all the men I find in Salt Lake City."

"I didn't say that."

"No, but you will have to say that from now on."

She spun on her heels and left him standing by his chair, cursing miserably to himself as he mopped the cold sweat that stood out on his forehead.

Cutthroat knocked once on the door to the darkened funeral parlor, then pushed it open and walked inside. He closed the door behind him, making no effort to move softly or conceal his presence.

"Who's that?" called Tyler from the other side of the curtained doorway. "Is there someone there?"

"It's me," called Cutthroat, as he started carefully through the dark parlor to the doorway. "Lem Flynn."

A match flared behind the curtain, and a moment later the stronger glow of a kerosene lamp sent beams of light around the curtain, giving Cutthroat a little more light to see by.

He brushed the curtain aside and stepped into Truman Tyler's cramped living quarters. Tyler was sitting up in bed in his longjohns. He did not look happy to see Cutthroat.

"What is it?" Tyler wanted to know. "Isn't this pretty damn late to discuss a funeral?"

"Depends on whose it is."

"Now what the hell do you mean by that, Lem?"

Cutthroat unholstered his Colt, aimed it casually at Tyler, and cocked it. He smiled then by way of answer, his hooked nose cutting the full line of his mouth.

"Oh God," moaned Tyler, flinging himself farther back up onto the bed and holding his right arm up to protect his face. "No, Lem, for Christ's sake, don't point that at me like that!"

"You got a sixgun?"

Tyler nodded, wide-eyed.

"Where is it?"

"Over there," Tyler told him, his voice quavering. "On the dresser next to my hat."

Cutthroat uncocked his revolver and dropped it into his holster. "Good," he said, reaching for Tyler's sidearm. He pulled the Colt from its stiff holster and checked to see if it was loaded. It was. Like all tenderfoots, Tyler had filled every chamber with a round. He was lucky he hadn't blown off his foot before this. But then, it did not appear that the undertaker had much occasion to wear his weapon. It probably frightened him too much. If he wore it, he'd only have to use it sometime.

Cutthroat turned to look at Tyler, still smiling—but there was no longer any trace of mirth in the smile. "Holloway says you're about to crack, Tyler—spill the beans. He thinks you'd be better off dead, so you won't be able to testify about all them bodies in boot hill."

Tyler gasped and pushed himself still farther up onto his bed, his eyes so wide that Cutthroat could see the whites all around his pupils. "I told Holloway I wasn't going to bury any more of his bodies, that I wanted out. But . . . but I was only trying to scare him! I wouldn't tell anyone! I swear. Please, Lem! Don't kill me!"

"Oh, I ain't gonna kill you."

Hope flickered for an instant in the undertaker's eyes.

"You're gonna commit suicide," Cutthroat went on mildly.

With one quick stride, Cutthroat returned to the bed and grabbed the neck of Tyler's nightshirt. He pulled the struggling man close and rammed Tyler's own Colt into his mouth, then thumb-cocked it. Tyler tried to scream, but nothing came out except a crazy gargling sound. Cutthroat rammed the Colt still farther into the back of Tyler's mouth. The man gagged and retched violently, his frail body twisting convulsively. Holding Tyler's head in place with the gun, Cutthroat snatched up a pillow and pushed it down onto the mortician's face.

Then he pulled the trigger.

The mess didn't bother Cutthroat, but there was a momentary flicker of irritation in his eyes as he struggled to get the fingers of Tyler's right hand around the Colt's grips. At last, satisfied, he left the parlor by the front door and hurried across the street to the Lucky Seven.

He was like a kid again, thinking of that raven-haired young wench waiting for him up there in that fancy crib. He hoped she was still scared.

Chapter 14

Other than Biff, who was dead, two members of Longarm's posse had been wounded, but neither man's wound was likely to prove fatal. Longarm had stayed at the Kid's ranch long enough to bury the two outlaws. Now, as he and Big Bill led the posse back through the canyon, he could not help but think of the four other outlaws that—according to the reports given to him by his men—were sprawled above him on the steep slopes, waiting for the vultures to find them in the light of a new day.

The narrowest portion of the canyon loomed ahead. The moonless night was as dark as the inside of a whore's heart. Longarm could feel rather than see the sheer walls of the canyon leaning over him as he rode. He glanced back past Big Bill at his two wounded men. Both of them were tough railroad men. They had joined the posse with a lighthearted eagerness, determined to do their bit to rid Antelope Junction of the element they felt was ruining it. Now, however, nursing their painful wounds as they rode, they were grimly silent and a whole lot more sober.

The night was suddenly punctuated by a gunshot from the slope above them. The high *spang* of a ricocheting round sounded close behind Longarm. Then came a second shot. This time Longarm felt the bullet breeze past before digging into the dirt of the trail.

"Up there!" Big Bill cried, pointing. "I just saw the son of a bitch's gun flash!"

Longarm's Colt Model T fairly leaped into his hand as he followed Bill's pointing finger and sent two rounds up into the darkness. But a moment later, from a closer vantage point this time, came a third shot. A horse screamed in pain and terror and, whinnying pathetically, collapsed on its side. Luckily it belonged to one of the posse members who was not wounded, and the fellow was able to leap clear.

"Hold it right there!" the outlaw shouted down at them. At once Longarm recognized the voice. It was Weed Leeper. "Don't none of you ride no further! I can see you better than you can see me. All I want is a horse. Get off your mounts and walk back the way you come from!"

"Do as he says!" Longarm told the others. "Dismount!"

Big Bill and the posse member without a horse helped the two wounded men down out of their saddles. Then, cursing bitterly, they all began to file back through the canyon.

"Keep going!" Weed Leeper called from above them, his voice sounding much closer. "I can see every damn one of you."

That was a lie, and Longarm knew it. He ducked swiftly in under an overhanging shelf of rock, waited a moment to see if he had been detected, then moved cautiously back through the darkness as the others continued on. In a few moments he had reached the abandoned horses. He heard gravel sifting down from just above him. Ducking back, he waited until Weed Leeper, scrambling frantically to retain his footing on the steep slope, dropped to the canyon floor only a few yards away.

"Hold it right there, Weed," Longarm said, his .44 trained on the man.

With a violent curse, Weed spun around to face Longarm, gunfire lancing from his fist. The round shattered the root system of a stunted pine just above Longarm's head, showering him with loose dirt. As he ducked back and tried to wipe the stinging dirt from his eyes, he heard Weed fling himself onto the back of a horse and gallop out of the canyon.

Still digging at his eyes, Longarm darted away from the canyon wall and flung two quick shots after the fleeing rider.

He could not be sure, but he was almost certain he saw Weed slump forward after the second shot. But Weed kept on riding, nevertheless, and soon the drum of his hoofbeats had faded away completely.

Longarm cursed aloud. With two fewer horses, it would be well past midnight before they reached Antelope Junction.

Longarm's gloomy estimate had been correct. It was only a couple of hours before dawn when he and his bedraggled posse arrived back in the tank town. The streets were deserted and dark, the only light coming from Doc Gibbs' office over the undertaker's parlor.

"Looks like the doc's still up," said Big Bill, as he pulled his horse alongside Longarm's.

"Good," Longarm replied wearily. "I hope he's sober. We've got some customers for him."

Big Bill nodded and turned in his saddle. The two men who had been hit were riding cantle behind the other two riders. Each wounded man had his head slumped forward onto the shoulder of his saddlemate. "Ride on over to the doc's place," the town marshal told them. "Longarm and I will give you a hand with those two."

"We'll need it," said the closest rider.

Longarm headed his horse into the tie rail in front of Tyler's place of business, and dismounted. Big Bill got down also, and the two lawmen helped the two wounded men to dismount. One of them awoke and was strong enough to negotiate by himself the outside steps leading up to Gibbs' office. But the other one remained close to unconsciousness. Big Bill slung this one over his shoulder and followed the other one up the steps with Longarm following close behind.

Doc Gibbs was asleep at his desk, his nearly empty lamp guttering fitfully. As they pushed through his door, he sat up, startled, his red-rimmed eyes blinking in surprise at their entrance.

"What in hell do we have here?" he managed.

"Two wounded men," Longarm replied.

Gibbs reached for a whiskey bottle on his desk, saw that it was empty, and flung it into a corner. Then he ran his hand distractedly over his bald head and made a conscious effort to pull himself together. "Put that one you're carrying down on the cot," he told Big Bill. Then, looking at the wounded man

157

who had walked in under his own power, he said, "You sit down in that chair over there while I take a look at your friend."

The wounded man nodded and sat down. He looked very pale and was obviously close to passing out himself, but Longarm knew he would be able to last until the doctor got to him.

Doc Gibbs got up from his desk and moved over to the unconscious man. In a moment his shaking but deft fingers had ripped off the man's shirt. Leaning close, he peered at the angry-looking wound in the man's side, poking at it carefully with his fingers. He straightened up after a moment and looked over at Longarm.

"He'll be all right, looks like. It's a clean wound and the bullet's gone right on through. Right now he's just plain exhausted."

Longarm heard heavy, hurried footsteps on the stairs outside the doctor's office, and a moment later Clinton Holloway burst in. The man was obviously distraught.

"Longarm!" he cried. "You've got to help me!"

Longarm studied the big man warily for a moment, trying to figure out what new perfidy he was planning. "What is it, Holloway?" Longarm drawled. "What's got you so riled up? The fact that Bill and I managed to escape the Kid's ambush?"

"Ambush? I don't know what you're talking about, Longarm. I did hear about your posse—after it left Antelope Junction. But I don't doubt that your failure to apprehend those you went after is responsible for what happened here tonight."

Longarm shrugged. He hadn't really expected Holloway to admit to anything. "All right then. What is it?"

"Truman Tyler's been murdered!"

"Murdered?"

"Who did it, Clint?" Big Bill asked, stepping closer. "You got any idea?"

"One of those men your posse flushed this evening—Cutthroat Flynn. Someone saw him let himself into Tyler's place and then heard a muffled shot. I went over and checked. It was terrible! The whole back of his head..."

"Spare me the details, Holloway," said Longarm angrily. "Where's that witness?"

"You think he'd testify against Cutthroat? He's already lit out, frightened half out of his wits. You won't get any testimony from him."

"What interests me now is why you're telling me this. You'd

be the one to benefit most from Tyler's death. The way I look at it, if Cutthroat murdered Tyler, he was most likely carrying out your orders."

"Why, that's a dastardly lie, deputy! I had nothing to do with Tyler's death."

"That so? Cutthroat and the Kid are beholden to you. From what I've been able to gather, you're the one settled them and all the other hardcases on their so-called homesteads."

"All right. I admit that now. But I no longer have control over any of them. I had no idea these men would be so dangerous, so impossible to manage. I've made a terrible mistake. But now I need your help. You've got to stop those two wild men at my place."

"Catching up to those two has been my intention since I rode in, Holloway. The Elko Kid is a wanted man, and I suspicion his sidekick is too. But I want your testimony on this murder of Tyler, for starters. That would give me something solid on Cutthroat as well as the Kid."

"My God, Longarm," the owner of the Lucky Seven gasped. "I...I don't dare. You have no idea what these two men are capable of. If they heard that I came over here to ask for your help..."

Doc Gibbs looked up from cleaning the shoulder wound of the sitting posse member. He was using a fresh bottle of whiskey and a bloody cloth. The wounded man was gripping the edge of the desk with his one good hand as beads of perspiration rolled down his drawn face.

"Never mind asking him," said Doc Gibbs, setting down the whiskey bottle. "I'll testify. I heard the shot from up here and saw Cutthroat leave. When Clint came over to investigate, I joined him. If I hadn't seen Cutthroat, I would have thought Tyler had shot himself. That's how Cutthroat wanted it to look, anyway."

"And you'll testify?"

"If I live that long."

"There now," said Holloway, obviously relieved to have the doctor take him off the hook. "With that settled, I suggest you two lawmen see to those two outlaws. They're still in the Lucky Seven, raising hell with my best girls. They've been at it for hours."

Longarm looked long and steadily at Holloway. "Sure," he said at length, "but you're coming with us, Holloway. You

159

show us where they are. I don't trust you, and I don't care if you know it. In fact, you'd *better* know it. If you make any funny moves, you'll find your fat ass full of lead. Do I make myself clear?"

The owner of the Lucky Seven was perspiring freely, his face beet-red in indignation at Longarm's blunt words, but he bottled his fury and nodded stiffly. "Yes, deputy. You certainly do. But that vicious statement—along with all those other wild accusations you've been making—was entirely uncalled for, and I hope when the time comes you'll be man enough to apologize."

Longarm laughed shortly and turned to Big Bill. "You ready to finish this business?"

"You bet I am."

Longarm looked back at Holloway. "Lead the way," he told him.

As Longarm followed Holloway across the dark street with Big Bill, it was obvious to him what the owner of the Lucky Seven was up to. Aware that Longarm was closing in on his operation, and seeing that the Kid and his gang had been unable to cut Longarm down, he had decided to double-cross the Kid in a desperate effort to ingratiate himself with Longarm. At the same time, the murder of the undertaker had gotten rid of a witness who would have been able to testify against Holloway and his use of boot hill, if it came to that. There was absolutely no doubt in Longarm's mind, therefore, that Holloway was behind Tyler's murder.

Only one lamp was still lit on the chandelier inside the Lucky Seven; it cast but a feeble glow over the gloomy interior. A faint sliver of light showed under the kitchen door beyond the stairwell. Dim light from another lantern filtered down the stairwell from the second floor. The saloon appeared empty, the chairs neatly placed on top of the tables, ready for the swamper come morning.

At the foot of the stairs, Holloway pulled up and turned to face Longarm. "The Kid and Cutthroat are in the room down the hall on your right. You can't miss it."

Longarm took out his .44 and prodded Holloway in the small of the back. "Keep on going up those stairs, Holloway. Take us all the way to the door."

The man swallowed unhappily. "That's not necessary," he

insisted, his voice a hoarse whisper. "You can hear them from here. They're in there, I tell you. What do you need me for? I've done all I can to help. It's up to you now."

The door leading from the kitchen swung open. A man with a sixgun in his right hand appeared in the doorway, his short, powerful figure silhouetted sharply against the yellow backlight. There appeared to be a slim blond lad cowering behind him, but what momentarily startled Longarm was the fact that the outlaw was naked from the waist down.

"Goddamn you, Holloway!" the half-naked gunman snarled. "You didn't tell me those two were in town already. You're double-crossin' us!"

"No, Will!" Holloway gasped, backing up hastily. "That ain't it! Honest! They surprised me!"

"Like hell they did!"

Longarm flung Holloway to one side just as the man in the doorway fired. The round smashed a balustrade, narrowly missing Holloway as the owner of the Lucky Seven fled up the stairs, screaming. The gunman fired a second time, and Big Bill groaned and went down, clutching at his right shoulder. Dropping low, Longarm returned the fire, pumping two quick shots at the gunman.

The first round splintered the doorjamb over his head, the second punched a hole in his belly. With a cry of dismay, the man dropped his sixgun and grabbed at his gut. Dark gouts of blood streamed through his clutching fingers as he staggered backward into the kitchen. Longarm saw the blond boy turn and dart out of sight. As the door swung shut, the last glimpse Longarm had of the gunman showed him sitting on the kitchen floor, his two hands still trying to hold his guts in.

Above them, Holloway was calling a warning to the Kid; he had obviously decided the advantage no longer belonged to Longarm, and was again changing sides. Longarm knelt beside Bill. The wounded man was holding his right shoulder and wore a look of pure astonishment. But when he saw the concern on Longarm's face, he managed a smile.

"Never mind me!" he said through clenched teeth. "This ain't much. Get up there before those bastards start pouring down on us!"

Longarm nodded grimly. Leaving the wounded man, he vaulted up the stairs and reached the second floor in time to see two armed men, the Kid and a lean, fearsome-looking companion, stepping out of a room at far the end of the hall. Unlike their companion downstairs in the kitchen, both men were completely naked.

This was the first time Longarm had laid eyes on the Kid's sidekick, the one they called Cutthroat. The moment he did, he remembered the old prospector's description of the granger who had shot him in the leg—and his own promise to the prospector to pay back the son of a bitch if he met up with him.

And this looked like the day.

He flung himself to the floor of the hallway, his .44 out in front of him. But before he could get off a shot, both men fired at him. One round tore off his hat, the other slammed into his .44, smashing it from his grip. Longarm glanced down at his right hand to see if he had lost any fingers. A red gash reached from his knuckles to his wrist. There was no feeling in the hand, but every digit was intact. He clenched his fist and saw the fingers close.

Grinning, the two men padded on naked feet down the hallway to inspect Longarm. The Kid looked scrawny and emaciated without the duster to cloak his figure. His skin had the pallor and sheen of a beeswax candle. Cutthroat reached Longarm first, his walleye staring blankly down at him, the big gun in his fist pointed casually at Longarm's head. As he halted over Longarm, he smiled and licked his chops.

"Get up, you son of a bitch," said the Kid, halting beside Cutthroat. "I been waiting a long time for this."

"So have I, Kid. The dodgers are still coming out on you."

"But no one's going to be chasing me after this, Longarm. I'll be dead and buried in boot hill. And as soon as I pull this trigger, there ain't gonna be no one to say that ain't me planted there."

The Kid cocked his pistol. At that moment, Longarm caught sight of an incredible apparition inching down the corridor toward them, a bloody sixgun in his right hand. Weed Leeper!

Longarm's desperate shot earlier that night had caught Weed squarely in the back. His entire shirtfront was a dark mass of blood. So drained of color was his face, it appeared to shine in the dim hallway. As Longarm watched, Weed staggered and fell to one knee, then pushed himself erect again, his wild, fevered eyes blazing.

"Kid!" Weed barked, his voice low and deadly.

Both the Kid and Cutthroat spun around to face Leeper. Weed's eyes were crazed now. He smiled as a thin ribbon of blood traced a path from the corner of his mouth. "You two set me up, made me crawl! I'm a dead man now, 'cause of you. So I come to take you with me!"

"No, Weed!" the Kid cried. "We didn't mean no harm! Someone had to stay back and slow down that posse!"

But even as he pleaded his case, the Kid was hauling up his iron. Weed fired point-blank at the Kid, then at Cutthroat. The Kid dropped like a rock, but Cutthroat managed to get off a single return shot as he was slammed backward. His foot caught Longarm's shoulder and he sprawled on his back past the lawman's prone form.

Cutthroat's round had struck Weed, catching him just above the belt buckle. The crazed gunman went down on one knee, but did not drop his gun. The sick smile remained pasted on his face. Incredibly, he managed to stand up and, using the wall as a support, pushed himself closer to the severely wounded Kid. Then he poured two more shots down into the Kid's naked body and continued doggedly on toward Longarm.

"I hear tell you was lookin' for me, deputy," Weed said, his voice a painful rasp. "I was the one killed that little slut Marie." He tried a chuckle, but began to cough, a weak, tearing sound that brought more bloody froth to his already crimsoned lips. "So now you found me," he managed.

As he spoke, he brought up his revolver and aimed it shakily down at Longarm, who rolled swiftly to one side as Weed's sixgun blasted, its slug punching a hole in the floor. Longarm kept on rolling until he was up on knee. Panting softly, Weed tracked Longarm with deliberate care and took aim a second time. But Longarm had already fumbled the derringer from his vest pocket. Switching it to his left hand, he fired up at Weed, emptying both barrels.

One neat hole appeared just under Weed's right eye. At the same time his other eye vanished, to be replaced by a wide, gaping hole. Weed's head was yanked backward, as if an invisible noose had settled over his head. The bloody sixgun in his hand detonated, the round smashing into the ceiling as Weed crashed backward to the floor.

Slowly, carefully, Longarm got up and walked over to inspect the dead Weed Leeper. He found it hard to believe that this sorry specimen of humanity could have exhibited such incredible tenacity of purpose. Evidently it was the Kid and Cutthroat who had forced him to stay behind to delay Longarm's posse. A dead man, Weed had come back to protest that suicidal mission. Cornered rats were dangerous, Longarm knew. But this had been a dead rat.

He was about to turn around to check on Cutthroat and the Kid when another gunshot sounded in the narrow hallway, its shattering explosion sounding like the crack of doom to Longarm's somewhat frayed nerves. He spun about in time to see Holloway spilling forward out of his office, the revolver in his hand dropping to the floor ahead of him.

Laraine Grover was standing in the open doorway behind him, a smoking Smith & Wesson .32 clasped firmly in her long, delicate hand.

Chapter 15

Laraine glanced at Longarm in horror at what she had just done. She was dressed in the same green dress she had been wearing the day before, an errant lock of red hair spilling across her forehead.

"He was going to kill you, Longarm!" she told him, her voice shrill, close to breaking. "He said he had to kill you. There was no other way."

He hurried over and took the revolver from her hand as gently as he could. The moment he touched her, she seemed to wilt. Before she sagged to the floor, he caught her up in his arms and carried her into Holloway's office and laid her down on a leather sofa.

She looked up at him, still distraught, her hand clutching at his shirt. "He said he could make it look like the Kid or Weed Leeper had shot you. I tried to talk him out of it, but he wouldn't listen to me. He laughed when I told him I'd stop him!"

"You just saved my life, Laraine. You don't have to say any more."

"You do understand, then."

"Yes."

She closed her eyes in relief, then opened them again to

gaze with sudden warmth up at him. "Thank God you are all right," she told him huskily. "I can't believe it. You alone surviving that awful slaughter out there in that hallway. I have never seen such a terrible sight."

She was becoming distraught again, her eyes widening in panic as she recalled the carnage in the hallway. Perspiration beaded her forehead. He bent low and kissed her on the lips, gently. "Relax," he told her. "It's all over now."

To his dismay she flung both arms about his neck and pressed her lips to his in a kiss he found incongruously wanton under the circumstances. He pulled away, his head reeling despite himself, and caught what he could only describe as an evil gleam in her hazel eyes.

"I've got to get Doc Gibbs to see to Big Bill," he told her. "He's been wounded. You just lie still there and try to forget what just happened. I won't be long."

She nodded. "Yes, Longarm. You go see to Bill. I'll be right here, waiting for you."

When he stepped back out into the hallway, he saw that Big Bill had pulled himself up the stairs and was now leaning on the bannister, a sick look on his face as he gazed on the bloody scene. He held his pistol in his left hand and had tucked his right hand into his shirt to give his shoulder some relief. Somehow he had managed to wrap what looked like a bar towel around his shoulder to stanch the flow of blood.

"Jesus, Longarm," he said. "You just had a war up here."

"You can thank Weed Leeper I'm still alive—and Laraine Grover."

Big Bill shook his head in disbelief. From below them in the saloon came a sudden burst of shouts and the sound of running feet. The battle had not gone unheard. The town was waking up prematurely to a grisly dawn.

Longarm tried not to take too deep a breath as he glanced down the hallway. A sickening stench was in the air. Two of the dead outlaws had voided themselves. He bent to check Holloway. The man was lying on his face. The bullet had entered high on his shoulder, but the wound did not appear to be fatal. Longarm rolled him over onto his back, picked up the revolver Holloway had dropped, and stuck it in his own gunbelt. The man's eyes flickered open. His lips moved slightly.

Longarm bent closer. "Can you hear me, Holloway?"

166

The man nodded feebly.

"You been shot bad, but I don't doubt you'll live. You going to tell me now what this is all about?"

"Laraine . . . ? Was it she who . . . ?"

"Yes."

"I'll tell you," he said. "I'll tell you everything, only get me the doc! I don't want to die, Longarm! Please! Get Doc Gibbs!"

"You won't die, I'm telling you. Just calm down till I get help for you."

At that moment the barkeep burst up the stairs past Big Bill, to kneel with evident concern beside the stricken Holloway. Surging up the stairs behind him came a crowd of hastily dressed citizens.

"Hold it!" Big Bill cried. "Hold it right there!"

But they paid the town marshal no heed as they continued to crowd on up the stairs, their faces eager, bloodlust lighting their eyes.

Big Bill fired his sixgun into the air. The detonation brought them to a hasty, scrambling halt.

"Tom! Perry!" Bill barked to the two closest men. "Go get some blankets to cover these dead outlaws. And the rest of you get back down them stairs!"

The two men turned and hurried back down to get the shrouds, but the rest tried to push past Bill to sneak a better look at the bloody, littered hallway.

"You heard me," Bill repeated, lowering his sixgun so that it was pointed at the growing crowd. "We got enough dead men up here so that a few more won't matter all that much! Now get back down there and wait!"

"Someone get Doc Gibbs!" Longarm called to the crowd.

But not a man budged from the stairwell. If there was blood up here, it was too strong an attraction for these men to pass up.

Ned, the barkeep, still bending over Holloway, looked over at the men crowding the top of the steps. "Drinks are on the house!" he told them. "Mr. Holloway just announced it!"

The crowd paused.

Ned pointed to one of the men at the top of the stairs. "Tim, you can serve till I get down there."

That did it. The crowd broke and streamed back down the stairs, hooting with delight as they went.

Ned stood up, glanced down the hallway at the litter of dead gunmen, then shook his head. "Jesus, if this town needed an undertaker, it needs one now."

"Where the hell's Doc Gibbs?" Big Bill asked, slumping wearily down on the top stair. "My head's beginning to spin."

"Let's go, Bill," said Longarm, helping the wounded town marshal to his feet. "I'll get you to your office, then go scare up Gibbs. You don't look so good."

"Reckon that's because I don't feel so good, neither," replied the marshal.

Ned called over to them, "I'll carry Mr. Holloway into his office. But you better hurry up with that doctor. Mr. Holloway just passed out again."

Longarm glanced back at Ned and watched as the burly barkeep lifted the owner of the Lucky Seven in his arms. He told Ned to put Holloway on his bed in his suite, and warned him that Laraine Grover was resting on the sofa in Holloway's office and should not be disturbed. Ned nodded, nudged the office door open with his massive shoulder, then eased his wounded employer gently through the doorway.

Longarm helped the weakened Big Bill down the stairs. From below them came the sound of breaking bottles and whoops of abandon. It was a kind of holiday for these men, Longarm realized. He had noticed that not a single man crowding the stairwell had resembled any of the hardcases that Holloway's scheme—whatever the hell it was—had imported to this town. The game was up, the outlaws undoubtedly realized now. More than likely, they were already preparing to pull out.

And these townsmen in the saloon below were celebrating the return of Antelope Junction to its citizens.

As soon as Longarm got Big Bill comfortable on the cot in his office, he hurried across the street and up the steps to Doc Gibbs' office. The two wounded members of Longarm's posse had left, and the doctor was asleep on his cot, a ratty blanket thrown carelessly over him, an empty bottle of laudanum resting on its side on the floor, inches from the doctor's outstretched hand.

Longarm shook the man gently. The doctor's eyes opened. He smiled. Longarm had seen that smile before—on the faces of Chinese workers asleep in opium dens. It was the blissful smile of those who had long since renounced the horrors of this world for the drugged fantasies of a better one.

"Doc!" Longarm called sharply, shaking him more violently. "Doc, wake up!"

Gibbs opened his eyes slowly, wonderingly, the soft smile still on his face. The smile vanished abruptly the moment he began to focus his eyes on Longarm. He groaned softly.

"Doc, we got two more wounded men," Longarm told him. "They need your help."

The doctor gazed blearily up at Longarm. "More wounded?"

"That's right."

He shook his head wearily. "Is there no end to it?"

"There will be now, doc. We've flushed the nest clean. But Clint Holloway's been shot in the back and Big Bill's got a nasty shoulder wound."

The man sighed. "I'll come. Just . . . just bring me a bottle from my medicine cabinet over there. There's a fresh bottle of laudanum."

"No, doc. No more of that stuff. When you get finished tending to Bill and Holloway, I'll buy you a bottle of whiskey. But not until then."

The man sat up and ran his hand over his glistening dome. "As you say, deputy." He flipped the blanket back and stood up shakily. "Just as you say." He smiled weakly. "You're the doctor."

Dawn was breaking over the town as Longarm led Doc Gibbs from the town marshal's office and back to the Lucky Seven. The doc had cleaned out Big Bill's shoulder wound and stopped the bleeding with a tight, efficient bandage. Then he had fashioned a sling for Bill's right arm. Despite his weaknesses, Doc Gibbs was a competent physician.

The Lucky Seven sounded like a Mexican revolution. Tim, the townsman Ned had designated, was still behind the bar along with another fellow. They were doing their best to satisfy the demand, but as Longarm thrust his way into the wild throng, he wondered why Ned had not come back downstairs yet.

A bearded townsman shoved a bottle at Longarm. "Have a drink, deputy!" he cried, lurching dangerously.

Longarm shook his head as he caught the man and prevented him from falling to the floor. Then he pushed his way past him

169

to the stairs. As he mounted them and looked down at the roistering sea of humanity below, he wondered what Laraine must be thinking as she tried to rest above this flood of noise. The very foundation of the building was shuddering from the pounding boot heels, the shouting, the clash of glasses and shattering bottles.

He needn't have worried. Laraine was gone from the sofa. As he looked around the office, the doctor walked on into Holloway's suite. A moment later, just as Longarm was about to follow after him, the doctor came out.

"I'll have that whiskey now, deputy," he said.

"What about Holloway?"

"He's dead."

"You sure, doc? That wound sure as hell didn't look like it was fatal."

"It wasn't. The man was either strangled or smothered to death. It makes no difference which, he's dead enough."

As Longarm started past him, the doctor restrained him. "God in heaven, deputy. Haven't you seen enough this night? I have. His face is purple, his tongue protruding from his mouth in an obscene display of bad manners." The little potbellied physician shuddered. "Please, deputy. That whiskey you promised. I need it now."

"I think I need it, too," Longarm replied, leading the way back down the stairs.

About a half-hour later, Longarm knocked on Laraine's hotel room door. She called out to him to enter. He pulled the door open and stepped inside. Laraine, dressed in a long satin robe, was standing before her bed, an open suitcase on the counterpane behind her.

"I was worried about you, Laraine," Longarm said. "You all right?"

"Yes, thank you," she replied, her voice tight. "I'm fine."

As Longarm closed the door behind him, Laraine turned back around and resumed packing. She moved efficiently, placing her things in the trunk neatly, then carefully smoothing them out before returning to the dresser. She seemed a mite too efficient for Longarm. It was as if she were trying not to think, just act. She kept her back to him when she spoke again.

"I must leave this terrible place," she told him. "I'm taking the morning train."

Standing by the door, Longarm said, "Holloway's dead."

"Yes, I know. I shot him."

"It wasn't your bullet that killed him."

She spun to face him. "What do you mean?"

"He was strangled. Or smothered."

Longarm said nothing; he just watched her carefully.

Longarm!" she cried. "Why are you looking at me like that? Surely you don't think I had anything to do with that!"

He moved closer to Laraine, then reached out both his hands to her. With a headlong rush, she threw herself into his arms. "As soon as you left, I heard the sound of those men downstairs drinking, carrying on like it was a holiday! I couldn't stand it! I left by the rear. But I had to walk down that corridor . . . past those bodies . . . !"

She shuddered and he held her closer, comforting her. "Tell me, Laraine. Did you see Ned carry Holloway into his suite?"

"Yes."

"Was he still in there when you left?"

"Yes. I slipped out as soon as he went past me into the suite."

Longarm nodded, stroking her red hair comfortingly. "It adds up, I reckon. I've been asking around, but no one seems to know where he's gone. He's just disappeared."

"But why? Why would Ned do such a thing?"

"I went back upstairs and checked the safe in Holloway's office. It was open—and empty."

"Then you think Ned . . ."

"Let's just say he had the opportunity—and the motive."

"You see, Longarm?" she cried, hugging him still closer. "You see why I must get out of this terrible place!"

"Yes. Maybe we'll both take that train."

"Oh yes, Longarm. Yes!" She found his lips with hers, and kissed him with the same reckless, passionate intensity she had exhibited in Holloway's office. Then she drew him urgently back toward the bed. "Please!" she told him fiercely. "I think I need you now. Do you understand how it is with me? All this death. I want life instead—the feel of your body once again!"

In a moment they were grappling on her bed, he to disrobe her, she to free him so that he could enter her. What followed was wordless and swift and violent. He impaled her without gentleness, with a kind of brutal insensitivity she appeared to crave. They were not making love. They were doing battle, it seemed. Her cries, when she finally climaxed, were shattering. Spent, exhausted, he pulled away from her at last and gazed down at her sprawled body—at the wild, unkempt tangle of her red hair spread like a torn flower upon the counterpane—and shuddered.

She saw him looking down at her and flung herself over onto her stomach and began to cry uncontrollably. Her pitiful, shuddering sobs filled the small room. As he had understood her passionate need a moment before, he understood now her sudden, overwhelming torment. She was a woman at odds with herself, unable to comprehend the titanic forces that ruled her.

He slipped off the bed, stepped back into his britches, and snatched up his hat. He knew, as he drew the door shut behind him a moment later, that his swift departure was what Laraine needed now.

Two weeks later, his right arm still in a sling, Big Bill Sanders chuckled as he raised his glass to Longarm's, then tossed his drink down the hatch. Even though the two men were in Salt Lake City, the Morgan Tyler Hotel was one place where Longarm could order all the Maryland rye he wanted.

"Guess maybe you're right," Big Bill said, still chuckling. "Now that all the steam has gone out of Antelope Junction, it ain't too much fun anymore. But Doc Gibbs ain't complaining. He says all he gets to treat now is baby colic and constipation, and that's just the way he wants it."

Longarm nodded. Aided by an influx of federal deputies, whom Marshal Vail sent in on Longarm's request, the town of Antelope Junction and the basin lands surrounding it had been cleared of outlaws. The miserable ranches they had started to homestead were now abandoned, and the town of Antelope Junction was settling back into what it had been before Holloway's arrival—a tired, dusty tank town.

Even boot hill had been cleaned up. The wooden markers over the graves were now accurate. This time the bodies of Weed Leeper, the Elko Kid, and Lem "Cutthroat" Flynn—among others—actually did sleep beneath the graveyard's rocky crust.

"Tell me, Longarm," said Big Bill, "ain't you any closer to knowing what Holloway was up to when he brought in all them hardcases to homestead the basin?"

"A mite closer, but I suspicion I'll be a damn sight surer before this day is out. One thing I know, and Billy Vail agrees with me, those outlaws were homesteading the basin lands on the understanding they would sell their claims back to Holloway when he was ready to deal. And what they got in exchange was a place to hide and a chance at a new identity. With themselves officially dead and buried, they could get themselves a new start."

Big Bill shook his head at the thought. "Glad they never got the chance for another start. They were bad enough the first time around."

"Guess you've got a point there, Bill. But don't forget, you've done pretty well with your new start."

"Sure. But I had to serve my time, don't forget. I had to earn the right for that new start. These men weren't earning it. They were part of a fraud."

"Reckon that's true, Bill," Longarm said, consulting his pocket watch. He put his watch back and finished his drink. Then he got to his feet. "Thanks for the drink. I'm glad to see that shoulder of yours is coming around."

"Time to go, is it?"

Longarm nodded. "I have an appointment with a very beautiful woman, Bill, and I don't want to be late."

Laraine pulled open the door of her suite before Longarm had a chance to knock twice.

"I was waiting for you, Longarm," she said eagerly. "Are you always so punctual? I was hoping you'd get here a little early."

"Met a friend downstairs," Longarm told her, striding into her suite and handing her his hat. "We had a drink together."

Laraine closed the door and turned to face him. She was dressed in a long blue dress that buttoned down the front. Its lines were simple, the waist narrow, the flare of the bust designed to set the lawman's pulse pounding. And that it did. As did the fact that Laraine had let her hair down, allowing its flaming luxuriance to flow down onto her shoulders.

She dropped his hat on the stand by the door, then walked toward him, arms outstretched. They kissed, not politely, but not passionately either. She was holding back, teasing him. "Drink?" she asked.

He nodded and sat down on the sofa.

"Maryland rye, if I'm not mistaken."

"That's right."

"You've been such a stranger, Longarm," she said, handing him his drink and sitting down beside him on the sofa. "I've felt so neglected."

"I've been busy cleaning up that mess in Antelope Junction."

She made a face. "Please. I don't want to think of that place ever again. It was like some awful nightmare."

"Yes." He sipped his drink. "That it was."

"Longarm, this sofa is so stiff and formal," she said boldly. "Bring your drink with you and follow me."

She got up and walked into her bedroom. With an amiable shrug, Longarm followed her. She stopped before her bed and turned abruptly. "Surprise!" she said.

It was a surprise indeed. As she walked with her back to him, she had deftly unbuttoned her dress. Now, as she turned to face him, the dress swung open, revealing that Laraine Grover had prepared herself for Longarm's visit without any of the usual feminine undergarments. No corset. No chemise. No bloomers. No garters or stockings. The only thing between Laraine and her dress was skin.

"You like?"

"Let me finish my drink. Then I'll tell you."

A moment later, on the bed, he was telling her—with his hands and his lips. But he took his time. Teasingly, he thought.

But he didn't fool Laraine.

"What's the matter, Longarm?" she asked, coiling a lock of his heavy, dark hair about one of her fingers. "You seem a little shy, all of a sudden. Are you . . . thinking of our last time together?"

"Guess maybe I am."

"I just don't know how to explain that, except to say that it was the most exciting time I've ever had. It was like something . . . had taken over me . . . and gotten into me," she finished, giggling and holding him close.

"I keep thinking of Holloway," he said, sitting up suddenly and resting his back against the bed's headboard. "And those basin lands. Laraine, what in hell did that man want with that wilderness of alkali, cheat grass, and jackrabbits?"

"What makes you think I'd know?" She rested her head against his chest and dropped her hand casually onto his sagging erection.

"He might have told you. You're a very lovely lady geologist. If anyone would know what he thought was out there, you might."

"Why do you want to know, Longarm?"

Longarm took a deep breath. "Do you have any idea what a deputy U.S. marshal makes in a month?"

"No. How much?"

"I'd be too embarrassed to tell you."

She snuggled closer to him and squeezed his erection impishly. "Then don't tell me."

"I figure Holloway was onto something. But it wasn't gold, like everyone thought—and like he tried to tell you. It was something else, but what, I have no idea."

"And you want me to tell you."

"If you could. You may know more than you realize. He might have let something slip."

She released his erection and pushed herself away from him so she could look into his face. "Why? I thought the case was closed. Holloway's dead, and those outlaws he brought in are dead or gone."

"That's right."

"Then what do you care what Holloway was after?"

"I told you."

"You mean . . . your small salary? You think perhaps you— and I—might be able to find what it was that Holloway thought was so valuable out there—and maybe sell it?"

He pulled her close to him and began stroking her hair. "Is that such a bad idea?"

"No," she said, her voice small as she snuggled closer to him. "Not at all."

He kissed her ear. She turned her head and they kissed on the lips. It was a long kiss, and when it was done, Longarm was finding his fifth member joining the party. "Mmm," she said, stroking his erection playfully. "Having you for a partner might be very exciting."

"Then you know . . . what Holloway was after?"

She pushed herself away from him and sat up on the bed. She looked at him for a long moment, while he feasted his eyes in turn on her pale, lovely nakedness. "This is more than I bargained for when I invited you up here," she told him.

She got up and walked over to her vanity and sat down on the bench before the mirror. Then—still as naked as a marble statue—she began combing out her long hair, thoughtfully.

Watching his reflection in the mirror, she said, "Have you ever heard of copper porphyry, Longarm?"

"Can't say as I have. What in hell's that?"

"It is a complex, low-grade ore containing sizable quantities of lead, zinc, silver—and yes, even a little gold, as a bonus."

"It's valuable then."

"Only if it is mined in a certain way."

"What way?"

"Open-pit. There's an open-pit mine in Butte, Montana, that is proving to be very profitable."

Longarm nodded. He remembered reading about it somewhere, now that he thought of it. "So that's what's out there in that basin? Copper porphyry?"

"Yes."

"And that's what Holloway was after."

Still combing her hair, she turned on the bench to face him, her pale breasts thrusting impudently at him. "Yes, Longarm. That's why Holloway was trying to buy up those lands." Her hazel eyes showed the excitement she was feeling. They were brilliant with greed.

"That kind of a mining operation would take big financial backing, wouldn't it?"

"Of course."

"Did Holloway have it?"

"He was getting it. But his backers pulled out after all this terrible publicity."

"How did he learn about this copper porphyry, Laraine?"

"I don't know."

"Yes you do."

"Why, what do you mean?"

"It was you who told him. In fact it was you who brought him to Salt Lake City from Butte."

"You know?"

"I've been doing some digging this past week."

"All right. I admit it." She spread her milk-white thighs slightly, so casually that it could have been a mistake—but wasn't. Then she smiled. "I brought Holloway into this. But Holloway was a fool, a blundering idiot, in fact. His plan was too elaborate. I knew it would fall through as soon as you arrived. But now the two of us can go ahead with our own plan. I have the deeds to that land, and I have found other backers. Together we can do it, Longarm!"

"No, Laraine," Longarm said, swinging his legs off the bed and sitting up. "Your days of planning are over. I'm sending a complete report to the Washington office, with your part in the scheme made as clear as I can. Then I mean to alert Quincy Boggs. I think the Mormons should be told what riches they have in their own backyard. I got a feeling they'll know how to put all that wealth to very good use."

She looked at him for a long moment, coldly. Then she smiled meanly. "I should have known what you were up to, Longarm—when a man built like you couldn't get it up."

"I'm sorry, Laraine."

"No you're not. You're probably congratulating yourself on your cleverness." She turned back to her mirror and began once again to comb her hair.

"That's not true. I am a man of the law, and I must do what is right, no matter how I might like to look the other way."

Laraine did not reply; she just continued combing her hair. The strokes, however, seemed shorter and angrier. As Longarm stood up to pull on his britches and shrug into his shirt, he felt a little disappointed that Laraine was not screaming and ranting at him for his duplicity.

"Do what you want, Longarm," she told him icily. "I have broken no laws."

"What about the murder of Holloway?"

"I had nothing to do with that man's death!" she snapped.

"You shot him."

"Only to save your worthless life."

"As you would have me believe."

She slapped the comb down and turned to face him, seething. Somehow she had managed to pull a small nickel-plated Smith & Wesson revolver from a vanity drawer. It was the same one she had used to shoot Holloway, and its muzzle was yawning up at Longarm before he could grab for his cross-draw rig, hanging on the bedpost.

She got up from the bench and walked toward him. He stood his ground. "I don't want to kill you," she told him. "But I will if you make me."

"I'd rather make love to you," Longarm said, smiling and reaching out to her.

She hesitated, momentarily confused. That instant was all Longarm needed. He slapped her gunhand, pushing the revolver away. It went off, its round spiderwebbing the vanity mirror. Longarm snatched the revolver from her and tossed it onto the bed.

Furious, she came at him with hooked fingers. For a moment he had all he could do to keep her claws out of his eyes. He grabbed her wrists and she tried to kick him in the shins. When she succeeded finally, she let out a shriek of dismay. She had forgotten she was barefoot.

The fight went out of her and she fell into his arms, sobbing.

"Please, Longarm," she pleaded. "Let me go. Don't turn me in. After all, I saved your life!"

"Did you? Is that what you were doing when you shot Holloway?"

"Of course. I could have waited and shot Holloway after he shot you, couldn't I?"

Longarm frowned. "Yes," he said. "I reckon that's true."

"You see, Longarm! You owe me, whether you want to admit it or not."

He pushed her away from him and looked for a long moment into her lovely hazel eyes, swimming now in tears. Then he shrugged. "All right," he said. "Get dressed. We'll go downstairs for a drink. It'll give me time to think."

She flung her arms around his neck and kissed him—the same woman who, a moment before, had been ready to pull the trigger on him. He returned her kiss, laughed ironically, then pushed her gently away and picked her Smith & Wesson up off the bed. He tucked it into his waistband, then strapped on his gunbelt and shrugged into his frock coat.

"I'll wait in the next room," he told her. "I suggest you put on some underdrawers this time."

As he walked into the next room and sat down on the sofa to wait for her, he could hear her moving quickly about the room as she dressed. To his surprise, she was humming.

Chapter 16

As they left the suite together and walked down the corridor to the stairs, Laraine kept her right hand tucked into Longarm's arm as she leaned her head against his shoulder. Her provocative nearness made him acutely aware of her perfume, a fragrance as subtly arousing as a woman's sigh in the dark. That, coupled with Laraine's low, seductive voice was eroding Longarm's resolve.

After all, as she was not at all shy in reminding him, she had saved his life. Furthermore, she was a woman whose passion was as violent and insatiable as that of any woman he had ever pleasured. The thought of that volcanic capacity shut away in some dank prison cell went against every bone in his body.

She had made a mistake in allying herself with a fool as inept and bloody as Holloway turned out to be. Obviously that plan to import outlaws to take out those homesteads had been his plan, not hers. Had she known what bloodshed would follow, there was certainly a chance she would not have gone along with it.

And again, she had saved his life. Holloway had found out in Doc Gibbs' office just how determined Longarm was to bring him to justice. As Laraine had told Longarm, Holloway felt he had no choice in the matter. He had to kill Longarm.

"You'll see, Longarm," Laraine said, squeezing his arm gently as they came to the foot of the stairs. "Ours will be a lovely partnership. You know how to satisfy a woman, and I know how to take care of a man. We'll be rich, Longarm, and happy. Very, very happy. I promise you."

He patted her hand.

As they started across the lobby to the lounge, she said, "What's the matter, Longarm? You haven't said much. I hope you haven't already made up your mind. You have not forgotten your promise—to think this offer of mine over." She leaned closer. "To let me do my best to convince you."

"I haven't forgotten my promise, Laraine."

"Fine. Order me a scotch, dear heart. We'll sit over there in that corner booth. It's nice and cozy."

"No, Laraine," he told her, coming to a halt and gently disengaging her hand from his arm. "We'll sit over there, at that table in the corner, where Big Bill and Marshal Deegar are waiting for us."

There was a familiar figure sitting beside Deegar, manacled to the sheriff's wrist. When Laraine saw him, she gasped. For a moment, Longarm thought she would turn and run.

But then she straightened her shoulders and marched resolutely across the lounge beside Longarm, pulling up in front of the sheriff's prisoner.

"Ned! You fool," she said to him. "What have you told the sheriff?"

The burly barkeep swallowed hard. "Everything."

She closed her eyes for a long moment, then turned to Longarm. "That drink, Longarm. Please. I need it now. And make it a stiff one."

A moment later, when he came back with the double scotch for her, she was sitting at the table across from Big Bill, her face pale and drawn, her eyes downcast. She took the drink gratefully.

"Thank you, Longarm."

Longarm sat down and looked across the table at Marshal Deegar. "Well?"

The sheriff nodded. "Ned here confirmed just about everything you guessed. When I told him I got the information from Miss Grover, he broke down and sang like a bird."

Ned looked across the table at Laraine. "You mean you hadn't been arrested, Laraine?"

"No."

"But . . . they knew everything."

"Not everything," corrected Longarm. "I only just found out for sure what in hell it was that Laraine and the rest of you were after."

"But Holloway's murder!" Ned blurted. "They knew all about that. They even knew why we did it."

"The titles to those homesteads," Longarm said, turning to face Laraine. "That was what you took from Holloway's safe, wasn't it?"

She sighed and shrugged. "Yes."

"How did you figure that, Longarm?" asked Deegar.

"That had to be the motive. We couldn't find the outlaws' deeds anywhere, and they should have been in Holloway's safe."

Longarm turned to Laraine. "You turned all your charm loose on Ned soon after he went to work for Holloway, didn't you? And when you saw him carrying Holloway into the office, you had no trouble convincing him what had to be done."

The only sign of emotion Laraine showed was the whitening of her knuckles as she clutched her glass.

"And I suppose you told him what you just got through telling me? Something about what a lovely partnership you and he would make, and how Ned really knew how to satisfy a woman, while you knew just how to take care of a man." Longarm chuckled ironically. "And I guess you do at that, Laraine."

With a snap of her wrist, she flung her scotch into Longarm's face.

Deegar sprang to his feet as Longarm took out his handkerchief and casually mopped his face. His eyes stung and he had to blink continuously, but despite his discomfort, he could not keep a smile off his face.

"A real tigress, that's what you are, Laraine."

"I'll take her in now, Longarm," said Deegar. "What are the charges?"

"Complicity in murder and conspiracy to defraud, for openers."

"Let's go, Miss Grover," Deegar said.

Laraine got up and looked down at Longarm. "You're a

fool, Longarm. The next time you get your paycheck, think of me—and what we could have had together."

"No," he told her. "I'll think of Holloway instead."

It was an hour or so later that Longarm said goodbye to Big Bill and stepped out of the hotel, feeling rootless and uneasy— an uneasiness that seemed to return with increasing poignance every time he remembered how Laraine had looked as Walters led her away. Just before she had reached the hotel door, she had turned to glance back at him. There were tears in her eyes and a look of disbelief on her face. She still could not understand how Longarm could turn her offer down.

And during many a weak moment from this day on, Longarm realized, he would find it difficult to believe himself.

"Longarm!"

He turned to see Audrey Boggs, just leaving a hack, hurrying across the sidewalk toward him. She hugged him delightedly, then stood back, a puckish grin on her face.

"Longarm! What have you been up to?"

"What do you mean, Audrey?"

"I mean Emma and Marge Fulton."

Longarm frowned. "Emma Fulton? Marge?"

"You don't even remember them do you? For shame, Longarm!"

And then he recalled the two Mormon widows who had nursed him after his shoulder wound. He grinned down at Audrey. "I remember. How do you know them?"

"They're friends of Emilie!"

"Emilie?"

"Yes. And guess what, Longarm! She's back. She's visiting us. And she wants me to bring you home right now."

Longarm groaned. "Now listen. Whatever those two women told Emilie, I'm sure they exaggerated."

"No they didn't," she said. "Not one bit. Come on now. Pa's expecting you for dinner tonight—and you mustn't disappoint Emilie. She has news about Emma and Marge. They've remarried, you know."

"To Lem Hanks?"

"Yes, that's the man."

"I hope he's up to it."

"You were, Longarm."

Longarm took a deep breath and looked down at Audrey.

Her impish smile, framed by blond curls, told him all he needed to know about her plans for him—and for Emilie. He sighed. There was really nothing to do but submit.

"All right, Audrey," he said, taking her arm and escorting her to a hack parked at the curb. "I think maybe you're right. And I sure in Sam Hill don't want to disappoint anyone else today."

Audrey didn't understand what he meant entirely. She just laughed and climbed into the hack ahead of him, then snuggled close to Longarm as he gave the hackie her father's address. It wasn't long before she was in his arms, her cool, delicious lips doing an excellent job of making Longarm forget a very dangerous, redheaded geologist.

SPECIAL PREVIEW

Here are the opening scenes
from

LONGARM AND THE BLUE NORTHER

thirty-fifth novel in the bold
LONGARM series from Jove

Chapter 1

He swung his legs heavily over the side of the bed. He sagged there with his head slumped forward between his shoulders, aware of oppressive midday heat, fiery sunlight rimlighting the drawn window shades, and most of all, aware of the naked girl sprawled in exhausted sleep on the rumpled mattress. He grinned faintly. She breathed through her parted lips, making a faint whistling sound that pleased him because it was as real and natural and honest as she was, as sincere as her total fatigue. She was a girl who believed it was more blessed to give than to receive, and when she gave she did it with all her heart and mind and gristle and sinew. A living, loving doll who truly enjoyed pleasuring a man. Exerting every ounce of his willpower, he kept both his mind and his eyes off the radiant mounds and hillocks and planes of her ceramic-smooth body, but she called to him with fearful polarity, like some lovely succubus, a singing Circe, a ten-dollar whore, the hope of heaven—none of which she was.

"God, you're pretty," she whispered at his back.

He didn't turn his head. "I've still got to get dressed."

Her voice teased him like fingers scratching lightly at his

back. "Even with your clothes on, you're pretty special, Long-arm."

"You got any idea what time it is?"

"I got an idea I don't care, and give me two minutes at that mast of yours, and you won't care..."

"It must be past noon."

"Half the day gone. All the more reason for coming back to bed. Too late to conquer any worlds today."

"I was due downtown at least three hours ago."

"What's downtown?"

He laughed and shook his head. "Beats me. But I sure as hell better go see, or I won't be able to keep myself in even the style I've had to grow accustomed to." He drew a deep breath. "Will you be here when I get back?"

She didn't answer and he grinned again faintly, knowing this was another of her tricks. She wasn't going to waste her breath reassuring him, if it went against her wishes. Let him suffer, let him wonder, let him worry and hurry back to find out for himself.

Sighing expansively, Longarm stood up. He heard her whispered intake of breath, but still did not turn to look at her. He could feel himself growing erect, just knowing she wanted him. Clamping his teeth tightly together, he took up his longjohns from the floor and hopped around, putting them on.

He was a tall man, lean and muscular, with the hard-boned body of a slightly aging athlete. There was youthful vigor in his dark eyes and in his manner, though his face was seamed and brewed coffee-brown by raw winds and pitiless suns. Well over six feet tall, he towered like a bronze giant over the average male of the 1880s. The average enlistee in the recent unpleasantness between the States had been only five feet two. But Americans were getting taller, eating better, and winning a few of the battles against epidemic and disease, and Custis Long was a promise of what the best among them could be.

For a moment before he buttoned his longjohns, Longarm fingered at the pursed stitches that closed the latest wound he'd collected along the way since he'd long ago lit out from his native West-by-God-Virginia, in search of something he'd never found—though he came damned close to it, wrestling in that bed with Bonnie—and embarked on a trail that had brought him, with tortuous turns and twists, to this place and this latest job as a deputy U.S. marshal, earning the grand salary of one hundred a month plus expenses.

He grinned crookedly. Who'd ever have tabbed Custis Long as a man who'd reach such affluence on the lee side of the law? His grandma had always had a saying that pretty well covered the situation. "Nobody in this life truly knows what he's going to be," his grandma had said, "until he's already become it— and by then it's too late." A great old lady. Life had dealt her a few hands off the bottom of the deck, but had never fooled her.

"Damn." A stabbing lance of such terrible intensity sliced through his gut from the ill-healed wound that he had to bite his lip to keep from crying out.

"What's the matter, honey?" Bonnie was truly concerned. She writhed on the bed, sitting up, but he remained facing away from her.

"Nothing, Bonnie. I just remembered something." Remembered? He'd never forget. Sometimes in the night he awoke in a cold sweat, thinking about it. Night shot, from the sneaking dark. He'd felt the impact of the rifle slug and glimpsed the muzzle flash at the same instant. He was knocked off his horse, and hellfire pain flamed through him as he fell. The first stunning numbness of the slug's impact was immediately replaced by a white-hot branding iron that chewed into his belly and made his toes curl with the agony. He'd still been conscious when he hit the ground, and then the pain overwhelmed his brain and knocked him out. At the moment he'd been thankful for the soft black pit of unconsciousness into which he plunged.

"That nasty old gunshot wound hurting you?"

"Only when I breathe."

She exhaled heavily, in deep sympathy. "I felt it last night."

"Oh? Was that you? What were you fooling around up there for?"

"It's bad. Not half healed. You ought to be in bed."

"I'll bet you say that to all the boys."

"Where'd you get it?"

"The bullet? On a job." He remembered the way he'd come slowly awake, after God only knew how long in darkness, a woman's soft hand on his fevered forehead, a woman-scent that was strange and pleasant to him, and him hurting so bad he couldn't care; not really care, with a hard-on and all. Jesus, he *had* been sick. Light lanced through his eyeballs and seared straight to the burning slash in his belly. Every move, no matter how slight, was like the stab of a merciless bowie knife in his side. It was not that it was the first bullet he'd survived; it was just that they never got easier. "A man don't get used to them," he said aloud.

"Come, let mama kiss it," said the warm, teasing voice from the bed.

He laughed over his shoulder. "Mama's too anxious." But his gunmetal eyes gleamed with reflected sunlight and inner warmth. He ran his hand through his close-cropped hair that bushed cigar-leaf brown between his fingers. His proud, well-trimmed longhorn mustache wriggled pleasurably. But the pain wasn't ready to release him yet. He had to go through it all, the recalled shock of impact, the ragged cut of the slug ripping its way through his flesh; the final flooding return of all the pain—of that bullet and all the slugs before it—and all of them ahead of him. And for what? A hundred lousy bucks a month and a pension in twenty years, plus all the lead he could carry, for God's sake.

"Why do I do it?" he said aloud, under his breath, mostly to himself. "What in hell am I doing here?"

Bonnie's voice chilled slightly and she stirred impatiently on the mattress. "What *are* you doing here?"

"Just lucky, I guess." He exhaled heavily. "Hell, Bonnie, I didn't mean you. It has nothing to do with you. I meant this latest memento of law and order. Law and order. Who gives a damn?"

"Not me. Just give me a warm bed and plenty to eat, and I'm fine."

"You're better than fine, baby. You're perfect. I really am lucky."

"Prove it."

"It's at least a month old and I'm still alive. I reckon I am lucky." He was remembering that saddlebag medic who had cleansed his wound, dug out the slug, and sewed him up.

"You're a lucky man, Marshal Long," the sawbones had said. "Lucky it was a high-velocity rifle that went right through you clean as a whistle, and not a pistol or a shotgun—they'd have torn you up. You're lucky you got a nice clean hole through the fleshy part of your side." The doctor had gone on talking through the pain singing its dirges inside Longarm's fevered mind. "Why, you are lucky. You couldn't of picked a better spot for a body wound, if you had to have one. No inflamation. Yessir, I'd say you're one lucky hombre."

Longarm had laughed through surges of pain. "Damned if you don't make it sound like I got a prize instead of a bullet hole, doc. . . . I don't think you can sell me that one. This ain't the first slug that's winged me, you know."

The doctor nodded. "I saw your scars."

"And I reckon it won't be the last. I just don't see how a man can be so effing lucky as I am."

The doctor shrugged, unmoved. "You're breathing. Still on a payroll. Two or three months it'll be completely healed."

"Two or three months?"

"Just be patient, Marshal. Be patient and keep your bowels open."

It had been a full week before Longarm had been able to stand erect and totter around like a senile old man. And when he'd reached for the gun he'd holstered at his side, he'd gagged with pain and felt as if the top of his head were coming off.

The doctor had no sympathy. In fact he'd cursed Longarm for trying to get around at all. "You stupid bastard. You trying to undo my work? You trying to make me look bad, you son of a bitch? Hell, that bullet went through two muscles that wrap around from your belly to your backbone. Those muscles stretch near to ripping every time you move. You got to give 'em time to repair. You're in good shape, but hell, man, you can't get shot like you did without a *few* side effects."

He shook off the hurting memory and turned. catlike, from old habit, taking up his brown tweed pants from a chair. These trousers were just one size too small and he struggled, pulling them on until they fit as snugly as an extra layer of skin. It made moving in brushland a lot easier and a lot smoother, and that could save your life. The beginnings of an erection didn't make buttoning his fly any easier, but he managed to curse it shut. Then he bent over and found his boots where he'd tossed them under the old oakwood dresser. He sat on a straight chair and pulled on the low-heeled cavalry stovepipes. This soft leather footwear wasn't as perfect as Indian moccasins, but was more suited for running than riding. This was the way he wanted it. He spent more time afoot than he did in the saddle, and in these shoes he could outrun any cowpoke in fancy foot-pinchers.

Her voice snagged at him, playful and yet determined. "Must you go, Longarm?"

He didn't look up. Hell, he didn't dare look up. He was only human. In fact, he was human as hell, and this girl had been born tempting; he bet the doctor that delivered her had stroked her bottom instead of slapping it. He didn't even have to look at her to see her clearly in his mind's eye. She was etched there, a moving angel of beauty, and all woman. She was tall, slender, with thick dark masses of curls about her face and neck and shoulders. Her eyes were taunting and saucy, and yet somehow as young as hell all at the same time, a deep violet gray, gleaming and bold and inviting. Her features were delicately cut, her bottom lip was full, made for kissing or nursing, and Jesus knew he wanted all she could give him. That body was firm, luminous with the faint wisps of daylight in the hot, dark room. She lay across the bed as she lay across his mind, driving him out of his head. With Bonnie, it was as it must have been with early man, finding a naked woman in his cave, and making fires with her long before matches were needed. He took in a deep breath and held it for a long time.

"Yes, I do have to go." He turned his back to her and slipped his arms into his gray flannel shirt. He fixed the string tie into a passable knot and tucked his shirttails into his pants, sucking in his breath. He took up his gunbelt and strapped it around his waist, adjusting it to ride on his hipbone. The rig holding his double-action Colt Model T .44-40 was cross-draw, and he wore it high; everything he did was part of his skill, the result of his learning the hard way. He drew the revolver effortlessly and held it out in front of him, feeling Bonnie's eyes on him.

He forced himself cautiously to inspect this most important tool of his craft. The barrel was cut to five inches and had no front sight, because he'd learned that revolver barrels can catch in open-toed holsters of waxed and heat-hardened leather.

"Like it or not, I got a job to do," he said between gritted teeth. "Whether it makes any sense to you or not. Hell, right now it makes no sense to *me*. But I *am* a lawman. That's all I am. That means I've got to go anywhere they send me, whenever they send me. That means I go if the rain is raining or the sun is shining, or I've got a bed full of the sweetest woman-flesh ever clustered in one place in this sad old world.

192

That means I've got to go whether I can make you understand it or not."

"I could show you what really matters."

"I know what really matters, but I can't make a living at it."

She smiled tauntingly. "You get tired too quick."

"The hell. I read somewhere that a girl, no matter how insane she is for it, can't stand up to a man that's a good healthy sex maniac."

"Like you?"

"Like me."

"You're the one with clothes on. Come on, I'll prove I can take it far longer than you can dish it out. I could die trying."

He grinned. "I'll bet you could."

She sighed and lay still as he continued to resist her. He gave the Colt's cylinder a quick, close inspection, satisfied with five cartridges and an empty chamber. He had no intention of accidentally losing a foot, jumping from a horse, wagon, or moving train.

He shoved the Colt into its holster and finished dressing in his vest and frock coat. Into his left vest pocket he placed his Ingersoll watch, after winding it and holding it to his ear from boyhood habit. He left the watch chain dangling. Then he reached under the mattress at the head of the bed and took out a fist-sized, double-barreled .44-caliber derringer with a small brass ring soldered to its butt. He clipped this ring to the loose end of his watch chain and tucked the mean little pistol into his right breast pocket, the chain draping innocently across the flatness of the vest front.

Watching him, Bonnie exhaled heavily. "So you really are going, no matter what I do . . . or what I promise to do?"

He nodded. Positioning his snuff-brown Stetson carefully on his head, tilted slightly forward, cavalry-style, he turned and smiled down at Bonnie. But the naked girl wasn't looking at his face. She was staring at the revealing bulge of fabric at the crotch of his tweed trousers.

"Poor baby," she said. "What a sin, having to go off to work like that."

He bent swiftly and kissed her lightly on the mouth, liking the taste, but moving away before she could entwine those arms about his neck. He let his gaze linger over the beautiful rises and valleys of her body. She writhed slightly, wanting him to look at her, wanting him to like what he saw.

He grinned down at her. "I'll be back to kill you."

She sighed and smiled, nodding. "I'll be waiting here to die," she said.

Longarm turned the corner at Cherokee and Colfax, passing the U.S. Mint on his way to the Federal Building. The high-slung sun tilted slightly westward, glittering in windows and glinting in puddles of standing rain.

He went up the steps and passed people hurrying out to lunch, talking and gesturing as they hurried. At the top of a marble staircase, Longarm paused outside a large oakwood door, gleaming with gilt lettering that read: UNITED STATES MARSHAL, FIRST DISTRICT COURT OF COLORADO.

When Longarm pushed open the door and entered the outer office, he could hear Billy Vail yelling from the inner sanctum. "George! Damm it, George, ain't that son of a bitch showed up yet?"

The red-faced clerk winced, clinging to the newfangled typewriter on his desk as it were his only security.

Longarm gestured sharply downward toward the lean-shanked clerk, silencing him. The pink-faced junior bureaucrat only nodded, hanging on to the typewriter as Vail's voice rattled the windows. "Goddamnit, George, answer me when I speak to you—whether you know the answer or not. If I waited for you to know anything, I'd never hear from...Goddamn it, George, where are you, and where is that son of a bitch?"

Longarm pushed open the inner office door and leaned lazily against its jamb. "What son of bitch is that, chief? Any particular son of a bitch you got in mind?"

Vail's head jerked up and his eyes widened slightly. He looked at the deputy marshal, nonplussed for less than the space of a full breath. Billy Vail had sat across too many poker tables at high stakes, stared along the gleaming barrels of too many outlaw guns, lied to too many irate politicians, ever to reveal any inner confusion he might have felt.

The marshal half-crouched behind his pinewood desk as if about to pounce, outrage still gleaming in moist residue in the irises of his pouched eyes. At least fifteen years older than Longarm, Billy Vail wore his ill-healed scars like proud badges from long-past violences in memory-dimmed hellspots. He figured he'd ridden all the backtrail at least twice. He resented that he ws falling victim to the one foe he could never outwit, outfight, or outlast: age. He resented that because of age only, he had been promoted out of harm's reach, away from the heady excitement of danger and conflict and encounter. He never even wore his gun to the office anymore. All his old enemies were in distant jails or faraway graves somewhere; he had outlived personal peril. Balding, desk-tethered, he was going to lard in belly and jowls, but in his imagination he remained as slim and hard and efficient as Longarm, and arguably faster with a gun. Foes learned that when Billy Vail drew his gun, he meant to use it. Sometimes he worried about Longarm; there was no better lawman, but Longarm had a way of thinking about things, and thought could put a lawman in deadly peril.

Vail's voice rasped like small-bore fire in the austerely government-issue-furnished office. There was no carpeting because Vail's grade didn't rate rugs, but the floors were polished to a high sheen because he had a cleaning budget the auditors expected him to use. He was permitted exactly three chairs—one swivel, one straight, and one red morocco armchair for guests—and two filing cabinets. A single window opened upon a sunstruck slice of the plaza. A thirty-eight-star American flag and a banjo wall clock shared wallspace with a map of the western half of the United States and a faded, framed photograph of the President.

"This here goddamn office opens at eight o'clock in the morning, Mr. Custis Long."

"Seems reasonable, gives you and George somewhere to go mornings."

"Don't bray jackass at me, Long. I show up at eight o'clock, I expect my deputies to show up at eight o'clock when they ain't on assignment."

"You must lose a lot of good men that way."

"You like your job, Long?"

"I've had worse."

"Damn right you have. Here we pay you like a goddamn Persian prince, and give you an expense account so you can rob us blind—"

"You ever eat a ten-cent breakfast, Billy?"

"When I could afford it. You get your steaks. You got it pretty goddamn easy, coming in here in the middle of the goddamn afternoon, needing a haircut, but smelling like bay rum or a whorehouse."

"I'm here, Billy."

"Yeah, and look at you. Look at your fly hanging open—"

Longarm grinned crookedly. "My fly's shut tight, Billy."

"But it could be flyin' open, that's the point," Vail said. "You'd screw a mare if you got hard up."

"You ain't tried it, Billy, don't knock it."

"Your screwing is your business. Your taste in partners is up to you, but not on government time. Is that clear?"

"I think everybody on this floor is pretty clear on that, Billy." Longarm walked over and sank into the leather chair. He tried to bit back a yawn, but could not do it. Billy Vail's face flushed red, watching Longarm admit his fatigue—on government time.

"I got an assigment for you."

"Sure. How else could I earn my princely pay?"

"You know what the pay for most men is right now, Long? Less than two bits a goddamn hour."

"That doesn't include getting shot at, either." Longarm removed a two-for-a-nickel cheroot from his jacket pocket. He bit off the end of it and struck a sulfur match with his thumbnail. He stared across the desk at Vail through the drifting flame. "Mind if I smoke?"

"Filthy habit," Vail grumbled, but he didn't say no.

"I've earned some time off, Billy."

"The hell you say."

"You want to see the gun wound in my side?"

"Hell, no. I've seen gunshot wounds you could stick your fist into. You're startin' to pamper yourself, Long."

"The hell. An inch higher, that bullet could have smashed my ribs and ripped down into my intestines. An inch lower, it shatters my hip and cripples me for life. An inch to the right, it would have gutted me—belly and kidneys."

"What the hell, an inch to the left and it'd have missed you clean."

"Think how sick you're going to be with me collecting disability retirement."

"Over my goddamn dead body, you will. Now you listen to me, I'm going to take your word that you ain't up to snuff— even though I know you been out screwin' yourself blind. I got a nice easy little assignment—"

"Those are the most fearful words you could say to me, Billy." Longarm shook his head and sat forward in the chair, aware of the stabbing pain in his side.

"A piece of cake. A Sunday-school social. Hell, it's something even George could handle."

"Let George do it then."

"You'd hate me for not giving you a paid vacation, Long. Hell, that's what this amounts to. A short ride from Denver. A little look-see. A little fresh air. A little paid vacation, that's all I'm asking."

Longarm held up a calloused hand. "Stop. You're scaring hell out of me. The nicer you get, the sicker I get. I been on your little paid vacations before. They're a lot like a one-way trip to hell."

"Somebody's been cutting fence." Billy Vail sat down in his swivel chair, then got up and went to the slash of sunlight at his window.

Longarm shrugged. "Somebody's always cutting fence when his cows get hungry. You know that, Billy."

"This here is government drift fence they're cutting."

"Ridin' fence is for line riders, not a lawman."

Vail grinned at him coldly. "If I say you're a lawman, then by God you're a lawman. If I say you ride line, by damn you're a line rider." The rotund chief came back to his cluttered desk and shuffled some papers. "Hell, old son, this is just an easy ride down south to the Arkansas Divide. How lucky can you get?"

Longarm laughed at him. He blew a ring of smoke and watched it drift slowly toward the ceiling. "I've been on some of these prime vacations you arrange, Billy, and I'll tell you how lucky I've been. I've been lucky to get back alive."

Vail looked as if he might swell up and explode, but he only shook his head and smiled again, though the smile never reached his eyes. "Now listen, son. This here is no tough assignment. I wouldn't do that to you, and you with a bullet in your side."

Longarm grinned wolfishly and shook his head. "There is just one thing wrong here, Billy, and that's the difference between what you and me call tough assignments."

Longarm realized he was in trouble, that he had spoken the wrong words. Vail nodded, face still flushed. He came around his desk and perched on the side of it, gazing at Longarm, eyes

197

unyielding. "Tough assignments? Hell, I'll tell you about tough assignments. They don't hardly have then anymore, what with this country getting so civilized and people growing softer all the time. I can tell you about a tough assignment. I was caught once by them half-human little runt Paiutes up in the Basin country. Hell, I suffered every pain and indignity a man can suffer and survive. But I survived. We were tough in those days. Hell, once me and Doc Withers had to chop and build and then seal an Alaskan ice hut with melted snow and then crawl inside it to keep from freezing our balls off. We slept with our sled dogs for blankets and hugging each other close like we was newlyweds. Tough assignments! Shit, you don't know the meaning. Hell, I recall me and Doc Withers crossing a desert, taking turns riding the only horse left alive to us. I'd ride three miles, leave the animal tied up, and walk three miles whilst Doc took his turn in the saddle. But we made it, Long. By damn, we made it."

Longarm gazed at him in mock awe. "I'm real inspired, chief. I swear I am. And I'd take this assignment, but the truth is I got a hangnail—"

"Don't you smart-talk me, Custis Long. This here little job has got to be done, and by damn you're going to do it. That's U.S. Government drift fence they're cutting down there. U.S. property. Just like destroying any other government property, it's against the law."

"What have those folks got against government bobwire?" Longarm inquired in his most innocent tone.

Billy Vail opened his mouth to answer him seriously, then stopped and drew his hand across his mouth.

After a long moment of silence in which Longarm peered at his red-hot cigar tip as if it held the secrets of the universe, Billy Vail sighed and conceded, "We do have a couple little problems down there."

"I'll bet you have."

"Nothing to grab leather over, Longarm. Little things." When Longarm did not speak, Billy winced faintly and continued as if on a totally new tack.

"You know, the Goodnight-Loving cattle trail runs over the Arkansas Divide, and Texas herds are still moving up into the Wyoming-Montana ranges."

"Thought the Sioux Indian Wars stopped those long drives."

"Well, them feedin' ranges up there is opened up again after the pacification of the Sioux. Indians ain't your problem. Gettin' feeder-cows to graze, that's the problem of the ranchers and the old-time herders. Keepin' them bastards from cuttin' government bobwire is your problem. It's that simple."

"If it's that simple, why are we in on it?"

"Because we got our goddamn orders to be in on it, that's why. That trail across the Divide is a public right-of-way, and nobody disputes that, and herders are welcome to push their cows along it—"

"Only the cows have grazed out any grass on the trail side of the fence and worn it down to dust and 'dobe," Longarm cut in.

"The public right-of-way is a good two miles wide between the government drift fences. A good two miles. I admit the trail narrows down to little more than a wide road in settled country, like around the settlements of Sun Patch and Dirty Fork. . . ."

"Dirty Fork?"

"Named for the mess some Indians made at a trail crossing when they came on some white people in wagon trains. Dirty Fork is not much of a town anymore, but they do depend a lot on passing herders for any income."

"So the local authorities down there in Dirty Fork and Sun Patch aren't cooperating with the government in trying to stop the bobwire-cutting?"

Vail gazed at the backs of his hands. He nodded. "That's right. Some of them ain't been real cooperative. The government is supposed to collect a modest grazing fee on every head eating public grass inside them fences."

"But they know damn well they can't do it. They know no Texan or anybody else is going to drive his cattle on a barren, dusty trail whilst grass waves green and lush on the other side of a damfool wire fence."

"All right. We concede that much. The government is supposed to collect, but nobody bothers to try to collect on casual grazing of passing cows. At least they never have before. But with the ranges shrinking southeast of Denver on the High Plains and along the Divide, Uncle Sam has had to set aside choice range for future homesteaders and local ranchers that are willing to pay grazing fees—usually no more than about two bits a head."

"Two bits?" Longarm whistled between his teeth. "With a

big herd, that can add up to a lot of greenbacks. No wonder they're having trouble collecting from Texans ridin' with bellies stuck to backbones."

Vail shook his head. "Ain't the collecting that's worrying the government, Longarm. You ain't been listening. Like I say, there ain't no way to collect from drovers passing through on open range. That's why the Interior Department has strung bobwire fences west of and parallel to the Goodnight-Loving Trail. Hell, it had to be done if there was to be any decent public lands left. Passing cows are welcome to grass east of the fence."

"Only there ain't nothing but dry stubble on the trail side of that bobwire." Longarm shook his head, totally out of agreement with Interior Department policy.

"Damm it, Longarm, you ain't a loyal government employee, that's your trouble. How trail drovers feed their cattle ain't our problem here. Protecting government property is our problem."

"Bobwire fences."

"In this here instance, yes. Bobwire that protects government-owned lands."

"All I've got to do is stop Texas drovers from cutting fence when the only grass on a dry, dead trail is *west* of that fence, where grass is greening up and lush? Come on, Billy, what would you do if you were a Texas trail boss who already hates them damnyankee bureaucrats up in Washington anyway?" He shook his head. "Right. You'd do just what they're doing. You'd cut fence."

"Maybe. Maybe I would," Billy Vail conceded after a moment. "But there's more to it than that."

"The story of my life." Longarm shook his head wearily.

"Them cuts made by passing drovers cause one hell of a lot more trouble than the Texans can be made to understand. Hell, nobody's begrudging the stolen grass. And Interior can afford to restring bobwire fences as long as the Glidden people keep turning it out by the running foot. Them drovers cut where they move in and they cut again when they finally move out on the trail again."

"What's wrong with Interior Department riders?"

"You mean them range inspectors?" Vail snorted derisively. "They don't have no real power to stop a man takin' a crap on government lands."

"But I can stop them?"

"I expect you to—with a modicum of trouble. You see, Longarm, the big bad trouble ain't the cuttin' of drift fences—goin' in or comin' out."

"I figured it was more than that—a modicum more," Longarm said.

Vail nodded. "The big pain is the growling and yelling of the legitimate local ranchers that *do* graze their cows on government land—with a permit. These legitimate ranchers have come to depend on the drift fence to keep their cows where they expect to find them, come roundup. They figure that's part of what they pay Uncle Sam for—to keep the cows on the graze. And you know very well, Long, a settled local businessman that pays for his permit to graze his stock is going to resent furriners passing through and fattening beef on grass that the local rancher has bought and paid for, plus cutting bobwire so the rancher's cows stray."

Longarm stuck his tongue in his cheek. "I see. It gets more interesting by the minute, Billy. All I got to do is head off a fence war between ranchers and trail drovers?"

"It won't be that bad, Long. Hell, you'll work with the sheriff at Dirty Fork. A Virginia gentlemen and former town-tamer named Lawson Carr."

"I've heard the name. If Lawson Carr is sheriff down there, why don't he stop the wire-cutting and the trouble with the drovers?"

"Carr's doing all he can. He's a good man. But he can't enforce an unpopular law down there, especially not right now."

"What's wrong with right now?"

"Well, Longarm, it's election year. I mean a sheriff is a local politician first, I don't care how good a man he is."

"Sure. I see. You don't get any local cooperation because local authorities don't want to make the good ol' boys who control all the votes mad in an election year."

Vail exhaled heavily. "Well, I can see how the moccasin pinches Carr's foot. He is up for reelection. Even if he's the best sheriff in Colorado history, he ain't going to be much good if he ain't reelected."

"What you're saying is I can't expect any cooperation from Carr?"

Vail swung his arm at an invisible adversary. "No, dammit,

I ain't saying nothing of the kind. You'll get every cooperation from Sheriff Lawson Carr. Within reason. I ain't saying that at all. I ain't even saying there *is* any big trouble between drovers and local ranchers."

"You just want it stopped before it explodes."

"It ain't that bad. You got authority where Interior's range inspectors don't. You can *act*, election or no election. I've got some warrants here that you can fill in and serve."

"On who?"

"Hell, how do I know? Anybody who spits on the sidewalk. You don't like the part in a man's hair. If he talks back to you. Hell, even if by chance you happen to catch somebody red-handed, cuttin' some Glidden wire, you might even cite *him*. I don't have to tell you your job, Longarm. We just don't want any trouble exploding down there in an election year. You may run into a few muleheads. Knock some sense into them. Hell, sometimes trouble in a place like this is nothing more than politics. Why, the Lincoln County War was Republicans against Democrats, Catholics against Protestants, for God's sake."

"I was there," Longarm reminded him.

"I know you was there. And I know you know how these things start and how they get out of hand. Hell, there wouldn't likely be a Colorado if them Protestants hadn't gotten themselves run out of the Midwest. Texicans called themselves rebels, but the truth was most of them was Irish Catholics, and Austin got his land grants from Mexico because the Mexicans figured that Irish-Catholic Texas would be a buffer between them and the Comanche–United States threat. Austin *was* a Catholic, but he still turned against the Mexicans. All I'm saying is that we got a little wire-cutting that can be nipped in the bud before it *does* flare into something big that nobody can handle without bloodshed. All I want you to do is to ride down there and spread the gospel. They're destroying government property, and that shit has got to stop."

MORE ROUGH RIDING ACTION FROM JOHN WESLEY HOWARD